Mikey led h
electricity, snappi
memory of the elec.. ... . to a halt.

"Whoa." She looked it up and down. The column reached from the ground to just above her head.

"In Frama-12 they know me as General Takka." He seemed unfazed by the anomaly. "If anybody questions your authority, just tell them General Takka sent you."

She couldn't pull her gaze from the shimmering thing.

"I know you don't like people bossing you, Windy, but when you get there, try to treat Queen Bogen with respect. Also, water is sacred. Offer a canteen to Her Majesty. Let's see, what else do you need to know? Oh yeah, mel-yew are good. You can trust them. And most important, don't forget the oracle's prediction. When the sea is smooth, the lurkin will attack. Are you paying attention? Windemere."

She snapped her head toward the little boy who sounded way too grown-up. "Wait. This is, like, really real? I'm doing this?"

"You're a warrior. It'll be easy for you."

She chewed her lip. Her mom had given her that title because she fought adversity, not giant spiders.

She walked all the way around the glowing column. "No offense, but this looks like it could kill me. I can't help anybody if I'm dead."

Frama-12

by

Aud Supplee

Winnie and the "Wizard", Book One

Frama-12

Cover Art by *Kim Mendoza*

The Wild Rose Press, Inc.
PO Box 708
Adams Basin, NY 14410-0708
Visit us at www.thewildrosepress.com

Publishing History
First Edition, 2022
Trade Paperback ISBN 978-1-5092-4358-7
Digital ISBN 978-1-5092-4359-4

Winnie and the "Wizard", Book One
Published in the United States of America

Dedication

To my husband and best friend, Brian; my sister and cheerleader extraordinaire, Sharon; my nephew, Eric, who was the inspiration for Mikey; my favorite bro-in-law, Joel; my awesome critiquing buddies, Gretchen, Alexandra, Stan, and Steve; and finally, to all the supportive staff and friends at TCHS-Brandywine.

Chapter 1

Winnie's Mom dreams never ended with the soft whisper of "Windy," her mom's pet name for her. They usually ended in the cruelest of ways, with Mom gently fading out, leaving behind an empty porch chair facing a lake.

Winnie heard the name again. Or maybe a breeze through the seagrass outside her open window played tricks with her ears. Before she could drift back to sleep, a tiny hand jostled her shoulder. Her eyes blinked open to a dark room that smelled faintly of salt air.

"Windy?" The small voice belonged to her little stepbrother, Mikey.

"Hey, bud," she said in a sleep-groggy voice. "Couldn't sleep?"

The hint of moonlight that shone through her window showed Mikey's silhouette, shaking his head. The little boy sniffled.

"Need some water? Or—" She swallowed hard, not really wanting to suggest it. "—do you want me to get your mommy?"

"Which one?" He sniffled again.

She had never expected that. "How many do you have?"

"Doesn't matter. What I need is to get strong really fast."

"Oh. Well." She sat on the edge of her bed. "That

might take a while."

"It *can't*," he whined. "The oracle just sent me a message. Bad things are in the sea."

Now she understood. The oracle was part of a fantasy game he'd invented called Frama-12. Late at night, though, anything seemed possible. Like her mom being alive or Frama-12 being a real place. Winnie gave him a side hug. "It was just a dream."

He slumped onto the bed beside her. "The oracle promised I'd be bigger when the lurkin marched on the castle."

Due to her warrior code, plus the fact the kid was cute, she often played Frama-12 with him. In the game, he played General Takka. She pretended to be the quarrelsome Queen Bogen. The object was for Takka to convince the queen to strengthen their army so they could defeat the evil lurkin. Obviously, the game had consequences. Winnie's recurring nightmares of giant attacking spiders for example.

"The oracle foretold it," Mikey said. "My human form was supposed to be taller, stronger, and smarter. But they're coming sooner than she calculated."

She gave him another hug. "It's okay, buddy. I get confused when weird dreams wake me up too."

He let out a huff. "Windy, this is for real, and I'm not strong enough to help. Or old enough. Or cunning enough. The oracle messed up."

"How can oracles mess up? Aren't they supposed to be, like, all-knowing and all-seeing?"

"The queen will never listen to me if I go to her in this form. She'll think I'm a baby."

"As your queen, I say—"

"You're only the pretend queen. I meant the real

one."

She had hoped a few words of comfort would send him back to his room. At this rate she'd get no extra rest before her alarm went off. And she wanted to run ten miles today.

"I'm going to tell you a secret. I'm a warrior."

"You are?" he said in an awed whisper.

"I don't advertise it, but yes. When I'm called to duty, I fight. Since my form is bigger than yours, I'll go to the queen and fight in your place."

Skinny arms wrapped tightly around her. "Thanks, Windy!"

"But not right now, okay? I'll go to war after lunch or something."

"Not right now. When the time tear opens again."

She laughed. "Whatever you say. Good night."

****

Winnie had never visited a castle in her life. That's how she knew she was stuck in another dream. How else could she explain standing in a high-ceilinged throne room with eerie candlelight flickering off its golden walls? She'd never dress like a warrior princess either, not even on Halloween. Yet she stood at stiff attention, wearing tights and a leather battle tunic. Not that she minded. Whenever she dreamed about the castle, she didn't feel like gangly Winnie Harris, adjusting to a growth spurt. She felt like General Windemere. The Great.

Currently, though, she felt like General Windemere, the Annoyed. She gazed over the sea of shadowed heads at the raised platform on the opposite side of the room. Polo, the court's wiry little jester, strummed his lute and sang, "Queen Bogen of the vogan, squatting on her throne. Eats her squiggs and wiggly thiggs, while spitting out their bones."

Windemere nervously rubbed a thumb over the hilt of her side dagger.

"Our brave and noble queen," Polo sang, "oft readies for the hunt. Seeking thrills and many kills of hoppers, wags, and glunt."

She quivered with frustration. This ballad had twenty-seven very long, very tedious verses. She leaned toward the knight on her left. His head barely reached her elbow. She lightly thumped his breast plate.

"Sound the trumpet," she murmured from the corner of her mouth. "I have an urgent message for the queen."

The knight peeked through the narrow slit in his fishbowl-shaped helmet. "Begging the good general's pardon," he whispered back, "but our queen is never disturbed during her evening's amusement."

"She will be now," she said through clenched teeth. "We're being invaded."

The knight turned his back on her. A general. Not just any general. A great and mighty general with critical news. Windemere did what any offended general would do. She shoved the insubordinate soldier into the guard beside him. Metal clanked against metal. Both frail men crashed to the floor in a creaky heap.

Polo stopped singing. He shaded his eyes with a tiny hand and peered toward the back of the throne room. "Does someone think he's more important than our queen's entertainment?"

Ignoring him, Windemere strode forward, head held high. "Your Majesty, the lurkin are about to attack the castle."

A thunderous boom sounded outside.

She cried out, "They're through the gate!"

None of the shadows moved.

"Don't just sit there," she commanded. "Defend yourselves."

"Vogan do not fight," spoke a pompous female voice from the front of the throne room. "We are royalty."

The ornately carved door behind Windemere crashed open. She spun around. An army of mandible-snapping spiders, fifteen feet tall, lumbered inside. They were accompanied by the boisterous strains of Wagner's "Ride of the Valkyries."

"That can't be right," she murmured.

Her mother appeared at her side. "Windy, you're a warrior. You need to help these people."

An eight-legged creature scuttled toward them. Winnie jumped awake. Two more bars of "Ride of the Valkyries" sounded from the smart watch her dad had given her. She pressed a side button, stopping the alarm, then took a deep breath to settle down. Something had to be done about those spider dreams. She fumbled in the dark for her clothes, thinking less-than-stellar thoughts about a certain little stepbrother and his fantasy game.

Uncool. After changing into a T-shirt and running shorts, she gripped her sneakers by the laces and tiptoed in stocking feet through her dad's beach house. Halfway through the living/dining room area, her left foot landed on a small, sharp lump. Not expecting to be stabbed in the foot so early in the morning, she let out a gasp and leaped straight up. On the way down, she landed on it again. She wanted to howl at the injustice but refused to wake everybody in the house.

She puffed and removed the offending object. By the feel, she'd been poked by one of Mikey's homemade fantasy toys. It was part man/part horse, but in a way mythology had never intended. He called it a "palum."

He kept a whole herd of them in a plastic bag. He'd created them by cutting up little plastic horses and green army men, then fusing the pieces together with hot glue. Winnie had supervised, never guessing she'd get speared by one.

Good thing Mikey was cute or she would've exacted revenge. She limped to the kitchen area and slid her feet into her shoes. As the pain faded, her thoughts switched to her fantasy of one day qualifying for the Boston Marathon. Today was day three of her training.

She took two gulps of orange juice directly from the carton. After four lunges and six hamstring stretches, she scampered down the wooden steps and onto the deserted beach. She jogged in semidarkness across dry beach toward the water. Once she reached the damp sand, she pumped her legs in time to the hiss and roar of the surf. She breathed deeply, savoring the cool salt air, and soon relaxed into an easy rhythm.

The crazy idea of jogging all the way up the Eastern Seaboard to New England made her grin. Four hundred and fifty miles. Now that was a long-distance run.

She might have kept going till she wore out if she'd had her cell to call Dad for a ride. Unfortunately, he'd made her leave her devices at home. She got to keep the smart watch after promising she'd only use it for the alarm and to tell time.

"We're going on an electronics-free vacation," he'd said. "It'll be fun," he'd said. What kind of fun involved living two weeks with no phone, no internet, and no TV? Sounded like child abuse to her.

A wave splashed onto the beach, sending foam over her feet. The distraction of glancing down cut off her negative thoughts. She looked up but not soon enough to avoid a weird column of sparks straight ahead. She plowed into it.

The flickering lights merged into a glowing web that wound around her, squeezing her breath. She gnashed her teeth and clawed at the snare. The hold tightened. She fought harder, lungs burning for air. A warrior never gave up. She'd learned that from her mom.

Through a growing buzz in her ears, distant voices said, "Live long our Mighty Queen!"

The snare let go. Her legs buckled. Before she collapsed, she saw eyes without a face, gazing back. If they hadn't been such a bright emerald green, she might have thought her mom was watching.

In time, Winnie's brain ambled toward consciousness. Light seared through her closed eyelids. She knew by feel that she lay on her back. Warm granules prickled her neck. More grit had attached to her elbows and bare calves. It had to be sand. *Where am I?*

She became aware of the sound of waves splashing against the shore. Seagulls squealed overhead. *The beach?* With effort, she sat up. She rubbed her aching head. Something weird and dangerous had tried to suffocate her. Her eyes snapped open. Was it still out there? She warily peeked through her bangs. Nothing.

At least she didn't see any glowing specks or hear electric sparks. She tentatively raised her right arm. Only warm sea air tickled her skin. She took a deep breath and stood on wobbly legs.

Two female joggers, dressed in matching pink tank tops and black shorts, glided gracefully past. Farther down the beach, an old man in a floppy hat watched his black Lab frolic in the surf. A typical morning at the beach had begun. Typical if Winnie ignored the memory of the invisible snare.

She moved cautiously toward home. At the bottom step of her cottage porch, she paused. Had she imagined the electric web? Had it been some bizarre trick her brain played on her for jogging on too little sleep? Trying to figure it out on an empty stomach made her head hurt. She gave up on the mystery and entered the screened porch. Through the cottage's open doorway, she saw Dad and Mikey sitting at the table, eating toast and cold cereal.

Mikey said to Dad, "I told Kip I'd show him my people today."

Winnie's stepmother, Maria, plump body wrapped in a pink bathrobe, stood in the tiny kitchen area, pouring coffee into two mugs. Everyone else wore shorts and T-shirts.

"Windy!" A loving glow shone from Mikey's wide-set brown eyes. "You can meet Kip too!"

She smiled back. She didn't even mind that she didn't know who Kip was. Mikey always lifted her spirits.

"You're a little late, aren't you, Win?" Dad stared more closely at her through his black-framed glasses. "Is that sand on your arms?"

She blinked down at the grit she'd forgotten to brush off. "Maybe. A little."

"Hon, did you fall?" Maria asked.

Winnie clamped her lips together. *Be civil, be civil. You promised Dad.* Still, she couldn't help frowning. Only librarians and old people were allowed to call her hon. She shrugged. "Sort of."

"What?" Maria set the two steaming mugs on the table and fluttered to her. "Let's see. Are you hurt?"

Winnie ducked away. "I'm okay, honest. Thanks. Just need to, you know, have a little breakfast." She slid into the chair opposite Mikey and grabbed the box of Oatie-Ohs. She dipped her hand inside.

"Get a bowl, Win," Dad said.

"Did you twist your ankle?" Maria handed a coffee mug to Winnie's dad and sat opposite him with hers.

Winnie shifted her shoulders. "Think I fainted."

Dad eyed her with concern. "Did you eat breakfast before you went out?"

"Orange juice."

"Oh, well, there we go, then," said Maria. "Low blood sugar."

Dad frowned at Winnie. "If you want to train for a race, you have to give your body the proper nourishment."

"After breakfast," Maria said, "you can sweep up the sand you just brought in."

Her sympathy sure didn't last long. All Winnie needed were a couple of nasty stepsisters, and she'd be living in a fairy tale. She took a few slow breaths, reminding herself that, as stepmoms went, Maria wasn't that bad. She simply wasn't Mom. *Don't go there.* She had bigger things on her mind anyway. Like that strange web that had grabbed her.

"Dad." She helped herself to another handful of sweet, crunchy cereal. "Ya know that wall runners hit when they do marathons?"

"Never experienced it personally," he said. "Win, get a bowl."

"Do you have to run a whole marathon, or can you hit it at any distance?"

"It was the time tear," said Mikey.

"A bowl?" Dad raised his eyebrows at her. "How far'd you go?"

"Windy," said Mikey, "it was the time tear."

She put down the cereal box. "The what?"

"The distance, Win," Dad cut in. "How far did you run on an empty stomach?"

"Tear in the time fabric," Mikey said in a casual tone. He took a dainty bite of toast. He always did that to avoid the crust. "Think of time as a great big blanket covering the universe."

"That's so creative!" Maria's dark eyes glowed with pride. "Maybe I should have named you Michelangelo."

Winnie rolled her eyes. She still remembered the time Maria had gushed over Mikey's creativity when he pushed a box of Band-Aids across the table and made car noises.

"Everybody knows blankets cover the universe," Winnie retorted. "I saw it on the Science Channel. I think it was called, 'In Search of the Cosmic Bedspread.' "

"I'd like to watch that one." Obviously, Mikey hadn't learned how to recognize sarcasm yet. "They're right. The universe is like a bedspread."

"I never know what you'll think of next." Maria affectionately tousled his shiny black hair. "I can't decide if you're going to be a scientist or a novelist."

"Or be totally made fun of when he starts first grade this fall," Winnie mumbled.

"Windemere," Dad said, "let's have a little less attitude."

Winnie let out an annoyed breath of air. "I happen to know stuff. And I know kids pick on kids they think are different. I'm trying to protect him."

Mikey held up his skinny arms. "Guys, listen. Bedspreads and the time fabric can get holes. But if you catch a time tear before it closes, you can jump into a whole nother world."

"Like Frama-12?" Winnie mentioned his game as a joke. His solemn nod took the fun away.

"Mikey," Maria said, "speaking about those bedspreads with holes in them. Didn't I notice a rip in yours at home?"

The little boy shrugged. "Maybe. Sharp things can tear regular bedspreads."

Winnie froze. She had hoped nobody would notice that.

Maria and Dad turned toward her. "What kind of sharp things?" they asked in unison.

"Oh sure." Winnie frowned at them. "Everybody look at me now."

And Maria did with a raised eyebrow. "Who had a better way to cook spaghetti sauce and ended up splattering it everywhere when the lid blew off the pot?"

"And who decided," Dad chimed in, "that the best way to get rid of dryer lint was to stuff it in the back of

Mikey's closet and tell him it was a dirt-making machine?"

"That one worked, Clive," Mikey said to Winnie's dad.

Winnie folded her arms. "What does everybody do? Keep a list?"

Dad shook his head. "When there's a mishap, you're usually nearby."

"I tore the bedspread," Mikey blurted.

Dad's and Maria's heads swiveled toward him. So did Winnie's.

"Well," Winnie said, recovering first. "It was probably an accident."

It definitely had been. Back home, a slip of the scissors had made the tear. She'd been cutting out a magazine article on marathon training. Her solid navy bedspread was identical to Mikey's. Since she just received a lecture for tracking muddy sneakers across the kitchen floor, she'd thought it prudent to secretly switch the bedspreads.

"Accidents happen," Mikey said.

Maria and Dad exchanged glances.

"Be more careful next time, champ."

Mikey bobbed his head up and down. "I will, Clive. Sorry."

Winnie's shoulders stiffened with indignation. Dad never called her champ when she wrecked things. Although she had to admit Mikey had just saved her from a lecture. That was why, when he invited her to meet his new friend, Kip, she accepted. She owed him a favor. Kip was probably imaginary anyway.

If she'd been keeping track, that was when the real trouble started.

Chapter 2

Kip Skyler drifted on the calm sea, arms and legs splayed over the black rubber of a borrowed inner tube. A gentle breeze wafted by. Wispy clouds overhead softened the sun's heat. He had to admit he didn't feel half bad. True, he was still grieving the tragedy of finding Randy stiff in his cage two days ago. At least he didn't want to chuck all his props and give up magic forever. Even without his beloved rabbit, he still had the look, the talent, and the patter. He even had the exotic accent...well, exotic enough. If only he could conjure the courage to tell his dad he wanted to pursue magic as a career.

His inner tube rolled with the soft waves. Kip closed his eyes, relaxed by the gentle motion. He was on the verge of sleep when a high-pitched voice called his name. He gazed toward shore. A tiny boy and a tall girl stood together on the private beach. The boy waved frantically at him.

He waved back, recognizing the little chap from yesterday. What was his name? Mickey? No, Mikey. As a lark, he had shown him his vanishing and reappearing coin trick. The little kid's wide-eyed wonder reminded him why he liked performing. Mikey had even called him a wizard.

Kip paddled back to shore and ambled to his beach towel.

Mikey raced toward him. "I brought my people." He swung a small plastic bag. "Remember? I told you I would."

Kip slid into his T-shirt, vaguely recalling the offer. At the time he'd had no idea what the kid was on about. What captured his attention now was the athletic girl who joined them. She seemed closer to Kip's age than Mikey's. And they looked nothing alike. Maybe his babysitter?

"Who's your friend?" he asked the boy.

Mikey swayed his bag in the girl's direction. "That's my sister, Windy!"

She rested her long fingers on Mikey's shoulders in a possessive way. "And you're Kip?" She sounded surprised but not pleasantly so.

Clearly, she didn't fancy him. Yet. He flashed a confident smile. The one he'd practiced in front of the bathroom mirror. No smile volleyed back. The only movement came from her short brown hair when a gust of warm air whipped through it.

He tried again with a deep bow. "Pleased to meet you, Windy."

"It's Winnie." Her eyes narrowed suspiciously. "Is Kip short for something?"

"Stage name."

His full name was Kenneth Paul Skyler. Not that he'd admit that to her. He loathed his given name. It sounded like he had a lisp. *Hi, my name ith Kenneth.* Ken was a doll's name. Kenny sounded infantile. Five years ago, on his tenth birthday, he'd dubbed himself *Kip*. He'd been answering to it ever since. When he performed magic, he became *Kip the Amazing*.

At five foot seven, he was taller than most of the

girls in his class at school. This girl stood eye to eye with him. She gave him a superior stare that made him feel awkward.

Mikey broke the silence. "Want to see my people now?"

He turned toward the little boy. Anything to avoid the girl's scrutiny. "You've got people in the bag, mate?"

"Toys," the sister clarified.

"Ready?" Without waiting for a reply, Mikey knelt and upended the bag.

An assortment of plastic horses and green army men bounced onto Kip's beach towel. At least that's how they first looked. He bent over to examine an unexpected collection of oddities. Some appeared to be a combination of man and horse. "Coo, Mike! Whatcha done to your horses?"

"They're palum. Nobody makes palum toys. I had to make my own."

Even the normal soldiers had been amputated at the knees. Kip lifted one. "What happened to this blighter?"

"That's a mel-yew. Nobody makes them either."

"Mel-what?"

The girl rolled her eyes. "Don't even ask."

"Mel-yew. They're the warriors in Frama-12. I call them Minute Men 'cause they're shorter than a minute."

"Characters from a game he created. When he grows up, he'll make a fortune selling it. Right now, it's in the planning stages."

Mikey turned to Kip. "Windy's going to save us from the lurkin by going to Frama-12 in my place to be the general."

Kip straightened to attention. He grinned at her and saluted.

Windy nudged her brother with her bare foot. "Let's not get into that with strangers."

"It's okay. Kip's a wizard."

The girl didn't look convinced. Kip gladly accepted the challenge. Sunlight glinting off a delicate gold chain around Windy's neck gave him an idea. His quick peek behind her back, while she focused on her brother, revealed the clasp. He smiled, recognizing it as one he could easily unfasten. He'd practiced multiple times on his Mum and Gran, and they never noticed. He rubbed his palms together to warm them. Just as his Mum and Gran had been fooled, Winnie would never feel it go. The moment he made it reappear, she'd be his friend for life. Little kids weren't the only ones impressed by his sleight of hand.

"I really am a wizard." Under the guise of pulling a quarter from her ear, he snatched the necklace. It only took a flick of the wrist. An unexpected heart-shaped locket was attached to the chain. Luckily, it fit snugly in his palm.

He held out both closed fists to Mikey. "Where's the quarter?"

The little boy pointed at Kip's right fist. He uncurled his fingers to show an empty palm.

"Then it's over there!" Mikey pointed at Kip's left hand.

He slowly opened one clasped finger at a time for effect. There lay the girl's gold chain and locket.

Her right hand flew to her throat. Her cheeks reddened. Kip expected that. Surprise, disbelief. Any second now, she'd laugh. Yes, Kip was the master.

Instead of smiling, though, she clenched her fists and scowled.

Kip cocked his head, confused. She wasn't supposed to snatch the locket out of his hand. He intended to give it back. She wasn't supposed to spin on her heel and run away either. In all of his years performing, he had never frightened away an audience. At least her brother remained.

Kip faced Mikey. "What was that all about?"

The little boy stopped sifting through his playthings to squint through the sun's glare at him. "That's just Windy. She gets like that sometimes. There's a picture of her mom inside her necklace. She showed me once."

"I don't understand."

Mikey gathered the horses and dropped them into his bag. "That's a memory you almost stole. Her mom died."

Kip slapped his forehead. How could he have been so stupid? "I should go to her."

"I wouldn't. She had a rough morning. See that?" He stood and pointed to a section of beach fifty yards away. "That's where she got tangled in the time tear." He took six giant steps away from the ocean and poked a piece of driftwood into the sand. "This is where the time tear will rise late tonight. It shifts a little."

Kip looked from the girl's retreating back to Mikey. "The what?"

"The doorway to my home world. I marked it so you'll know where the time tear will be when it starts to rise. The queen doesn't have a court wizard. And Windy might like the help."

Kip wasn't sure what the little blighter meant. At

the moment it didn't matter. His nagging conscience focused on Windy. The poor girl was an orphan. He had to put things right.

"Wait for us by the towel, right? I need to speak with your sister."

"She might not want to talk to you."

Who wouldn't want to talk with me? Kip signaled to Mikey to stay, then dashed after the long-legged girl. She had a hefty lead. He lowered his head and sprinted to catch up. Despite giving it his all, he still lagged behind by a good ten paces. If she didn't stop soon, he'd never reach her. "Wait," he called out.

Windy skimmed to a halt. She spun around, hands on hips. "What do you want?"

Kip hunched over, gasping for breath. "To apologize. Mikey explained about the locket."

"If your mom's still alive, you'll never understand. My mother died when I was nine."

He choked on his own breath. That young? To cover how startled it made him, he coughed a few more times and thumped his chest.

"Do you have asthma?" she asked.

Was that a note of concern in her voice?

The girl frowned. "We didn't run that far."

Maybe not. "Swallowed a bug," he lied. Now that his breathing had returned to normal, Kip straightened. "I'm sorry. Ya know, about your mum. I never meant for my trick to upset you. I pinch watches mostly."

"Who do you think you are? The Artful Dodger?"

"I'm a magician, actually."

"You're a menace." She unclenched her balled fist, exposing her locket. "This was the last present my mother ever gave me."

"I'm truly sorry, Windy."

Her jaw tightened. "That's not my name. I told you, it's Winnie."

"Thought that's what Mikey called you."

"He's allowed." She glared from Kip to the area directly behind him. "Where *is* Mikey?"

"Waiting by the towel."

"He's only six. We can't leave him alone!" Winnie raced back the way they'd come.

Kip sucked in a deep breath of air and hurried after her. He panted, barely keeping up. In the distance, he saw his inner tube and beach towel. As they got closer, he could tell that Mikey's toys were missing. So was Mikey.

Chapter 3

A year ago, when she learned that Maria might become her stepmother, Winnie had felt betrayed. Nobody was allowed to replace her real mom. If that wasn't bad enough, Maria had a son, ending her reign as an only child. How could she still be Dad's number one with all these extra people in the family?

Then she met Mikey, so small, so vulnerable. If anyone needed a warrior's protection, it was that sweet boy. From their first meeting, Mikey had instantly accepted her as his champion. He didn't just trust Winnie—he believed in her. She couldn't help but love him.

Now he was gone. Winnie knew he would be. That's what usually happened whenever she had something too good to be true. She lost it.

Positive thoughts, positive thoughts. She glanced up and down the beach, hoping to spot him. Her little brother had to be on land. *Please, God, don't let Mikey be in the water.*

But he wouldn't be, would he? He had said bad things were in the sea.

"I told Mikey to stay right there." Kip's Cockney voice sounded shrill.

Her hand tightened around her locket. "Yeah, little kids always do what they're told."

"Windemere!"

Dad's voice shot an electric charge of guilt through her. Not now. Why did he call her now? She had to find her brother first.

"Mikey's gotta be nearby," Kip mumbled.

Dad called again.

Panic gripped her. How was she supposed to hide what she'd done with Dad standing on the porch, watching? "Just a sec," she called back.

"Now!"

Winnie jumped. Dad never shouted.

"Keep looking," she said and jogged to her beach house. She stopped just outside the closed porch door. Dad's penetrating stare blazed at her through his glasses and the screen.

"Uh, Dad? I think we...I think I lost Mikey."

He folded his arms across his chest. "I know you did. Come inside."

Her stomach flopped over. Did that mean she was already too late? "Don't we, I mean, shouldn't we look? I don't think he went far."

"He's with Maria. She took him with her to the store."

Relief splashed over her. Everything was fine after all. She called to Kip, letting him know that Mikey was safe. The boy's narrow face broke into a wide grin. He waved, gathered his things, and loped away.

"Inside." Dad opened the screen door.

His serious tone ended her good feelings. She joined him on the porch, her head bowed.

"Maria was out here, sweeping," he said in a quiet voice. He rarely raised it when he got mad. "She saw you abandon Mikey."

Her head snapped up. She bit her tongue to keep

from shrieking a denial. Kimber, her best friend, had daily screaming matches with her parents. The whole family blurted words so cruel they made her shudder. In Winnie's home, she and her dad knew better. Nobody lived long enough to shout cruel words at them.

With a steady voice she said, "I didn't abandon him."

Dad raised an eyebrow. "You left Mikey alone. Maria's furious and rightfully so. What were you thinking?"

"I was thinking about this." She opened her hand, revealing her gold locket and chain. "That guy, that *Kip*, took it. I didn't even feel it go."

She could still picture his smart-aleck face. What could she do but grab her locket and run? Her mom's picture was inside. Five years, seven months, three weeks, and four days had passed since her mom died. Winnie still missed her.

Dad gently lifted the locket from her palm.

"Open it." When he saw the picture inside, he'd understand. Even though he'd remarried, she knew he missed Mom too.

"I know what's inside." He turned the locket over. " 'Warrior,' " he read from the inscription etched onto the back.

She lowered her eyes. Mom had been the true warrior. Toward the end, as she fought for each breath, she had still been able to keep every promise she made. Even her last words had been the truth. "I'll always love you and Daddy," she'd said. "I'm going to go to sleep now. I'm sorry, but I probably won't wake up."

"I was with her when she had the locket engraved."

Dad's voice intruded on her memory, jerking

Winnie back to the porch.

"She wanted it to say, 'To my little warrior,' but there wasn't enough room."

"That's what she called me." But he already knew.

"We're both warriors," her mom had told her. "Just because I lost my war doesn't mean you should give up the fight. Always remember that." Winnie had promised she would. That was why she lived by her own warrior code.

Dad handed the locket back. "Doesn't a warrior protect her people?"

"Yes." That was rule one of her code.

"Were you protecting Mikey by leaving him alone at the water?"

Anger surged through her, but she refused to let it show. "Mikey would never go in. He won't even dip a toe in unless somebody holds his hand. Everybody knows that."

Bad things are in the sea. She didn't add that part but knew Mikey believed it.

"Not the point, Win. Maria wants to talk to you when she gets back. If she decides to punish you for your lapse, I'll stand by it."

Winnie already hated that she'd accidentally left Mikey alone. Did she really need a nonparent to punish her? She kept that injustice to herself, clenched her teeth, and marched to her room. She didn't slam her door. She didn't even close it. She stood at her mirror to return her locket to its rightful place around her neck. The chain's simple mechanism should have taken two seconds to connect. Her fingers trembled so badly she tried five times before the two ends finally attached.

With her locket resting safely under her T-shirt, she

moved to her window. It overlooked dunes, seagrass, and an expanse of sky. The tall grass, swaying in the breeze, had a calming effect. Her mind drifted toward nothingness. She didn't know how long she stared out the window. Long enough to forget she hadn't closed her door. Long enough for Maria to return.

"Clive sent you to your room?" Her voice sounded impressed.

Winnie twisted around. Her stepmother stood in the open doorway.

Be civil. For Dad. "Come on in."

Maria entered, carrying an oversized, individually wrapped chocolate chip cookie. She held it out. "Compliments of Mikey. He said you needed this to, and I'm quoting here, 'build up your strength.' "

Chocolate chip cookies were Winnie's weakness, especially the big, soft, gooey kind. She leaned forward, accepting it. "Thanks." She unwrapped it. "I didn't really do anything wrong." She took a bite.

Maria's dark eyes flared. "It could've been disastrous. Can't you see that?"

Winnie didn't want to see it. She wanted to be right. At the same time, she didn't want to give the intruder any parental ideas, like grounding her. She kept her mouth shut, except to take another bite of that delectable cookie. The chocolate chips melted on her tongue. At least her mouth felt happy.

To stall for time to answer, she pointed at her chewing mouth. She hoped her stepmother recognized the universal sign for *I'd love to respond, but it's rude to speak with my mouth full*.

Maria put a hand on her hip and waited.

Winnie kept chewing. "This is so good. Seriously."

She took one more big bite.

"For what it's worth, Mikey doesn't think I should be angry about what happened."

Good ole Mikey.

"He insisted he knew I was watching, which made him safe all along. He also said someone stole your mother?"

"Somebody did, but I got her back." She set the cookie on her bureau, wiped her hands on her shorts, then pulled her locket from under her shirt. "My mom's picture. Want to see it?"

Her stepmother agreed, which surprised her. She thought she'd run away from it.

Maria examined the smiling photo for a full minute. "Remember how you felt when you thought your locket was gone?"

She nodded and gave Mom's photo one last loving look before closing the locket again.

"Then you know how I felt when I saw you leave Mikey by himself," Maria said gently.

Winnie's shoulders slumped. She did know. "It'll never happen again. I promise."

Maria peered deeply into her eyes. "Can I trust you to take good care of him if I go to dinner with your father tonight?"

Winnie gave a solemn nod. "I took babysitter training at the Y last summer." Her promise, as a warrior, to protect Mikey went unsaid.

"Good." Maria swept out of the room.

Three hours later, Maria, dressed for the night out and surrounded by a cloud of sweet perfume, called to Mikey in a high-pitched voice, "Kiss-kiss."

Mikey stopped playing with his "people" long

enough for a hug. He returned to his game with red lipstick smudging his cheek.

Dad leaned over Winnie. "I know you'll be responsible." He kissed the top of her head, then followed Maria out.

After a mac and cheese dinner with Mikey, Winnie lay sprawled across the love seat with a bag of microwaved popcorn and a paperback by Agatha Christie. Her little brother sat on the floor, mumbling softly to his toys.

The sound of rain spattering on the roof gave the beach house a cozy feel. An unexpected clap of thunder made her jump. She looked at Mikey who peered warily at the ceiling.

"Kip is camping on the beach."

"Is that what he told you?"

He shook his head. "I'm fey."

She puffed out a breath of air. "Why do you say stuff like that? You don't even know what fey means."

He gave her a superior look. "Otherworldly."

Lightning briefly lit the night sky. Another crack of thunder followed.

"I hope nothing bad happens to him."

She snorted. "It won't."

Okay, secretly, she thought Kip's Cockney voice sounded cute. It also reminded her of a street urchin from the Dickens novel she'd read in English class.

Heavier rain pummeled the roof.

"Since he's magic," Mikey said, "when he goes through the time tear…"

She closed her book. "I hate ruining it for you, but nobody's magic, especially Kip. And time tears are only part of your game."

He dropped his toys into his bag. "Remember that wall you hit this morning? That was a doorway to my world."

"You're forgetting that I stayed right here."

"That's because portals rise with the sun. It couldn't transport you because most of it was above you." He carried his bag to the love seat.

Winnie sat up to make room. "Whatever." She reopened her book.

"Bunches of worlds exist next to each other, like a layer cake on its side."

"First bedspreads, now layer cakes. Maria's right. You have a wild imagination."

"Instead," he said over the loud rain, "instead of calling it Frama-12, you could call my world Layer-12 or Frame-12. Your world is Frame-11. We're side by side. That's why Maggenta sent me here."

She pretended to read.

"Windy. It was never a game. It was practice. My true name is General Takka."

"Buddy, you were born right here like everybody else."

"My *essence* traveled here, not my form." He slapped his chest. "I came to this world to grow inside the vessel we call Mikey."

"Is this a new twist to the game?"

He folded his arms and scowled.

Outside, a cloud dumped a vat of water over the roof. A minute later, the rain eased up. His annoyance seemed to lessen with it. He let out a deep breath. "Ages ago, one of your species visited Frama-12."

She rolled her eyes. "Do tell."

"He wasn't just powerful. He was craftier than

anyone in my world. The council believes our only hope to defeat the lurkin is to have someone just like him lead our army. Except someone not as deceitful."

Thunder grumbled in the distance as the storm rolled away.

"Gotta give you props, bud. You're a storytelling genius."

He shook his head. "It's not a story. It's a prophecy. The lurkin plan to march through a time tear to invade this world. Since I was already a general, I volunteered to grow inside a human vessel and learn your wily ways."

She laughed. "Wily ways? I love it!"

"I was supposed to return to my world in human form and lead Queen Bogen's army against the lurkin. But this form"—he pointed at himself—"was supposed to be older."

She couldn't help grinning. "Most little kids want to get older so they can drive. You're the only person I know who wants to grow up for a game. And speaking of your game, I have nightmares about your *lurkin* attacking the castle."

He gaped at her. "The lurkin attacked the castle?"

"I only *dreamed* they did because that's the only game we ever play together."

"Tell me about your dream. Please, please?" He pressed his hands together, like a typical little kid eager for a story.

She grabbed a handful of popcorn. "It starts off in a castle, and a tiny bald jester starts singing." She popped the puffy kernels into her mouth.

He dipped his hand in the popcorn bag. "Sounds like Polo."

28

She almost choked. "How'd you know his name? And don't say you're fey again."

"You're not having nightmares. I think your mind has been traveling to Frama-12 in your sleep. Time is different over there." He still looked like Mikey, but his voice deepened. "Since your mind has already been to Frama-12, you'll know where you are when your body goes there."

"How am I getting there? You just said the time tear is in the sky."

"It'll rise out of the ground one more time before it mends."

She didn't want to believe, but that wall she'd hit seemed real. So did the lurkin dreams. *Get serious. It's just a game.*

No matter how hard she tried, she couldn't stop wondering. One question stayed with her all the way to cookies and milk time. She had to ask. "Are lurkin giant spiders?"

Mikey/Takka shrugged. "I only know they'll attack when the sea is smooth."

"And I agreed to fight them." Of course, back when she made that promise, she'd believed they were playing a game.

He bobbed his head up and down. " 'Cause you're a warrior."

She couldn't argue that. What if her recurring dream really was a premonition? "In my dream I saw little knights in armor."

"I told you the mel-yew were small."

"If that's supposed to be your army, they're too weak. I knocked one over with a push."

"You have to convince the queen to strengthen her

forces. Just like we played."

"But in our games, I always played the queen."

He smiled. "You were a really good queen. You'll make an even better general."

She looked away. What if he truly was an alien from another world trapped inside a kid's body? No wonder he'd made that weird comment about cosmic bedspreads.

Mikey lifted his glass of milk. Somewhere between taking a swallow and returning the glass to the table, he became a little boy again. His milk mustache definitely made him seem more kid than general. Winnie still shivered. The kid might be right.

Chapter 4

Over dinner, Kip's dad announced, "Your mom called."

Kip nodded and chewed. And chewed. Broccoli, the veg *du jour,* was half raw.

"Not that I'm sending you away or anything, but we were both thinking you might do better staying with her after we get back from vacation."

No surprise there. His parents had been periodically swapping custody for the past three years. Spending extra time in a home with fresh laundry, a tidy house, and properly cooked meals definitely had its appeal. "All right."

"Once you settle in at Mom's, you can start work."

The undercooked broccoli almost made a U-turn. "Work?"

"If you want to buy a car the instant you turn sixteen, you'll need money."

"But that's a full year away."

"Then it's time to start saving. Mom got you a job as a bag boy at Tully's. Isn't that great?"

Great? Had his father no compassion? "I can't start a job now. We had a death in the family. I need time to soul-search."

Dad's smile dissolved into a frown. "It was a rabbit. You can soul-search while you're putting milk and bread into grocery bags."

Kip sprang to his feet. "He wasn't just a rabbit. He was me best mate."

Dad pointed his fork at him. "That's the other thing, Son. Your mom and I have put up with that silly accent long enough. It's time you started using your real voice again."

Those words, not quite an order, not quite a threat, struck Kip with more force than an unexpected blow to the stomach. He turned away so Dad wouldn't see how much it hurt. "I'd like to be excused now. I'm camping out tonight." He spoke in the only voice he knew how to use.

"It's going to rain," Dad called after him.

Kip finished packing as the last of the sun vanished behind a heavy gray sky. He smelled dampness in the air, but a little rain never hurt anyone. Especially when one owned a new tent. He hefted his gear over his shoulder and marched straight to the piece of driftwood still standing upright in the sand.

Too bad Mikey's reason for putting it there had been make-believe. If anyone needed to escape to another world, it was Kip. How could his parents be so heartless? Hiring out their only son as a bag boy. And they both wanted him to change how he talked? Why couldn't they accept him for who he was?

He yanked the driftwood from the sand and unfolded his tent where the stick had been. The tent quickly took shape. After pushing in the last peg, he crawled inside. Sleeping bag and pj's here, battery-powered lantern there, snacks and gym bag full of magic props close at hand. By the time the first raindrop spat upon his nylon roof, he was nestled inside, practicing his one-handed cut with a deck of cards.

A gust of wind slapped against one wall. Rain spattered. Thunder boomed. Maybe the wind would scoop up his tent and blow him into another world. His parents would feel sorry then. Bag boy. It wasn't right.

The storm had nearly played itself out by the time he flicked off the lantern. The soft rain quickly lulled him to sleep.

He dreamed he worked at a circus as a magician. Just as he was about to make his sequin-clad assistant, who looked a lot like Winnie, disappear, a rogue elephant stampeded into the ring. It sat on his chest, squeezing the breath out of him. Kip woke gasping, his head throbbing.

Lying in the dark, he became aware of an unnatural stillness outside. He propped on one elbow, cocked his head, and gave a listen. Silence. The rain had stopped, so why couldn't he hear the crash of moving surf?

He tried to check the time on his mobile phone, but the screen stayed black. "I just charged this," he muttered. A clacking noise distracted him. It sounded like metal boots marching toward his shelter. The sound stopped just outside. Light spilled over the outer walls of his tent.

He sat upright, heart revving. He fumbled into his trousers, pulling them over his pajama shorts. These weren't robbers, were they? On a private beach?

"Come out slowly." The voice sounded as though it spoke from inside a tin can.

He reached for the tent's zipper with a trembling hand. He'd rather face them head-on than let them attack the tent while he was still inside.

He poked out his head. "I haven't any cash on—"

He cut himself off and gaped at the dark stone walls that surrounded him. His nostrils filled with the smell of moss and rising damp. Where'd the beach go? And who were these little blighters in metal suits of armor? Some held flaming torches while others pointed spears at him.

They outnumbered him seven to one. He unfolded himself from his tent. The tallest soldier barely reached his elbow. He could probably take them on. They were nothing more than a band of miniature men. Minute men! He sucked in a breath of moldy air and choked. Either Mikey had been right about the portal, or Kip was having an incredibly realistic dream.

"How did you get in here?" A knight's reedy voice echoed against his metal helmet.

Kip slowly rubbed a hand through the rumpled curls at the back of his head. "Blimey." This felt like no dream he'd ever had. Louder he said, "I believe it was a time tear? If you're familiar with the term."

The tiny men turned, looking from one to another.

The leader spun back toward him. "Were you sent by General Takka?"

"Yes." If that's what they wanted, then he jolly well was. Dream or not, he'd play it out.

"You've come to stop the lurkin, then?" asked the leader.

"That would be me." Any job was better than bag boy.

The knights leaped as one and let out a muffled cheer.

"Then you must meet with our queen," said the leader.

"My thought exactly. Is it all right if I get a few things first?"

34

Without waiting for an answer, he ducked into his tent, pocketed a few magic props, and slid back out.

He followed the knights through the lower regions of a castle. At least that's what it seemed to be. They led him up a stone staircase along candlelit corridors until they reached an oversized room. Its tapestry-covered walls glowed under bright fluorescent fixtures. Because it had to be a dream, the odd mix of primitive and modern lighting made perfect sense.

"Please be comfortable, General. The Regal and Majestic Queen Bogen shall meet with you shortly."

He stood alone in a room lined with benches and chairs, each covered with plush maroon material. He bounced onto a comfy bench beside a table filled with snacks. He helped himself to a glass of red liquid that tasted strawberry sweet and lemony tart. The cheese and biscuits were superb. Or maybe the fact he hadn't eaten in hours simply made him hungry. Either way, he'd gobbled all the cheese by the time a bugle fanfare sounded outside the door. Kip jumped to attention. She might not be his queen, but he would still pay respect to the little woman.

What entered on springy steps, however, was far from tiny. In fact, it looked to be over seven feet tall. Kip pressed his lips together to keep from gawping at the queen's large, white, webbed feet. Long, muscular legs of dry, warty, white skin shown from beneath a gold-and-purple robe. Her lumpy face had a long, thin mouth and twin pinpricks for nostrils. Two bulging, pink eyes stared from her crowned head. He couldn't say what she was—the result of a scientific experiment gone wrong? She reminded him of a pro wrestler crossed with an albino frog.

He cleared his throat. "Your Majesty?"

"You are an odd-looking creature," the queen said in a pompous voice.

Considering he was the stranger here, he bowed deeply. "Odd, perhaps, but able to recognize great beauty when I behold it, Your Majesty."

A tan frog man bounded into the room. "Queen Bogen! Your Majesty! You should have waited for us! You might have been in danger." Three other giant frogs, walking upright, crammed through the door behind the first one.

"Zyke, you worry too much. This creature is Takka's champion. How rude of me. I haven't even asked your name."

"Kip the Amazing, Your Majesty." He conjured a bouquet of paper flowers and offered them to her.

The queen accepted them with a bow. "These are quite lovely, but they won't protect us from the lurkin, will they?"

"True, Your Majesty. But if I can make things appear—" He pulled four red sponge balls seemingly from the air. "—doesn't it follow that I can also make them disappear?" One by one, he palmed the balls. "I'll do the same with your lurkin."

The queen clapped in delight. "Our dear Takka hasn't sent us a general but a wizard! Master Kip the Amazing, allow us to personally escort you to your laboratory."

A wizard! Now there was a job title a thousand times better than bag boy. *I hope this isn't a dream.*

He followed the queen and her entourage to a laboratory, high in one of the castle's towers. The large round room proved to be drafty, and every object, including the fireplace, lay under a thick coating of dust.

Kip sneezed. Okay, maybe it was only ten times better than bag boy.

"Forgive the condition," the queen said. "We haven't had a wizard in ages. Our servants will tidy up for you. In the meantime, take stock of what's here and give our cook a list of any special ingredients you may require."

The queen and her staff departed, allowing him to inspect his laboratory in private. The tower room held tall, curved shelves crammed with potions and leather-bound books. He picked his way across the room, through broken glass and bird droppings. An antique volume, thicker than any he'd seen at a library, lay open on a table by a little round window with no glass. He blew the dust away to reveal a script fancier than hieroglyphics, more baffling than Hebrew.

Unable to make sense of it, he turned away and pulled a random book from the nearest shelf. He eased into a dusty overstuffed chair and opened it. Each page offered colorful illustrations on how to hold the arms while reciting incantations. He puzzled over a picture of a rodent turning into what appeared to be a cabbage. All it took was a wave of a wand. Were these mere illusions or real magic?

He flipped through more pages, growing frustrated. "What's it all mean?"

"You need a familiar," a voice chirped.

Kip snapped his head toward the sound. A black bird, the size of a raven with a short, curved, orange beak, stared back from its perch on the sill of a second open window.

He gaped at the bird. "Did you just say something?"

"I just said you need a familiar."

In a world where the queen was a frog, why shouldn't the birds speak?

"Aren't familiars usually cats?"

The bird glided to the arm of his chair. "I am a kak."

"Actually, what I said—"

"Kaks have been wizards' familiars since the beginning of time," the bird chattered. "Of late we've had no wizards. I blame Maggenta. You are the new court wizard, are you not?"

"Just now got the title," he said with pride.

"Then we shall become great friends. Bauble!" The bird hopped onto his shoulder and nipped at the gold hoop in his left earlobe.

"Oi!" He batted the bird away. "Leave it be. It's attached to me ear."

"It shines so."

"You can't have it."

The bird fluttered back to the chair arm. "Bad as the cook, you are," it muttered. " 'Leave it be, Willum,' he says to me. 'Don't step in the flour, Willum. Stop eating that pie, Willum!' "

"Your name's Willum, then?"

The bird cocked his head and stared up at him with one yellow eye.

"Right. Stupid question. I'm Kip, by the way."

Willum shook his shiny black head. "No, no, no. You need a proper wizard's name. I've always fancied the name Blundoon."

"Sorry, but it's Kip. Kip the Amazing."

"Oh, Kip *the Amazing*," Willum said with a head bob. "That's all right, then, as long as you've got the amazing bit at the back. What amazing things are you studying in that book?"

"Nothing. I can't read it."

"Even after you drank the enlightenment potion?" Willum toddled from one end of the chair arm to the other. "It must be a book of confusion."

Kip eased the book closed, intrigued. "Enlightenment potion?"

"Was it stolen?" The bird flitted to a high shelf. "No, here it is." He tipped over a vial with his beak. Kip leaped up, catching it before it reached the floor. He pulled out the cork stopper. It smelled like black licorice.

"You're sure this is an actual enlightenment potion and not poison?"

"Who would put poison in an enlightenment potion bottle?"

Kip's curiosity allowed him to accept the bird's logic. A tiny drop couldn't do any harm, surely. He put a dab of the clear liquid on his finger and touched it to his tongue. It tasted spicy hot. When the burning dissipated, his mind sizzled with clarity. He raced back to his book and flipped to a middle page.

The words seemed to flow directly into his subconscious. *At no time should you attempt this incantation during an electrical storm.*

He turned to the cover and read out loud, "Incantations for the Mischief Maker." He set the book on the floor. "Willum, is there a book on how to make things disappear?"

"I didn't drink the enlightenment potion, did I?"

the bird said indignantly. "Read the titles. What manner of wizard are you anyway?"

"A new one."

The bird let out a squawk. "What? An apprentice without a master?"

"Don't be cheeky. I have powers." To demonstrate, he made a quarter appear.

"Bauble!"

He tossed it into the air. The bird caught it in his beak and flew out the window.

"Oi! I thought you were me familiar."

He probably didn't need one just now anyway. The ability to read the books more than made up for his familiar's lack of loyalty.

He skimmed more titles, eager to begin. He was going to like it here. A lot.

Chapter 5

Usually, a Frama-12 dream didn't come two nights in a row. Yet here she stood in the castle, foot impatiently tapping during Polo's boring ballad. This time, she simply hollered, "Spiders are coming!"

"That's one way of doing it," Mom's amused voice spoke from nearby.

Winnie pivoted toward her. "You're back! And you're in my dream!"

Her smiling mother appeared on her left. "I'm in a lot of your dreams."

"Yeah, but when you are, I don't know I'm dreaming. This time I do."

The castle's ornately carved door behind them crashed open. Dozens of spiders, over twice Winnie's height, lumbered inside. Before they completely surrounded her and her mom, a small hand touched Winnie's shoulder. She jumped awake, disoriented. "What happened?"

"It's time." Mikey shook her arm. "Get dressed."

"Why?" she whispered to an empty room. She let out a sigh and checked her watch. He'd woken her twenty minutes earlier than yesterday. She changed into running clothes. Jogging in the dark might be fun. She carried her sneakers to the kitchen area where Mikey stood in the light of the open refrigerator door. He filled a food-storage bag with fried chicken and dinner rolls.

"What are you doing, bud?"

"Helping you get ready."

She gave a bewildered head shake. Nobody took snacks on a long-distance run. "Whatever." She reached for the orange juice and took two swallows from the carton. The refrigerator light illuminated a pair of round canteens in canvas carriers on the dining table. They hadn't been there last night.

She pointed at them with the juice carton. "Where'd they come from?"

"Mommy used to hike. Fill them with spring water."

She complied. Staying hydrated made better sense than carrying a bag of chicken.

"Get the binoculars from the second drawer. You'll need them too."

"For what? The sun isn't even up yet."

"It's up in Frama-12."

Play along. It's just a game. But was it? A ripple of unease rolled through her. Still, she pulled out the binoculars and draped the long black strap around her neck. She crisscrossed the canteen straps over her shoulders.

"This should last until you reach the castle." He twist-tied the plastic bag of chicken to her belt loop. "The queen will feed you when you get there."

She looked from her supplies to him. "This is just practice, right?"

"What time is it?"

She peered at her watch. "Four-oh-eight. Right? It's practice?"

"We have to leave now."

She clomped down the steps behind him. Her

canteens and binoculars sloshed and clanked all the way. She felt ridiculous following a barefoot kid dressed in yellow choo-choo jammies across the dark beach. At least none of her friends from school saw her.

Mikey led her to a wide column of static electricity, snapping and shimmering. Yesterday's memory of the electric wall sent her skidding to a halt.

"Whoa." She looked it up and down. The column reached from the ground to just above her head.

"In Frama-12 they know me as General Takka." He seemed unfazed by the anomaly. "If anybody questions your authority, just tell them General Takka sent you."

She couldn't pull her gaze from the shimmering thing.

"I know you don't like people bossing you, Windy, but when you get there, try to treat Queen Bogen with respect. Also, water is sacred. Offer a canteen to Her Majesty. Let's see, what else do you need to know? Oh yeah, mel-yew are good. You can trust them. And most important, don't forget the oracle's prediction. *When the sea is smooth, the lurkin will attack.* Are you paying attention? Windemere."

She snapped her head toward the little boy who sounded way too grown-up. "Wait. This is, like, really real? I'm doing this?"

"You're a warrior. It'll be easy for you."

She chewed her lip. Her mom had given her that title because she fought adversity, not giant spiders.

She walked all the way around the glowing column. "No offense, but this looks like it could kill me. I can't help anybody if I'm dead."

"Time tears are safe."

She whipped around to face him. "Are you kidding

me? Last time I hit that thing, it knocked me out for an hour."

"And you woke up again. You'll be fine. Want me to show you?" He stepped toward it.

She grabbed his shoulders and pulled him back. "I'm supposed to protect you. I promised my dad *and* your mom. If anybody goes in, it has to be me."

He let out a despondent sigh. "Nobody would believe that I'm Takka anyway."

She shook out her arms and did a few neck rolls to prepare herself.

"One last thing," he said. "Time is important."

She stretched down, touching her toes. "How long have I got?"

"Less than two months."

She stood upright. "What? School starts in three weeks."

"That's two months in Framan time, not this time. In this world the time tear will mend in about four hours."

"Four hours? What can a warrior do in four hours?"

"You'll be living in *Framan* time."

"Uh-huh," she said doubtfully. "And will this time-tear thing wait till I'm done?"

"No. It moves. When you're ready to return, you'll need the oracle to help you find it."

"And how do I find the oracle?"

"She'll find you. Good luck, General."

"I'll need it." Louder she said, "Where will you be while I'm gone?"

"Waiting right here for your safe return."

"I don't think so, bud. You need to wait inside."

Thankful for a delay, she rested a hand on his shoulder and turned with him toward home.

He dug his heels into the sand. "We both have jobs to do. Mine is to wait. I'm the anchor."

"Little kids, even with generals inside them, can't be outside when it's dark. Especially with this thing glowing on the beach. I promised your mom I'd keep you safe."

"You have to trust that this is right."

"Well, I don't. Maybe we should go back and rethink this. In my dreams I wore a knife."

"Then you'll get one at the castle."

Her insides rattled. This was wrong on so many levels, but if she didn't enter the weird sparkly thing, Mikey might jump in ahead of her. She was a warrior after all. "You have to promise to go back home. I can't do this unless you promise."

"I promise."

Winnie took a deep breath the way she did before jumping off a high dive. She breathed out, inhaled again, and plunged in.

Just like yesterday, the electric web wound tightly around her, stealing her breath. Before she passed out, she saw those emerald eyes again, watching her with that same loving glow. Then she fell into darkness.

****

Déjà vu. That's what Winnie's firing synapses told her during her gradual ascent toward consciousness. She recognized the heat, the warm granules prickling the back of her neck, the grit attached to her elbows and bare calves. Oh yeah, she'd been through all this before. Just like before, her head ached. Hot, bright light seared through her closed eyelids. Sound, however, wasn't the next sense to return. This time her nose woke up first. With a vengeance. She inhaled a stink that could mean only one thing—garbage pickup day. Who knew vacation trash could reek this much? It smelled worse than sauerkraut stewing in a pot of sweaty hiking boots and dead skunks. It was enough to singe the nose hairs. Maybe the sanitation workers were on strike.

Through closed eyes she sensed a shadow blocking the sun. She guessed it was Mikey. Cozy relief flowed through her. It was just a game after all.

She slowly opened her eyes. A palomino pony's flared nostrils snuffled at her chin. That wasn't right. Chincoteague lay hundreds of miles south of Dad's beach house. *I must be dreaming*.

She slowly raised her arm. Her fingers brushed over a velvety nose. She'd never had such a vivid dream before. The pony snorted, spraying droplets of pony snot all over her face. The hoof-steps galloped away. She sat up, wiping her face, eyes wide.

A long swath of vacant gray sand stretched out before her. Gray? When had it turned gray? And where were the joggers? Where was the old man with the floppy hat and his romping dog? The early risers, searching for shells? Something else was missing. The sound of waves splashing against the shore.

Her head pounded with a pain sharp enough to disprove the dream theory.

She stood, turning to her left where the ocean belonged. An expanse of gelatinous green-brown goo had replaced blue-gray water and rolling waves. She gasped, accidentally inhaling that putrid stink. She hacked and sputtered, clenching her eyes shut again. At least now she knew where the icky smell came from.

She turned away, facing not familiar sand dunes and beach houses, but a tangle of palm trees, oversized ferns, and stubby bushes. Where was she? And what had happened to the pony that just slobbered on her?

The rancid breeze stopped blowing from the jellied ocean. Without that overpowering stench, she could think. If this really was Frama-12, why hadn't she landed in the castle? Every dream had begun in a castle. Where was that queen she was supposed to respect? Where was Polo?

A bush straight ahead rustled in the calm air. Winnie gripped the canteen on her right, poised to use it as a weapon.

Fat green leaves parted, revealing a pony's nose. She instantly relaxed her grip. Now she knew where the pony had gone. A second furry head poked from the brush, followed by another and another. Dozens of golden equine faces blinked out at her. A whole herd of them stood behind the bushes.

If something was going to greet her in this weird place, she'd rather have it be horses than an army of giant spiders. She held out her hand and made gentle kissing sounds, hoping to coax them into the open. Slowly, the tallest one edged through the parting leaves. Its coloring reminded her of the palomino she'd ridden in summer camp. But it walked upright on two horse legs. Its long horse neck was attached to a human torso with human shoulders, arms, and hands, all covered in horse hair. Its long tail swished at a cloud of tiny flies.

More horse/man hybrids eased into the open. Soon males and females, ranging in height from Winnie's knees to above her head, surrounded her. Except for their differing sizes, they looked almost identical. Only the white markings on their horse faces varied. But that wasn't the weirdest part. Winnie recognized them from the toys Mikey had made at home.

She shifted from one foot to the other. "Are you, uh, palum by any chance?"

The two-legged horse creatures looked from one to the other. Several turned to their neighbors and mumbled. When the whispering stopped, the tallest one lowered his long neck in a deep bow. "We are indeed palum."

"Whoa, for real? Then this really is Frama-12?"

"Frama-12," said the leader in a clear, precise voice. "Indeed, this is Frama-12."

"Plus, you speak English!"

"Anglish?"

"Maybe I'm speaking Framan. Anyway, I'm here to see your queen? Bogen?"

The herd bowed their heads. "Live long our Mighty Queen."

She remembered Mikey had mentioned something about giving the queen one of her canteens. She patted the one hanging at her left hip. "I brought her a present."

The palum raised their heads.

The leader, who stood horse-head and shoulders above Winnie, stepped into the circle with her. "You come with gifts for our Mighty Queen?"

She nodded. "Is Queen Bogen a palum too?"

The leader's eyes widened. "Our Mighty Queen is a voga. We are but the dust beneath her feet. I am Pall, of the palum. If I may inquire, what are you?"

"I'm a person. And a friend."

"A kind person-friend that brings gifts to our

48

queen."

"Except I don't know where to find her. I think she's expecting me too."

"Indeed, indeed." Pall bowed again. "Our Grand and Mighty Queen always is expecting gifts from friends. She is very well thought of."

"I'm also here to stop the lur—" A gust of odorous wind blew past. She grimaced at the smell, then peered through the palum circle at their ocean.

"You admire our jumping sea."

A pair of palum colts, their heads barely reaching Winnie's knees, raced to the ocean. They laughed as they stumbled and wobbled over the surface. Several yards out, they began to jump on the jellied ocean as if it were a trampoline.

"Some sea. No wonder water is sacred here."

The palum bowed again. "Sacred water," they said in a reverent tone. "Good water, guarded by the Brothers Ky."

"That's what I brought the queen. Sacred water."

"Indeed, indeed," said Pall. "You are an honored friend of our Mighty Queen."

"Live long, our Mighty Queen," the herd chanted.

"I probably should see her now. I'm, ya know, on a timetable."

"Indeed. A runner will direct you to our Mighty Queen's castle straight away."

She nodded absently, still captivated by the gelatinous ocean. It held the two colts' weight even when they did backflips on it.

"How much weight can your jumping sea hold?" she asked.

"You wish to wait for the jumping sea?"

49

Winnie slipped out of the circle. She pressed a toe into the ocean's rubbery edge. It reminded her of dirt-colored gelatin. She took a tentative step, then another. She bobbled forward, cringing with each step. If the gelatin wasn't completely set, she might sink waist-deep into greasy sludge.

"Playmate!" The palum colts bounded toward her. The pliable surface held all three. Mikey's warning suddenly came to mind. *When the sea is smooth, the lurkin will attack.*

Their sea was already smooth. If the lurkin lived on the opposite shore, all they had to do was march across to reach them. Winnie lifted her binoculars and focused on the horizon. Even though the jostling colts blurred her view, an empty expanse lay before her. The invasion hadn't begun. Yet.

A thunder of hooves galloping closer pulled her attention to the beach. Three palum tore through an opening in the brush. "Harrik on the way!" they said. "Harrik on the way!"

"Mind the colts," Pall ordered.

Nostrils flared. Ears pinned back. Hooves stomped the sand. The palum herd huddled closer together. Adults gripped their young. Even the colts by Winnie's side pressed close to her.

"What's a harrik?" she mumbled.

Chapter 6

A ferocious screech filled the air. A ten-foot-long snake shot from the tallest tree. A pair of massive silver wings kept it airborne. The colts at her sides fought for balance on the quivering ocean. The snake soared toward them.

It unhinged its great jaws and zoomed closer. Without thinking, Winnie flailed her arms at it. "Get out!"

The harrik cocked its head, sizing her up with one black eye. As huge as it was, nothing larger than a palum colt would fit in its wide mouth. It broke off its attack and rocketed upward.

"That's right. You just keep going. Nothing for you here."

It let out another fierce wail and flew at her and the colts again. She swung her canteen, smacking the snake over the head with it. "I said, get out!"

The harrik let out a pained shriek and flapped back into the woods.

"Ha!" She pumped her fist. "That's what I'm talkin' about."

For the first time, she felt like an actual warrior.

The colts nuzzled their noses against her. She petted their soft fur and cooed at them. "You're safe now."

"Indeed, indeed!" Pall called from the beach. "You

are a good and true friend to the palum as well as our Mighty Queen!"

Two palum trotted onto the ocean. They lifted Winnie onto their muscular shoulders and carried her back to the beach. They gently returned her to solid ground and to the herd's loud cheers.

"Person-friend." Pall bowed. "What do you name yourself that we may respect and honor you properly?"

"Winnie Harris."

The joyous mood changed in an instant. The palum stamped the ground. Some snorted.

Pall's ears pinned back again. "Harrik?" he snapped. "What new forms do the harriks take now to steal our young?"

"Not harrik, *Harris*. I didn't come to steal your young." She backed away from the advancing herd. "I just saved two of them."

The mob stopped to mumble to each other.

"You have no wings?" asked Pall.

She spread her arms. "Do you see any?"

Pall spoke to the crowd. "Harriks have wings."

The herd bobbed their heads in agreement.

"Have you a tail?"

She turned all the way around for them to see.

"Harriks have tails," Pall said.

"So do palum. Does that make you a harrik?"

Pall swished his blond tail. He turned to the others. "This is no harrik."

She breathed easier.

"We misunderstood. One must be ever on the alert for harriks, which prey on the young and defenseless. Please speak your name again. We have heard wrong."

"Winnie." Last names seemed beyond their grasp.

"Ah, indeed. We must honor our gallant person-friend, Whinny."

Four palum with bulging biceps carried tall drums from behind a row of bushes. They thumped the skins. The others formed a circle, prancing to the lively beat. A few stopped dancing to gather flowers and greens to place at Winnie's feet.

Maybe she really was a warrior. Who else got this kind of attention? Still, she felt weird being the object of their celebration. She smiled to hide her embarrassment. Just standing there, grinning like an idiot, seemed worse, so she joined in. When the palum shook their manes, she shook her hair. She leaped and shimmied, trying to imitate their prancing steps. No one seemed to mind that she swayed to the left when they swayed to the right, or that she bowed when she should have leaped. Their full acceptance made it easy for her to laugh at her mistakes. She even laughed when she lost her footing and landed on her behind.

"I think I'll just watch from down here."

The beat whomped faster. The dancers never lost their fluid motion even as the steps grew more complex. Winnie bobbed her head to the rhythm. She absently untwisted her canteen's cap and took a drink. The drums immediately silenced. The dancing stopped. The palum mumbled gravely again.

"You are an untrue friend who sins against our queen," Pall said.

She eased the canteen from her lips. "Huh?"

The same palum stallions that had lifted her in triumph now yanked her to her feet.

"What did I do?"

"You must see the Brothers Ky." Pall turned to a

third palum. "Inform the brothers we bring a heretic."

With a nod, the palum galloped into the forest.

"Wait a minute!" She tried to shrug away. The hands clutched tighter. "I'm supposed to see the queen."

Pall shook his mane. "Not now. The Brothers Ky will deal with you."

"Will they take me to the queen?"

"They will take you to the dungeon."

"I'm a warrior. I'm supposed to lead your army!"

Pall turned his back on her. The palum guards tugged her onto a wide trail that cut into the woods. She scuffed along the dirt path, dazed by her sudden change in status. How had she sunk so quickly from hero to criminal? Were the horses crazy? If she hoped to help the queen, she had to escape and find the castle on her own.

A sudden downpour filtered through the wide leaves, soaking her and her captors. At least they'd left the smelly ocean behind. Her wet head cooled her mind enough to think clearly.

"Where are we going?" she asked.

"Brothers Ky," said the palum on her right.

"What does it mean? Who are they?"

"Pious mel-yew," said the one on the left.

Maybe it was all right after all. Mel-yew were supposed to be good. At least that's what Mikey had told her before she left. Good people didn't put warriors in dungeons.

After a half-mile hike, Winnie and her captors veered from the main trail to a side path. It eventually opened into a clearing. Five crude huts, made of bamboo or something that looked like bamboo, formed a circle. Their doors faced a small, moss-covered pond. Three short men, wearing suits of plate armor, stood at attention by the water's edge. Winnie's eyes widened. The men reminded her of the little knights from her Frama-12 nightmares.

At the small settlement, a frail, robed figure stepped out of the nearest hut. He pressed his little hands together as if in prayer. The hands looked bony but human. Since the robe's dusty brown hood hid his face, she couldn't be sure what he was.

"Brothers Ky?" spoke the palum on her left.

"Of which I am one," spoke the little robed man. He shuffled closer. The pointed top of his hood came no higher than Winnie's elbow. "A runner informed me you were coming. What manner of heretic do you bring to us today?"

"Great Brother," said the palum on Winnie's right, "it has many names. One is person-friend, though a lie. Another is harrik."

"Harris," she muttered from the corner of her mouth.

"Harris. Another is—" He turned to his companion.

"Whinny," the other added.

"And heretic," the mel-yew monk spat.

She chewed her lower lip. The good guys weren't acting very helpful.

"Where is this sacred water your runner tells me about?" asked Great Brother.

Both palum eased their holds on her arms. Playing along for now, she slid one canteen strap off her shoulder. She handed the container to the monk.

"It was meant as a gift for our Mighty Queen."

"You there, on the left. Fetch Brother Bo and a

crystal," said Great Brother.

The palum trotted around the pond to another hut. He returned with a second robed figure, shorter than the first. The little man carried a crystal goblet.

The monks bowed to each other. Brother Bo held the glass while Great Brother uncapped the canteen and poured. It just looked like water to Winnie, but the monks let out reverent gasps.

"Praised be, praised be," Great Brother said as he closed the canteen.

Both monks dropped to their knees, rocked, and chanted, "Ahh-tee-ooh, ahh-tee-ooh."

The palum guards joined in.

Winnie looked from one to the other. "What's going on?"

Great Brother pointed a quivering finger at her. "Silence, heretic!"

She shrugged. "Just wondered."

The monks rose, leaving her canteen on the ground.

"Brother Bo, call the others. We have a heretic that must be stoned."

She gulped. "You can't do that."

Brother Bo held up the glass of water. "What of this?"

"Ahh-tee-ooh," they murmured respectfully.

Great Brother gently took the glass from him. Once free of it, Brother Bo scurried from hut to hut, calling to his fellow monks.

"I don't think you're allowed to stone me." Winnie straightened her shoulders, hoping to appear braver than she felt. "I'm the warrior General Takka sent to help you fight the lurkin."

"Another lie!" Great Brother said. "The one chosen by the general arrived weeks ago."

She shook her head. "That's impossible."

He held the glass to the sky. "This is the purest of sacred water that I have ever seen," he said in a reverent whisper. "Where did you find it, heretic?"

"For real, I have to see the queen now. That's how the dream goes."

More cloaked monks, short as the other two, emerged from their huts.

"Palum, you are dismissed," Great Brother ordered.

The palum guards trotted back down the trail.

"Brothers," Great Brother called out in a boisterous voice. "Witness the creature that dares drink the sacred water."

The monks crowded closer for a better look at her. She stood in stunned silence.

"I've sentenced it to a stoning."

The mel-yew monks nodded their approval.

"Gather your stones, brothers."

"Wait. I thought you were supposed to be good."

"We are very good. Heretics, on the other hand, are bad. We do what we must, and we do it quite well. You shall die."

"What? No. You have to listen. This was an accident. Where I come from, we drink water whenever we're thirsty. I forgot about the sacred water rule, okay? Can't I just say I'm sorry and promise never to do it again?"

"If it is meant for you to be forgiven, it will be so at the moment of your death."

"Mikey!" she shouted at the sky. "Get me out of this!"

"Your deity cannot help you now."

"He's not a deity. He's my brother." She called his name again.

"Silence, heretic. Die like a brave mel-yew."

"I don't want to die at all. It was only a little spring water."

"The spring!" the brothers cried out in unison.

"You've been to the spring under the castle, have you? You steal sacred water from the queen and then have the audacity to offer it as a gift? Stone this heretic!"

The Brothers Ky cheered. Winnie shivered and hugged herself.

One by one they examined the empty ground at their feet. And one by one their enthusiastic shouts died away.

"Where are your stones, brothers?" demanded their leader.

The monks scuttled through the clearing. To Winnie's relief, their search produced only a handful of pebbles. During a dispute over what new method they might employ to execute their prisoner, an orange bird flew to the edge of the pond for a drink.

That started another uproar. While the monks chased the bird, Winnie snatched her canteen by the strap and charged into the woods. Wet leaves, big as elephant ears, slashed across her body as she ran. She leaped over fallen logs, darted around trees, hurdled prickle bushes. She raced deeper and deeper into the woods. Gradually, the underbrush thickened, forcing her to slow to a brisk walk. She pushed her way through more brush. No one seemed to be following. Sweat rolled down her face in the humid air. She strode on, afraid to stop.

At a small clearing with long, lush grass, she paused to listen. Insects sputtered and hissed from the trees. Feeling safe enough to take a short break, she flopped onto her back in the damp grass at the edge of the clearing. She gazed up at the palm trees and fern-like plants that surrounded her on all sides. Fluffy, gray-blue moss hung from the taller branches. Gradually, her breathing slowed.

A bird, invisible behind the leaves, sang, "Dora-dora-dor-ree!" Another sang, "Figgy-figgy-figgy-no?" An occasional raindrop dripped on the leaves. She heard no shouts or charging noises. After a slow count to one hundred, she concluded she had successfully evaded the little monks.

She glanced around. She had escaped one threat, only to end up alone in an unfamiliar rainforest with no clue how to get out. At least the plastic food storage bag was still attached to her belt loop. What if the food ran out before she found a way out of the woods? What if she starved out here? She shook her head. *Think positive thoughts or no thoughts at all.* That was what her mom used to say.

Mom.

Winnie sniffled, missing her all over again. Then she did something she hadn't done in months. She ignored the outer world and fell into a memory.

Mom, looking frail, had sat in her favorite spot on a comfy chair facing the window. She watched a light snow settling over the pine trees in the backyard. Winnie perched on the chair arm, hoping for a day off from school so she could stay right here.

"Mom," she said slowly. She had a question she

needed to ask even though it embarrassed her to admit her fears to her brave mother. "Are…warriors ever afraid?"

Mom had taken Winnie's hand and kissed it. "All the time," she'd said in a gentle voice. "But fear never stops them from fighting. That's what makes them warriors. They never give up, even when they're afraid."

Winnie blinked away tears. She returned her attention to her foreign surroundings. If warriors never gave up, then she had to stay strong. She breathed deeply and sat up.

She gulped another breath of air, trying to relax. It didn't work completely. After a long drink from her canteen, she felt less scared and more annoyed. Mikey—or was it Takka?—could have done a better job warning her about this weird place. Who would have guessed she could get executed just for drinking water?

"Why didn't you give me an instruction manual?" she muttered as she untied the plastic bag. That first juicy bite of chicken woke her appetite and lifted her spirits. She gnawed the leg to the bone. The warrior inside pulsed with renewed confidence. That lasted until the bushes nearby rustled. Her muscles clenched. She snatched her canteen by the strap, ready to hit the unseen threat.

Chapter 7

The tall grass to her right parted. Winnie held her breath.

A floppy snout appeared. Its nostrils fluttered. A harmless-looking gray animal, resembling a tapir, pushed into the clearing.

She released her nervous energy with a giggle and tossed a piece of dinner roll toward it. The tapir shuffled forward. It briefly sniffed the roll, then scooped it into its mouth with its flexible snout. Three-quarters of a roll later, she had the little guy eating out of her hand.

She petted his fuzzy back. The tapir chewed contentedly.

"Too bad you can't talk. I have a zillion questions about this place."

"Ask away," spoke a chipper little voice.

The tapir darted into the brush. Winnie shot to her feet, clenching her fists. A frail, little, gray-faced humanoid slipped into the clearing. She guessed it was a male child, judging by its hairless head. He wore a crude tunic made from a chestnut-colored pelt. The boy, with his red-rimmed eyes and tiny mouth, looked about as threatening as a party balloon. This little creature had gotten her adrenaline pumping again? She doubled over, laughing at herself.

She straightened up, still grinning. "Who are you,

little man?"

"I am a mel-yew cub," he said in a cocky voice. "Grown-ups call me Cubby."

Did the Brothers Ky look the same under their robes? Just imagining those frail little men trying to hurt anybody sent her into another giggle fit.

The cub scowled at her. "Are you laughing at me?"

"No." She tried to look serious. "I was just thinking about your friends, the Brothers Ky. They wanted to kill me."

"Really?" Cubby's ears pricked up. His little eyes glowed eagerly. "What did you do?"

"Drank water."

His shoulders drooped in disappointment. "You're just a heretic."

"Not even a little bit. That was a huge misunderstanding."

He nodded. "Brothers Ky are always misunderstanding something. Their brains are almost as small as a palum's. At least palum don't eat skitters. Brothers Ky do sometimes."

"What's a skitter?"

"That creature you were just feeding. I wanted one for a pet, but Papa said I was too young. That's why I left home. Now I'm an adventurer."

"That's cool. Me too. Well"—she shrugged—"a warrior, actually. Ever hear of General Takka?"

"Everyone has. He was the greatest warrior in all of Frama-12. It was foretold that he would return in a new form, with a keen mind. He was meant to lead our army, except—"

"Except there was a miscalculation with the timeline," she completed. "That's why I'm here, by the way. I'm the one with the keen mind."

His little eyes widened. "Are you as good a warrior as General Takka?"

"I could beat Takka with one hand tied behind my back. Not that I'd want to," she quickly added. Her little stepbrother was weird but too sweet to hurt.

Cubby bowed. "What does the warrior greater than General Takka call himself?"

"Windemere. Except I'm a girl."

He looked up. "Females can't be warriors. They're too weak."

She lifted him by the front of his tunic until his feet dangled above the ground. "Do I look weak?"

"Forgive me, General, forgive me."

She lowered him to the ground. "You don't want to mess with warriors, especially when Takka sends them in his place." She gave him a gentle pat on the shoulder to show she had no hard feelings.

Cubby gaped at her. "He sent you too?"

"I'm the only one."

"There's another," said the mel-yew child. "When Takka couldn't fulfill the prophecy, he sent a wizard to make all the lurkin disappear."

"Hold up. If somebody's going around saying Takka sent him, he's lying. I know definitely that the only person Takka sent through the time tear was me."

He gasped. "Could this wizard be a lurkin spy?"

She spread her arms, indicating her foreign surroundings. "In this place anything's possible. If there is a spy, we need to warn Queen Bogen. Do you know the way to her castle?"

He straightened to attention. "Yes, General. Permission to join your army, sir?"

He looked much too small to be a soldier, but Winnie didn't want to hurt his feelings. "Actually, what I need most is an advisor who can keep me updated on all the Frama-12 bylaws and stuff. Would you be interested in the job?"

The cub bowed his head and scuffed at the ground. She recognized the disappointment in his pale gray face.

"It's a super important job."

He looked up. "Then I accept the position."

"Thanks. First order of business. Can you guide us to the castle without running into anybody who thinks I'm a heretic?"

"Oh yes, General. The Brothers Ky probably ordered the palum to find you, and they'll never look for you out here. Palum think the only way to cross the woods is by using the path."

"Not to be mean or anything, but are the palum, like, stupid?"

"The palum do much for us, but they are rather simple. This way, General."

The two marched from the clearing into the dense forest. At first, Winnie felt confident, having a guide. The woods seemed harmless enough with birds twittering and leaves rustling gently in the breeze. Then an eerie howl sounded in the distance.

She almost stumbled. "Are we, ya know, safe out here?"

"Safe from the palum but not from the snaps."

"What are they?"

"Creatures with big teeth and even bigger appetites."

They continued on through the humid forest in

silence. A green harrik glided by overhead but ignored them.

"These snaps," she said in a low voice. "What do they eat?"

"Anything that moves. Unless we kill them first."

"You don't throw stones at them, do you? 'Cause there aren't any out here."

"Our hunting party uses bows and arrows or spears." They pushed deeper into the jungle. "A tracker sneaks ahead and makes bait of himself. If he's fast enough, he leads the snaps onto the path where our hunters wait to ambush it."

"Sounds like a fun way to spend an afternoon," she retorted. "Frama just keeps getting better and better."

They hadn't gone far when Cubby froze. Winnie skidded to a stop to keep from tripping over him.

He blinked up with round eyes. "Snaps' den. I smell it."

All she smelled was damp air.

"We have to be careful," he said in a hushed voice. "And quiet."

Her insides clenched.

"We're lucky the wind is with us. There's a hunting party out today, but I don't know where it is."

The two crept forward, careful not to break any twigs underfoot.

"Snaps give a warning before they attack. They click their teeth. If you hear chattering teeth, you'll only have time to make peace with your maker before you die."

"Takka never told me that," she said in a harsh whisper.

He moved forward. She followed, edging carefully

through the forest.

He pointed to the mouth of a cave on their right. "Snaps' lair."

She willed her shaky legs to keep moving. After they'd passed the cave, leaving it hidden behind a field of boulders the size of garden sheds, she allowed herself the luxury of one deep breath.

The forest went still. The breeze stopped. Even the birds quit singing. A sudden clatter ripped through the silence. It sounded like an over-caffeinated woodpecker attacking a steel tree.

Cubby yelled, "Run!" and bolted.

Winnie burst after him, charging through low-hanging leaves.

A primal squeal pierced the humid air from behind.

She peeked over her shoulder. Between the trees a T-Rex-type creature with a chestnut-colored hide tramped into view. Its pointed yellow teeth clenched around a wriggling skitter.

"That's my tapir!" she cried out.

"Run for the path!"

She dashed after him. With a final burst of energy, she plowed through the leafy brush, sprawling on hands and knees onto a dirt road. When she looked up, a tribe of mel-yew, dressed in leather armor, faced her. Each held a cocked bow. A dozen arrows were aimed at her head.

"Move!" Cubby shouted. "They're after the snaps."

She slithered from the line of fire.

The snaps bounded onto the path. She ducked behind a thick tree and watched. Mel-yew hunters shouted a battle cry and pelted the monster with arrows. Most of them bounced off its thick skin. Its roar echoed through the forest. Hunters with larger spears stepped in, piercing its hide. The snaps bellowed. Thick, red-brown blood spurted from its wounds. Its long tail thrashed, knocking over three hunters. The last thing it bit, before its massive head crashed to the ground, was air.

Dozens of cheering hunters rolled the slain beast onto a large wooden cart. Four palum, their arm muscles bulging, pulled it forward.

"Freeden!" one of the hunters shouted.

Cubby scampered into the hunter's open arms. "Papa, we brought you the snaps!"

"We might not have been on the path to save you. You could have been killed."

"But you were. And look who I found!" Cubby clasped Winnie's hand and pulled her from behind the tree.

"You've done well, Son. A palum scout warned us about this heretic."

"Papa, this is the warrior the oracle promised."

His father glared. "The oracle promised a champion. Broon! Amado!"

Two mel-yew men shouldered their weapons and stepped forward.

"Guard this prisoner," Cubby's father ordered.

"Papa, General Windemere is a warrior even greater than General Takka!"

"Not another word. You're in enough trouble as it is. You know you're not to stray from the path."

Cubby shuffled beside the snaps cart, bald head bowed.

"I think I can explain," Winnie said.

"Speak again, and it's an arrow in your throat," a

guard snarled.

After witnessing what they'd done to a dinosaur, she didn't dare argue. She marched silently between her captors. Could anything else go wrong today?

Chapter 8

Frama-12's new wizard didn't want to lose faith, but hardly any of his incantations worked the way they were supposed to. Just the other day he had very carefully enunciated, "Dray-la-da-*la*-da-la," to levitate a candle. Instead, he temporarily put his familiar into a deeply suggestive state. The failure had one positive effect. Kip had mastered the convincement spell.

In his tower laboratory, he attempted the vanishing spell daily. It involved a combination of vowel sounds that he hadn't quite wrapped his tongue round. So far today, he'd only given his bunny-eared subject the hiccups. On the next go, it mutated into a long-eared pillow. He blurted the undo spell, snapping the hopper back to its original shape. Kip puffed in exasperation.

"You're not saying it properly," Willum squawked.

Kip glared at the black bird. "If you don't want me to turn you into a pillow, start giving me positive suggestions."

Willum swooped across the room and lit on Kip's left shoulder. "Here's a positive suggestion. Hoppers make delicious meat pies."

Before he could begin his fiftieth attempt, a rap at his door stopped him.

"What now?"

"The queen wishes to speak with you in her meeting chamber, Master Wizard," spoke a voice from outside the lab. "And, Master Wizard? Her Royal Majesty also requests that you bring your packet of magic cards."

Kip sighed. Another study session interrupted. He never should have taught her to play blackjack. The fact that he always won had yet to dampen her enthusiasm for the game. Not even her councilmen noticed that he used a marked deck.

"On my way." Maybe the distraction would clear his mind.

He entered the meeting chamber where the queen sat in her elaborately carved chair at the head of a felt-topped table. Her four-member council sat two to a side. Kip moved to the plain wooden stool at the other end of the table from the queen.

"Your Majesty. Gentlemen," he greeted with a deep bow and took his seat.

Midway through the first round, a voga messenger entered. "Your Majesty, a heretic has been captured this morning during a snaps hunt."

The queen studied her cards. "And what of the snaps?" she asked absently. "Did the hunters capture one of those as well? I don't suppose heretics are a part of the hunters' diet?"

"It is my understanding, Your Majesty, that the hunting party was successful. Apparently, the snaps followed the heretic onto the path where the hunters stood."

"Thank you for your report. Carry on. We are in the midst of a serious consultation."

"As you command." The messenger strode to the door, then turned back. "Your Highness, the hunters wish to know what should be done with their prisoner."

Zyke, the councilman on Queen Bogen's right, leaned toward her and whispered loud enough for Kip to overhear, "Heretics must be dealt with, Your Majesty. Mustn't upset the Brothers Ky, must we?"

The queen laid down her cards. "Very well. This session will have to wait. Master Wizard, accompany us to the throne room and observe our interrogation of the prisoner."

Kip grinned. He loved the queen's throne room. It looked like a golden auditorium. The entertainment, though a bit odd, was always good for a laugh.

"We will call upon your services should we decide to vanish the prisoner."

He stopped smiling. Vanish the prisoner? "Your Majesty, I don't think—"

"You mustn't bring attention to yourself. Remain hidden unless called forth."

She glided from the room, followed by her councilmen and then Kip.

The cavernous main hall's deep silence was broken only by the slap of his sneakers on the polished marble floor. Despite what might be coming, the surrounding splendor lifted his mood. He'd visited dozens of castles in England, but none stole his breath the way this one did. Hundreds of golden candles glowed from crystal chandeliers. Plush tapestries covered the walls. Each one depicted a scene from vogan history.

He especially liked the tapestry that showed a small figure, flying high above the castle, its shoulders clasped in the talons of a regal gray bird. When he asked about it, his guide had explained that was how guards flew on patrol. It made Kip appreciate Framan ingenuity. They didn't have cars or jets, but that didn't stop them from moving swiftly from one place to another.

Currently, only candles set into the golden walls lit the throne room. The castle generated its own electricity, but the queen preferred candlelight until showtime.

Kip eased into a dark corner. He wasn't too keen for her to learn he hadn't yet mastered the vanishing spell. If he stood quietly enough, the queen might forget he was there.

In the darkness, he heard more than saw the audience members settle into their seats. A spotlight snapped on, bathing the low stage at the front in dazzling light. Polo, the court's mel-yew jester, pranced to the stage on spindly legs, the light reflecting off his bald head.

"How many palum does it take to open the front door?" he said in a reedy voice. "One to lift the latch and five million to push the castle!"

The audience laughed heartily.

"Ever want to make a harrik go crazy? Hide in the bushes and go like this—" Polo let out a high-pitched whinny. "They think it's lunch." He flapped his arms, imitating a winged harrik. "They're looking for a colt in distress, and all they see are bushes. Makes 'em crazy!"

The audience hooted and applauded.

From Kip's experience, Polo's comedy act followed the same format. He offered silly examples of how the palum were strong yet stupid. He joked that mel-yew were smart yet weak. Polo always ended the set by praising the frog-like vogan for being both strong and smart.

Three-quarters of the way through the act, a pair of

mel-yew buglers entered the back of the room and played a fanfare. The spotlight swung toward them, sending blazing light over their golden bugles. As the last note echoed off the walls, a knight in shiny armor stepped between the musicians. "Your Royal Highness, the heretic has arrived."

"Send it forth," Queen Bogen said in her deep voice.

The spotlight splashed its brightness into the eyes of the tall, willowy prisoner. Kip's mouth dropped open. Winnie? How had she gotten here?

Two mel-yew knights in armor nudged her forward. She marched down the blue, plush carpet toward the throne with her head held high.

"Show respect for your queen." The guards poked the backs of her knees with the blunt ends of their spears. Winnie fell forward into a kneeling position. Slowly, she raised her head. She stared open-mouthed at the queen. Kip imagined he'd looked just as surprised the first time he laid eyes on the region's monarch.

The queen cocked her head and scrutinized Winnie. "What's the matter with it? Why is its mouth gaping so?"

"You're...you're a big white toad," Winnie blurted.

Kip clapped a hand over his forehead. Had the girl no diplomacy? Whoever heard of speaking to royalty like that? Besides, the queen was clearly a big white frog.

Queen Bogen blinked from Winnie to the guards. "What did it say?"

One of her guards stepped forward. "Your Royal Highness, it..." He cleared his throat. "Begging the

73

queen's royal pardon, it called you a white toad."

"Why should it do that?"

The guard turned to Winnie. "Her Grand Majesty, Queen Bogen, wishes to know why you referred to Her Royal Eminence as a white toad."

Winnie said directly to the queen, "You look like one. And you're all white."

"Your Majesty," said the guard. "It has just made the keen observation that Your Royal Highness is white in hue."

"What did it expect? Green with purple spots? We happen to be an albeeno voga."

"Albino," Winnie corrected.

"Did it just sneeze?" asked the queen.

"No," said Winnie.

Kip shook his head. If she wasn't capable of tact, couldn't she at least keep still? The fool was going to get herself banished. Or worse, the queen might call him forward. If Winnie recognized him, what might the queen think? That he, too, was an adversary? He'd worked too hard to gain her trust to lose it now. He closed his eyes, silently willing the girl to keep her mouth shut.

And of course she didn't. "I was just saying the correct pronunciation is al-*bi*-no."

The queen scowled at the guard. "Did it just address us directly?"

"Surely not, Your Highness," said the guard.

"Sure I did," said Winnie.

The queen's pink eyes bulged. She sputtered and gasped. "Such insolence. Keep it silent, or we shall order both your executions!"

Kip's heart thudded. The queen had never

threatened to kill anybody before. He swiped at the perspiration dampening his upper lip. If only he knew the correct pronunciation to cast an obedience spell on the blighted girl.

The tiny knight whispered something to Winnie.

She glared back. "That is the nuttiest thing I ever heard. Look, Your Majesty." She rose. "I'm supposed to be the general."

"What did it just say?" the queen demanded.

Winnie clicked her heels together and saluted. "General Windemere Harris, reporting for duty, Your Highness!"

The knight looked from Winnie to Queen Bogen. "Your Majesty, it appears to be under the delusion that it's some sort of milit'ry figure."

"Did it call itself Harry? We once knew a voga went by the name Harry. Ruddy boor, Harry was. He's dead, you know," the queen said with a conceited sniff. "Lost him to the hunt."

"I've heard about the hunt," Winnie said.

The queen sniffed again. "Our fame precedes us."

"Do you hunt snaps?"

"Grand Maker, no! Fancy us chasing after snaps. That's mel-yew work, hunting snaps. No, we hunt the hopper, a much more civilized sport."

"Hopper, wags, and glunt," Winnie recited.

Kip raised an eyebrow. How'd she know all that? She'd only just arrived.

Queen Bogen leaned forward. "It seems to know quite a bit about us. Is it a spy?"

"No, Your Majesty. I'm a warrior, here to train your army."

"We believe your assumption was correct, Sir

Knight," the queen said. "This creature is clearly demented."

Winnie frowned. "Does the name General Takka mean anything to you?"

While astonished gasps sounded from the audience, Kip frowned. All this time he'd been playing at knowing the bloke. Winnie spoke the name as if she actually knew who he was.

Queen Bogen turned her head toward the short table occupied by her councilmen. "Zyke, I believe we have a spy before us. Come and assist us with the questioning."

The tan voga walked with a springy step to the queen's throne. He cocked an eye at Winnie. "Interesting garb," he said. "Could you please ask it to explain that rather large medallion, my queen?"

"What, this?" Winnie lifted the binoculars that hung from the strap around her neck.

"When we are present, you will respond to questions addressed by us only!"

"I thought you just said I wasn't allowed to talk to you."

The queen slammed her scepter against the floor. "You've been speaking with us all along, whether we wished it or not. Now that we command it, you address our councilman. Is there no end to your effrontery?"

Kip shook his head, bewildered. He never had trouble communicating with the queen, but then he knew how to behave in a respectful manner. If Winnie had done the same, the pair might be having a friendly chat over tea instead of the absurd interview currently taking place.

"Sorry."

To Kip's ear, she didn't sound the least bit apologetic.

"If we choose to speak beneath us, the least you can do is answer us when we pose a query. Now then, what is that large, rather awkward medallion you wear round your neck?"

Winnie slid the strap over her head and held out the binoculars. "You look through the lenses," she said. "They help you see things that are far away."

"It's a trap, my queen," Zyke spoke into her left tympanum.

"Remove the medallion immediately!" Queen Bogen roared. "The heretic spy is trying to assassinate us!"

Mel-yew knights clattered toward Winnie. They pointed their spears an inch from her throat. Another guard snatched the binoculars. Kip sucked in a breath of air. If only he'd learned the incantation for the "spell of protection." All he could do was silently pray for the blades to come no closer to Winnie.

"Careful," Zyke said. "It could be some sort of exploding device."

The knight stiffened. The royal guests screamed and ducked under their seats. Zyke yanked Queen Bogen behind her throne. Even the guards let go of their spears and dropped to the ground.

Kip breathed relief now that Winnie's neck was no longer in danger. He waited for the outspoken girl to clear up the misunderstanding. She just shook her head and smirked.

Queen Bogen shoved her advisor aside. "Guard, take the medallion away. We refuse to cower behind the furniture all evening."

"I shall have it analyzed, my queen," the knight said in a nervous whisper. He tiptoed from the hall, armor rattling.

The doors closed behind him. The remaining guards returned to their feet. Everyone else came out of hiding.

Queen Bogen resettled onto her cushioned throne and pointed her scepter at Winnie's canteens. "Are those more bombs?"

"Seriously? It's just…oh. Wait. I probably should have told you this first." She held up the canteen on her right. "Takka told me to bring this as a gift, um, for the queen."

The queen straightened. "A gift?"

"Your Highness," said a guard, "the containers hold what the Brothers Ky claim to be water more pure than that of your spring."

"The prisoner just said it was a gift."

"Your Highness," Zyke said in a warning tone. "Mightn't we have it examined first?"

"We'll do just that." Queen Bogen raised her scepter. "Brothers Ky, come witness. Page, bring forward a crystal."

A mel-yew monk rose from the audience and bowed to the queen.

A young gray-brown voga page bounded to the front of the throne room with a crystal goblet in hand. The guards confiscated Winnie's canteens.

The page held the goblet while a guard poured the canteen's spring water into it. The monk immediately knelt and chanted, "Ahh-tee-ooh."

The others in the room whispered eagerly to one another.

The page handed the water-filled glass to the queen. She clasped the long stem with four knobby fingers and held it toward the light. When Queen Bogen raised the glass to her mouth, her subjects shouted in alarm.

"It could be poisoned, Your Highness," Zyke said.

"Impossible. Look at the liquid's clarity." Queen Bogen took a dainty sip, then drained the glass. "As we suspected. Not poisoned at all. We shall have another." She held out the goblet. The knight in charge of Winnie's canteens poured more water into her glass.

"You're welcome," Winnie said. "For the gift. Does this mean I'm not a heretic anymore since you drank it too?"

Queen Bogen paused with the glass partway to her lips. "You are our prisoner. This means you are forbidden to speak without our consent. However, since the question, ignorant though it may be, has already been posed, we shall explain. All water of this realm is guarded and preserved for us alone. And anyone we jolly well choose to share it with."

"That water isn't from your realm," Winnie said. "It's from my home. We're good now, right?"

"One gift cannot even begin to negate your crimes," said the queen.

Winnie chewed her bottom lip.

"Prisoners bore me. Do you have anything else you wish to say before we cast you into the dungeon for all eternity?"

"Your ocean stinks!"

"Now it's a critic," said the queen. "Take it away."

The Brothers Ky bowed. "Begging the pardon of Your Honorable Highness, could our brotherhood torture the heretic? Just for a bit?"

"Granted."

Kip forced his mind still. No one would torture a fellow human on his watch. Once alone with the queen, he'd use his newly discovered convincement spell to set things right.

Winnie's guards yanked her toward the back of the throne room. "Wait, please!" she cried out. "You can't do this. I know something about your wizard."

Kip gulped. He had hidden himself perfectly in the shadows. How'd she know he was here?

"Halt!" Queen Bogen ordered.

Winnie stopped fidgeting. The guards stiffened at her sides.

"What about our wizard?"

"He's an impostor. Takka only sent me."

Kip hissed under his breath. He planned to rescue her, and this was how she repaid him.

"The Brothers Ky shall postpone their torture of this prisoner," the queen decreed. "This is no ordinary spy. Take it to the questioning cell."

"By your command," said the head knight.

After the door banged shut behind them, the queen turned toward Kip's side of the room. "Master Wizard, we wish to have a word with you."

Chapter 9

Winnie's guards marched her to a high-ceilinged, windowless room. She scanned the area for paintings or tapestries, anything that might hide a secret passage to escape. Each of the four cream-colored walls appeared bare. She turned her attention to the furniture. Maybe if she hid well enough, her captors might think she escaped.

A long, narrow table and half a dozen chairs were the only objects in the room. Five plush chairs stood pressed against the far side of the table. A sixth, made of hardwood, stood alone in the middle of the room, facing the comfy ones. It had a tall, straight back. Attached to the rigid arms and legs were pairs of leather straps.

The guards shoved her into the hard seat. Her heart didn't start pounding until two guards gripped her wrists and used the leather straps to tie them to the chair arms. Two other guards tied her ankles to the chair legs.

She tugged at the sturdy straps. "You don't need to do this. I'm on your side."

Wasn't this supposed to be a civilized interrogation? How else could she explain she had come to save them? The guards said nothing.

"You're making a mistake."

The lights winked off. The guards' feet clacked on the floor as they marched out. The door banged shut behind them.

Winnie sat rigidly in the deep darkness. Her pulse boomed in her temples. Was there enough air in here? Before her suffocation fears got out of hand, cool air blew down from an invisible vent. She breathed it in, trying to relax.

A creaky-hinge noise sounded from the blank wall in front of her. Her mouth went dry. She didn't care anymore that a secret passage existed. Who just came in?

Soft footsteps shuffled inside. Through the blood pounding in her ears, she heard the shushing sound of chairs being pulled back. Someone coughed.

Winnie trembled in the dark. A blinding light splashed over her face. She clenched her eyes shut and held her breath.

"The medallion did not explode," an indignant voice spoke from behind the spotlight. It might have belonged to the queen's advisor, Zyke. "What is the purpose of the medallion?" His grumpy voice sounded more curious than threatening.

The muscles in her shoulders loosened a little. She squinted in the direction of Zyke's voice. "They're called binoculars. They magnify things when you put the small ends up to your eyes."

"Pah!" A hard object, presumably the binoculars, banged on the table. "Nothing but rubbish."

"It was designed for people with eyes closer together," she explained.

"An utter waste. How did you expect to assassinate the queen with it?"

"I didn't come to assassinate anybody. I'm here to help."

"By being a heretic?" said a different, more gravelly-sounding voice.

"By being a warrior," she said with more conviction than she felt.

Running away, or even wanting to, was not an option. This was her chance to be an actual warrior. Mikey/Takka had been right about the time tear and Frama-12 being a real place. Winnie had even recognized the throne room from her dreams. That meant her spider nightmare might also come true.

"I came here on Takka's behalf to help save your people from the lurkin."

"Takka sent us a wizard."

She shook her head violently. "He only sent me. That wizard has to be a fake. How many times do I have to tell you?"

"I happen to be a close acquaintance of our Master Wizard," said Zyke, "and I can assure you, the wizard presents himself as a much more believable champion than you do."

"What do you make of the symbols on its frock?" asked a third, baritone voice.

"It probably says something blasphemous," spoke the gravelly voice.

"Answer, spy," Zyke said. "Translate the symbols."

The blue lettering on her dirty white T-shirt glowed harshly in the light. "It says, 'Valaro X2.' "

"I expect Valaro X2 is the code name for vogan," said Baritone.

Winnie scowled into the brightness. "It's the name of a car model."

"Mm hm," said Zyke. "And I suppose car would be

the code name for—"

"It's not a code. My dad co-owns a car dealership with my uncle. Can we stop wasting time and get to the point?"

"It sounds angry," said Gravelly Voice.

"How do you expect me to feel? If we don't do something about the lurkin, they'll trample all over you!"

"Now we're getting somewhere," said Councilman Zyke. "If an invasion is imminent, how shall they proceed?"

"Just like your oracle says, when the sea is smooth."

"You're not telling us anything we don't already know."

"Your sea is solid. The lurkin can march straight across it to your beach."

"I say!" said Baritone. "I believe she's right."

"I am. I tested it. Now do you see why we have to get your army ready for the invasion?"

"We most certainly do," Zyke said. "Fellow councilmen, observe our enemy, the lurkin."

One of the voices called for the guards. "Take this spy immediately to the dungeon."

"What? No!"

Half a dozen armored mel-yew clacked into the room. One guard untied Winnie. Two others clasped her arms in their metal gauntlets. Four more surrounded her.

"I'm not a lurkin spy." She squirmed in their surprisingly strong grip. "I'm human. You need the crafty stuff in my head to defeat the lurkin. Takka said so."

"Enough!" Zyke's voice boomed. "If what you say is true, you will be freed. First, we must consult the oracle. Guards, escort the spy to the dungeon."

"I'm supposed to be your champion."

The mel-yew guards tugged her from the room. The afterimage from the bright light clouded her vision. She blindly stumbled along a corridor that sloped downward.

The stone floor changed to dirt. The sharp clank of metal boots turned to a muted thud. The air grew colder. It also smelled damp and musty. Before her eyes could adjust to the dim glow from hanging lanterns on the walls, they grew farther and farther apart with each turn.

At her prison cell an unexpected shove against the small of her back sent her sprawling onto a hard dirt floor. The harsh sound of metal banging behind her couldn't be good. She heard the decisive click of a key pushing a bolt into place. She scrambled to her feet and groped until she found the locked door. She clutched two cold bars and poked her head through the space between them.

"Hey!"

All she heard were fading footsteps, stomping away.

"How long do I have to stay down here?"

Chilly silence.

She pressed her forehead against one of the bars. This couldn't be happening. People didn't get thrown into dungeons anymore. She rattled the door, hoping to shake it open. The movement caused her snack bag to bump against her upper thigh. At least the guards hadn't confiscated her food. She sighed and opened the bag.

The homey taste of leftover chicken sent a twinge of longing through her. It also reminded her that Mikey had been right. Her food had lasted until she reached the castle. He'd just never said she'd eat it in a cell.

She paced while she ate. What time was it back home? Did anyone miss her yet? Did anyone even know she was missing?

Little skittering-feet noises scraped across the far corner of her cell. A rat? She hurled her chicken bone toward the noise, and it stopped. She poked her head through the bars again. From a distance feet trampled toward her. She stretched her neck for a better view. A soft glow shone from around the corner. It brightened as it came near. Voices broke through the silence.

"Ahh—" *Tramp, tramp.* "—tee-ooh." *Tramp, tramp, tramp.*

Brothers Ky. Winnie let out a groan.

She tucked her head back inside. Maybe if they didn't see her, they'd forget they wanted to torture her. She backed away and bumped into a solid, musty-smelling bundle. Invisible arms clasped around her waist from behind.

Winnie yelped and broke free. She rushed to the door. "Over here! Brothers Ky!" Miniature monks, even with rocks, had to be safer than whatever had grabbed her.

"Ahh—" *Tramp, tramp.* "—tee-ooh." *Tramp, tramp, tramp.*

"Here!"

Several monks scuttled toward her cell. Two held up lanterns.

"Why, it's the heretic," one brother said in a cheerful voice. "Hello and greetings."

"Do you have a key? I need to get out of here."

"A key? Sorry, no."

The rest of the parade broke rank and formed around her cell door.

"Here is the heretic, brothers." The leader sounded like a tour guide.

"Please help me. There's some strange animal in here."

"I shouldn't think so," the leader said with a chuckle in his voice. "Nothing lives down here for very long."

"No, I mean it. Something back there grabbed me." She jabbed her thumb over her shoulder at the shadowy back corner.

The monks waved their lanterns at her cell door. Bands of yellow light washed over an empty, wooden bench attached to the back wall. The chicken bone she'd thrown lay on the floor beneath it.

"You appear to be the only strange animal inside. Perhaps you've had a bit too much vill wine. I hear it makes those of weak character hallucinate."

"I didn't have any wine. And I'm not weak. I'm telling you—"

"Good day, heretic," said the leader. "We shall meet again at the stoning."

The group stepped into formation. "Ahh—" *Tramp, tramp.* "—tee-ooh." *Tramp, tramp, tramp.*

As the light disappeared around another corner, the voices faded. Something rustled from behind her again. She swung around, pressing her back against the door.

"Who's there? I have a knife." She hoped she sounded fierce. Her only "weapon" was a plastic bag attached to her belt loop.

A candle materialized in a knobby hand. A hunched creature dressed in rags and a foot taller than Winnie shuffled forward. Bulging red-purple eyes glowed from a toady face.

"You're a vogan."

"*Voga*," it corrected. "Vogan is plural. I am Maggenta, Sister of Twilight. I am the one they call the oracle."

Winnie's insides pulsed with hope. "You're the one who sends messages to Mikey, I mean Takka. Right? So you know about me?"

The oracle bowed her toad head. "I know very well."

"Finally. You can get me out of this mess."

Maggenta rubbed her warty chin and glanced away.

"Can't you?"

"You've broken quite a few of our laws. Why did you drink the sacred water?" she said in a stern voice. "You were so warned by Takka."

"He didn't say I couldn't drink anything if I got thirsty."

"It was foolish of you to quench your thirst with palum watching. They are very loyal to their queen."

"Their queen is crazier than they are."

"Enough," the oracle said. "While you are here, you must abide by the rules of the realm. If you had shown the proper respect to Queen Bogen the way your wizard has, you wouldn't be in this predicament."

"I've been trying to tell you guys there is no wizard."

"I've recently spoken with Takka. He claims a wizard from your world entered through the same time tear that brought you to us."

"My world doesn't have wizards."

"Takka asserts otherwise. He also informs me you need this." The oracle held out a bony arm. One of Winnie's canteens dangled from her wrist. "I couldn't wrestle the other from the queen. She's taken quite a fancy to your spring water."

"Thanks." Winnie uncapped it and took a long drink.

"Takka was disappointed that you'd been taken prisoner. However, he accepts full responsibility. He should have prepared you better. That helps us little now."

She lowered the canteen, shoulders sagging. "Don't tell me I'm stuck in here forever!"

"We requested a leader, not a prisoner. I'll see to your release."

"Finally. Thank you." She stepped up to the door, eager for the oracle to unlock it with a magical wave. An ear-popping force of wind hit her from behind instead. She spun around. All she faced was darkness.

"Hey! Aren't you supposed to let me out?"

"Your release is forthcoming," said a disembodied voice. "Use this brief time to contemplate on how to show respect for customs and laws of the land."

Winnie's back stiffened. "I respect customs, but come on. I can't drink water?"

"There is sufficient fluid in our food and prepared beverages. The water here is not safe for your consumption. This is no longer about water. I worry your stubbornness could lead to your downfall."

Winnie snorted. "I'm not stubborn. I'm just honest. That's what warriors are."

"You are a warrior with a queen now. That means you must take direction."

"If I promise to obey her, will you let me out now?"

"Patience," said the voice.

She sighed. "Wait. You said you spoke to Takka. Could I talk to him?"

After a long silence, the voice said, "To do so, you must first take a seat."

She frowned. "I'm a warrior. I can talk standing up."

"You misunderstood. To communicate between worlds, you must enter a sleep-like state."

"How was I supposed to know that?" she muttered, fumbling in the dark toward the bench. She'd barely sat on it when a wave of calm rolled over her. A moment later the cell dissolved, and she stood in an open field of long, amber grass.

"Mikey? Takka?"

A cyclone, no taller than she was, swirled toward her.

"Why did you not heed my words?" demanded a deep voice from inside the mini tornado.

She folded her arms. "Mikey, if that's you, quit the theatrics."

The whirlwind morphed into the little boy. "How'd you know it was me?"

"Lucky guess. By the way, you never told me not to drink the water."

"I said it was sacred. That means don't drink it."

"The queen drinks it. What about that?"

He gave her an indulgent smile. "She's the queen."

Winnie let the topic drop. "So you probably heard

I'm kind of in a dungeon."

"The oracle fixed that. Once you're out, remember, Queen Bogen won't trust you to lead her army if she doesn't like you. Try to be more polite."

She could be polite, but leading an army? She hadn't given a lot of thought to what that would involve. "I might not know exactly how to do that." What did she know about war? She'd gotten a C- in History.

"Humans are more resourceful than my people. That's why you're there in my place."

Her insides pulsed with uncertainty. What if she wasn't resourceful enough?

"Windy. You're the bravest warrior I know."

She didn't feel brave. She didn't feel like a warrior anymore either. Mikey and the field vanished. Winnie woke in her cell to the sound of multiple feet shushing toward her door. The bolt slid back. She jumped up just as the door opened.

She stepped out to freedom and four guards carrying lanterns instead of spears. A fifth person, dressed in shorts and a T-shirt and towering above the others, accompanied them.

"Kip? What are you doing here?"

He winked. "The queen's ready to speak with you again."

Chapter 10

The guards and a smiling Kip led Winnie back to the interrogation room. This time soft overhead lights replaced the blinding spotlight. The guards directed her to sit in the wooden chair again. At least this time, they didn't strap her in.

Part of the wall, which appeared solid, opened inward. Four man-sized toads entered through the secret door. They sat at the table facing her. Queen Bogen entered last, settling her toad-shaped bottom into the fanciest seat between three toad advisors and Kip.

Ordinarily, facing a bunch of toad people would have unnerved Winnie. Seeing Kip with them, though, turned the situation from scary to annoying. She still hadn't forgiven him for the stolen-locket incident. Everything about him bugged her. From the gold hoop, glistening in his left earlobe, to the way his hair, the color of an undercooked waffle, curled up so naturally. Even his long lashes got on her nerves.

"Your Majesty," said the tan toad man directly on the queen's right. "Are you satisfactorily convinced this creature is not a lurkin spy?"

Queen Bogen inclined her head. "Master Wizard, further allay Zyke's fears."

Kip leaped up. "I would be honored, Your Majesty."

Winnie just shook her head. How could he act so

nonchalantly in this weird world? He almost looked like he fit in.

"This particular wand," he said, as one materialized in his right hand, "possesses the ability to detect lurkin no matter what form they take."

The toad people "oohed" in delight. The green one even applauded lightly. Winnie rolled her eyes. She knew Kip didn't possess a magical bone in his body.

"If I strike the subject with it and she disappears, that means she's a lurkin spy." Kip strolled to Winnie's chair. "If she remains, we'll know she isn't." He thumped her on the head with his wand.

"Ow!" She rubbed at the sting on the side of her head.

"See? Still visible. In fact..." He held the wand to his ear as if listening for a message. "What was that?" He listened again. "Me wand just said that the young lady is indeed a general. She's called General Winnie, er, Winifred."

"Windemere," she said through clenched teeth.

"Right. General Windemere. Really? Is that a family name?"

"Mom's maiden name, if you must know."

"Smashing. Now, as I was saying, Your Majesty, Windemere is world renowned. Takka did, indeed, send this great general to us."

"Are you telling us he sent the both of you?" the queen demanded.

"Precisely, Your Majesty. Being as clever as Takka is, the good general wanted to provide Your Majesty with a backup plan in the unlikely event that the first one, i.e., me, failed. You see, under certain atmospheric conditions, me wand isn't always reliable."

The queen let out an indignant whiffle. "Not reliable?"

"It's quite all right. It works perfectly well indoors, as I've just demonstrated. Outside, where the enemy will be, it's a bit dicey, I'm afraid."

"We expect you to correct that before the enemy arrives." Queen Bogen turned to Zyke. "Our wizard and Takka approve this new general. Maggenta also recommends her highly."

Zyke grunted.

"We certainly understand your skepticism, Councilman Zyke." The queen thumbed through a short stack of papers in front of her. "When we examine the general's contradictory behavior since her arrival, we cannot help but question her intentions." She stared across the table at Winnie. "We've a report before us which states you introduced yourself to the palum as a harrik, then proceeded to save two of their colts from a harrik attack."

"I introduced myself as Harris, not harrik."

"Drinking sacred water, escaping punishment." Her bulging pink eyes frowned over the paper at Winnie again. "One doesn't dash off mid-stoning. It simply isn't done."

Winnie leaned forward. "They wanted to throw rocks at me."

"You did, however, redeem yourself when you returned a runaway mel-yew cub to its father. This report also states that you led a snaps to a hunting party. For that we are grateful. Mel-yew hadn't eaten properly in weeks."

Zyke coughed. "Begging your royal pardon, but she also made an attempt on your life."

Winnie huffed. "They were binoculars, Your Majesty."

"Did you or did you not intend to assassinate us with them?"

Her back stiffened. "You can't kill anybody with binoculars. Ask your new BFF, the wizard."

"That is true, Your Majesty. Binoculars are perfectly safe."

"Takka asked me to bring them," Winnie said to Kip. "What did he ask you to pack?"

He grinned. "Me charm and me wit."

"I can understand sending a wizard," Zyke said, "but a female warrior?"

"We had hoped for Takka's return," said Queen Bogen. "However, in our grave moment, we must not be too particular, must we?"

Winnie stood. "If you think you can handle your lurkin problem with a wizard whose wand doesn't always work, be my guest. I'll just go home."

"You must stay." The corners of the queen's lips lifted into an ingratiating smile. "We declare you General of All Armies. This title puts you in charge of our military advisor, Commander Fynn, and all of his subordinates. You also rank above our personal advisor, Zyke, and our Councilmen Jebb and Steed. You are authorized to give orders to the royal guard, civilian volunteers, and to the palum. In fact, General Windemere, our decree makes you almost as important as we are."

Winnie sat back down. "Okay, then. That sounds more like it."

"From heretic to general," the voga named Commander Fynn muttered in his gravelly voice. "Only in Frama-12."

"What about me?" Kip said. "Do I get to order anyone about?"

"Wizards don't give orders. They vanish unwanted enemies. You said yourself the wand doesn't always function properly. A warrior, on the other hand, can be relied upon." The queen turned to Winnie. "What is your first order of business, General?"

Remembering Mikey's Frama-12 game, she said with confidence, "We need to recruit more fighters. The army you have isn't strong enough to stop a lurkin attack."

Queen Bogen nodded. "Sadly, we are limited by the small mel-yew population."

"Your…um, Majesty? They aren't your only subjects."

Fynn bobbed his gray head up and down. "That is true, Your Majesty. A herd of palum may have small brains, but they have great strength."

"Denied," said the queen. "We mustn't go killing off the workforce."

"With all due respect, Your Majesty," Winnie said in her most polite voice, "I'm hoping to win this war with as few casualties as possible."

"And I'll fix me wand," Kip added. "That should count for something, right? Besides, I've been around longer. Shouldn't I get a decree as well?"

"Let's decree that the wizard has to be quiet. About those palum, we don't need all of them. Just a few to kick the lurkin."

"Yes, and that is where we run into difficulty," Zyke said. "The palum can't be trained to do anything but pull carts and carry heavy loads."

"Then what about vogan? They look strong. Why can't a few of them join the front line?"

"Front line?" sputtered the green toad named Jebb. "Never. We are royalty."

Winnie's muscles clenched. In her dream someone had uttered that same pompous remark. A moment later, the spiders had crashed through the castle gates.

"Being royal doesn't make you immune to the dangers of war."

"My dear general," Queen Bogen said sweetly, "is it not possible that the lurkin merely wish to reach the portal that will open up in our region? Perhaps they'd simply pass our subjects by if we let them march through the time tear. Then we'd be shot of them once and for all."

"Your Majesty, the time tear opens into my world. We don't want the lurkin any more than you do."

Queen Bogen sighed. "There we are, then. I suppose we must fight."

"Not us, surely, Your Majesty," said Jebb.

"Certainly not us. Someone expendable shall do it."

"What if I transformed a few dozen glunt into fighters?" Kip suggested.

Jebb gasped. "Queen Bogen, forbid that! Glunt are a culinary delight."

"If you ask me——" Winnie said.

"Which we didn't," said the fourth councilman, a beige toad with brown freckles.

The queen faced him. "Careful, Steed. You are addressing a general sanctioned by the oracle and by Takka."

Winnie smirked at Freckles. To the queen she said,

"Even if we just got a few of them, it would be good for morale if vogan, palum, and mel-yew all trained side by side."

"Just one moment, please," Steed demanded. "Vogan are superior. We do not stand beside palum. We stand above them."

Winnie stared down her nose at him. "Then we'll have to change that."

The four councilmen sputtered in protest.

"This is highly irregular!" Fynn, the gray military advisor, shouted above the din.

"Begging your pardon, Your Royal Highness," Zyke said, "but Maggenta has made a grave error, sanctioning this outsider. I cannot tolerate such blatant disrespect for the royal name of voga."

"Yes," Steed said. "She must follow our ways or lose her command."

"Never heard such blasphemy," Jebb muttered.

"Generals shouldn't be the only ones getting decrees. Wizards deserve them as well."

Queen Bogen banged her scepter on the floor until the room went quiet. "Maggenta erred only once when she sent Takka into the wrong time frame. We must believe the oracle when she tells us this human person is our salvation."

"Maggenta was wrong once," said Zyke. "She could be wrong twice."

"Highly doubtful. This discussion is over. We command that you follow our new general's instructions or be tried for treason."

All four councilmen pinched their mouths closed.

Winnie beamed, enjoying her position. "There's one more thing we should do as soon as possible. We need advance notice about the invasion. Since we know the lurkin are coming by sea, let's set up a watch post on the beach. The palum can man it. I'll give them my binoc—my black medallion."

"The palum will never learn to use your magnifying medallion," Zyke grumbled. "I had difficulty operating it myself, and I'm highly intelligent."

"I don't mind teaching them."

"Teach them?" said the green toad named Jebb. "They wouldn't even know they had bums if it weren't for their tails!"

Winnie, who loved horses, gave them her harshest stare. "Stop making fun of palum."

Queen Bogen straightened her papers. "We shall decree the recruitment of more mel-yew and station a palum lookout post on the beach as the general requests."

Winnie nodded, appeased.

"General, the army shall be assembled for your inspection first thing in the morning."

She stifled a yawn. "Thank you, Your Majesty."

"This concludes our meeting," said the queen.

"But, Your Majesty, don't I get a decree?"

"Very well, Master Wizard," the queen said. "We decree that you direct the general to her quarters. She looks tired."

On the way out, Winnie overheard the queen say in a low voice, "If the new general causes any more trouble, we'll simply lose her to the hunt."

She didn't know what the hunt was, but nobody was going to "lose" her. She pressed her lips together in determination. Warriors never got lost. The expression "forewarned is forearmed" came to mind. Winnie would be ready. She wasn't sure how, but she'd think of something. She hoped.

Chapter 11

Winnie didn't realize how exhausted she was until the queen suggested it. She plodded up the staircase behind Kip, ready for a shower and rest. They climbed dozens and dozens of shiny marble steps.

The colorful murals on the walls and the fancy curlicue carvings on the banister could only distract her so long. After three landings they had to be close, but Kip led her through a wide corridor to another staircase.

"Where are you taking me? To the attic?"

"Nearly there." He sounded way too cheerful.

They reached a landing with royal-blue carpeting. From there, they entered a wide room with the same color carpeting.

Upholstered benches built into the inside wall faced three wooden tables, and a pair of potted ferns, at the opposite side of the room. The first table held a crystal goblet and a clear glass bottle filled with cranberry-colored juice. A plate of orange cheese and a sliced baguette had been laid out on the second table. The third held a bowl, overflowing with red and green grapes. At the fruit table, Winnie plucked one from the bunch.

"Don't eat the green ones."

Too late. Sour juice splashed over her tongue. She spat it into the nearest plant pot. She hacked and thumped her chest.

"The red ones aren't nearly so bad, but they still take some getting used to. If you like sharp cheese, you'll love theirs. And the bread is divine."

Her stomach lurched at the thought of sharp cheese. Divine bread sounded promising. She grabbed a slice. The outer crust held just the right amount of crunch. The moist inside was still warm. She groaned in ecstasy.

"You do know your bread," she said with her mouth full. "I'll give you that."

The smell of freshly mown grass wafted through the arched windows that lined the room's outer wall. She followed the scent to the nearest window. Rolling green lawns lay beyond the castle's stone walls. Far beyond a band of trees stood a mountain range.

"This is amazing. I see everything!"

"Everything but the sea," Kip said.

Just remembering the ocean's putrid smell made her nose twitch.

"Bed and bath are in there." He nodded toward the open doorway on his right.

She peeked into the next room. The deep-red paneling made the room as dark as a cave. Only a hint of light shone through the stained glass french doors on her left.

He eased past her to a column in the middle of the room. Sconces with unlit candles encircled the column. "Interesting thing about this place," he said.

A casual wave of his wand made a flame appear at the end. "They've got electricity from solar and water power." He held the wand, which she assumed was a lighter, to the wicks, flaring them to life. "Oddly, they seem to prefer using candles to light their rooms."

A gentle glow from the lit candles fell over a platform supporting a king-sized, four-poster bed. Gold-and-blue curtains had been tied back to expose a comforter and wide mattress.

"I don't mind." She joined him in the enchanting room. "This place is amazing!"

"It is. I've a similar suite in the north wing."

She ran back to the front room for more bread so she could eat while exploring her suite. Two doors opened into deep walk-in closets. A third housed a bathroom with a toilet. Instead of a sink, the top of a cabinet held a pitcher with mint-smelling liquid and a washbasin.

Back in the bedroom, french doors opened onto a little white balcony with a table and two chairs, facing the mountains.

She gasped in delight. "It's like my own hotel room in the alps, minus the snow." She gripped the balcony railing and breathed in the cooling air.

"If you don't mind me asking," spoke the Cockney voice from behind her. "Where did you learn about General Whatzit? I mean Takka?"

She glanced back at him. "My dad married his mom. It's Mikey."

"That's who everybody's been going on about? Little Mikey is a general?"

"Kind of." She returned her attention to the balcony's view. "I don't completely get it myself. Takka's mind or something is inside Mikey's body. If you can put yourself into a trance, you can ask him about it. The oracle helped me talk to him when I was in the dungeon."

"Unbelievable. You go from prisoner to general,

and you get to speak with the oracle. I've been in this place three weeks now, and all I got—"

"Three weeks?" Winnie faced him. "I just saw you yesterday."

Kip frowned. "No, you didn't."

"Oh, right. Time acts funny here. When did you step into the time tear? I mean what time?"

He shrugged. "Middle of the night. I didn't exactly step in, though. I pitched me tent over the place where Mikey said it would rise."

"You came here on purpose?"

"So did you."

"That's because I'm a—" She stopped herself, unwilling to admit her warrior status. "It's because Mikey needed somebody to lead his army."

"Mikey asked for a wizard as well."

"He never said anything about a wiz—" She cut herself off again, eyes narrowing. "Are you here because of your magic tricks?"

"They're not tricks anymore. I've got me own lab now and books. I'm learning incantations that actually work. Good thing too. I needed to use the convincement spell on the queen after you tried to get me nicked for being an impostor."

She shook her head. "I hate to tell you this, but you are an imposter."

"I hate to tell you this, but you're not a real general." He stalked from the room.

"Whatever," she muttered.

From the balcony she watched the evening sky turn from pale blue to purple and pink. The colors softened her mood. Wispy clouds parted, exposing Frama-12's rising moon. Instead of a man in the moon, the craters formed the shape of a lady in profile, sitting on a rocker. The image wore a dress and a cowboy hat. *Whistler's Mother* in a Stetson.

The odd moon proved just how far from home she was. A deep ache throbbed in her throat. She'd felt that same pang her first night at sleepaway camp after her mom died.

"You have to be a kid," Dad had told her. "Going to camp is what kids do."

Before he drove away, he'd given her one last hug. "Look to the moon," he'd said. "Each night, just before bed, blow it a kiss. It'll bounce off and come right to me. I'll be standing outside, waiting to catch it."

She blinked through tears at Frama-12's lady in the moon. She kissed her palm and blew it toward the alien moon. After a quick washup in her miniature bathroom, Winnie dropped onto the fluffy mattress. She didn't even undress.

Chapter 12

In his lab, Kip whistled for his familiar. The bird flew in and lit on the desk.

"Do you know where General Takka is?"

"Which one?" Willum said in his usual confounding way.

Kip rolled his eyes. "If there's more than one, just tell me where all of them are."

Willum gave him a one-eyed stare. That look usually meant information came at a price. He pulled a dime from his pocket and tossed it into the air.

Willum caught it in his beak. He dropped the coin on the desk as if for a closer appraisal. "Not as big as the other ones."

"Sorry, mate, I've run out of quarters. So where are all these multitudes of Takkas?"

Willum gave the dime an indignant peck and flew across the room to the chair arm where Kip sat by the fire. "There are no multitudes. Only two shells and one essence."

Kip hadn't a clue what that meant. He nodded anyway. "Go on."

The black bird waddled up and down the chair arm as he spoke. "Takka's original shell is stored in one of the oracle's ice rooms, far from the castle to keep it safe. That would be shell number one. Shell number two—and attend to me here, young wizard—there are only two, which hardly counts as a multitude."

"Sarcasm doesn't become you."

"Shell number two," Willum continued, "is where Takka's essence currently resides. And that would be in the adjoining world."

"His essence. As in…"

"As in the part that can speak and think. The one in the ice room is simply a shell."

"Then Mikey could be Takka." And if Winnie could speak with him, maybe Kip could as well. For his own peace of mind, he had to confirm that Mikey/Takka indeed had invited him to Frama-12. He could peruse the titles on the bookshelves, but that could take ages. "I've another bauble for you if you can tell me how to contact Takka's essence in that other world."

Willum flew to his shoulder. "You won't find that in a book."

"Where will I find it?"

Willum nipped at the gold hoop dangling from Kip's earlobe.

"Oh, all right." He removed the earring and held it up. "Now will you tell?"

The bird flew out the window with his shiny prize clasped in his beak.

Kip added a log to the fire and waited. Once the bird hid his latest bauble, he'd return. He always did.

A quarter of an hour later, as expected, Willum swooped through the window. He lit on an upper shelf and waddled beside a row of vials. He paused occasionally to eye one or two. "Yes. Here it is. 'Trance enhancement.' " He tipped over a vial.

Kip sprang forward and stretched his arm, just in

time to catch it. "You really should warn me before you do that."

Willum cackled. "All wizards need quick reflexes." He fluttered down to Kip's worktable.

"Obviously, with you around," Kip mumbled. He held the brown glass container to the light for a look at the liquid within. It looked a little like water, but it was hard to tell without uncapping it and pouring some out. "Right. What's the procedure? Do I drink a bit of it? Rub it behind me ears? Use it in a potion?"

"Try reading the bit of paper attached to the back. It starts with the words, 'Directions for use.' "

Kip turned the bottle over. " 'Add two droplets to one cup rainwater,' " he read aloud. " 'Stir twice to the left and once to the right. Drink whilst lying down. Immediately conjure within the mind the image of the one you wish to contact.' " He turned to Willum. "That would be Takka, right?"

"Is that one of those rhetorical whatzits? Because I've only seen the Takka shell that has nothing inside."

Since most potions required rainwater, Kip had placed a barrel on the balcony just below his lab to catch it. He scurried down the stone stairs with cup in hand. Back in his lab, he dropped onto the cot he kept for nights when he worked late.

He swallowed the concoction, careful not to choke. Who drank while lying down anyway? He imagined Mikey at the beach.

He never felt the transition but soon found himself sitting on a beach towel, building a sandcastle with Mikey. "So here we are, then, wot?"

The little boy grinned, revealing his missing front teeth. "See? I knew you were a wizard first time I met you."

"That's me, Kip the Amazing. But you never told me you were a general."

Mikey lowered his gaze to the mound of sand between them. He added another handful to the top and patted it into place. "I used to be a general. Now I'm an anchor."

Kip gave him a gentle nudge. "No need calling yourself names, mate. You're fine just as you are."

Mikey laughed. "No, an anchor is a good thing. It helps travelers find their way back home. Did you see Windy yet? She can tell you all about it. We used to play a game called Frama-hopping and took turns being the anchor."

"We didn't get that deep into it, but she said you sent her to Frama-12."

"Actually, she volunteered to save our worlds from the lurkin."

Kip poked at their mound of sand. "She doesn't believe you invited me to come. You did invite me, didn't you?"

"I showed you where the time tear was going to rise. Why would I do that if I didn't want you to go there?"

Kip's mood brightened. "Brill. And if there's anything else needs doing, I'm your bloke."

"Help Windy, please. She might be too proud to ask."

"I've been working on making the enemy disappear. I could surprise her with that. I don't suppose you know the proper pronunciation to make the vanishing spell work, do you?"

Mikey shook his head. "Sorry. We didn't have

wizards when I lived there."

Kip's shoulders drooped.

"You'll figure it out. Just be careful how you use your magic. Wizards were banned before. Queen Bogen could forbid them again."

"Not a problem. The queen and I get on quite well."

The air around them began to shimmer.

"Ooh, I think me potion is wearing off. Any other advice before I go?"

"Don't let Windy forget she's a warrior."

Kip nodded even though he didn't see Winnie as the warrior type. Bossy, maybe, but a soldier? Never. Maybe she needed his help after all.

He returned to his lab, brimming with images of saving the world on her behalf. Once he perfected that vanishing spell, she'd have to believe in his magic. He leaped off his cot, eager to resume his practice.

Chapter 13

Winnie, age fourteen years, four months, and two days, found it perfectly natural to share a dock on the lake with a mom who died five years, seven months, three weeks, and five days ago. Winnie lay on her stomach, peering through the clear water at the dozens of orange, brown, and white pebbles on the lake bed below.

"Ya know how warrior has 'war' in it?" she said dreamily.

Mom said with a smile in her voice, "I might have noticed."

Winnie sat up, unable to look her in the eye. "I'm about to go to war. Against lurkin. Ever heard of them?"

"Don't think so."

"They're giant spiders."

"Sounds like you'll need a really big can of bug spray."

"Mom, it's not a joke."

"Just trying to lighten the mood." Mom hugged Winnie close.

She could always sense Mom's deep inner strength. She felt it now. Mom could do anything. She wasn't the one going to war, though—Winnie was. What if she didn't share Mom's warrior qualities? What if she failed?

Her eyes opened to daylight. Why didn't her alarm wake her before sunrise? She sat up with a jolt. Sunlight streamed through her open french doors.

Movement from her right pulled her attention to a small gray humanoid dressed in a long red chemise. The being had a large bald head and tiny mouth. Alien abduction!

Then she remembered she'd landed in Frama-12 yesterday. She flopped onto her back again.

A mel-yew leaned over her, looking concerned. "Are you unwell, General?"

Winnie sat up. "I'm fine." She rubbed a hand down her face. "Just thought I was someplace else."

The tiny person nodded. "A dream."

Winnie guessed it was a woman, judging by the simple dress she wore.

"I'm Nita, your servant." She curtsied. "I've brought breakfast and will serve it when you're ready, General."

Winnie had her own maid? Being a general in Frama-12 had perks.

"Nita, could I have breakfast on the balcony, please?" she asked, testing her new power. "I feel like eating outside."

Nita curtsied again. "As you wish, General."

From her balcony, she gazed down at the dew glinting off the lawn. A chorus of birds sang from the bushes below, announcing a fresh new day. She even smelled sweet honeysuckle in the air. If she breathed too deeply, though, she caught a hint of Frama-12's rotting ocean. She hoped the lurkin weren't marching yet. She wasn't ready.

Nita lifted the silver cover on the breakfast tray

she'd set on the balcony table. A heaping platter of scrambled eggs, along with a bowl of orange melon balls, lay beneath.

Winnie dipped a fork into the eggs. She took a bite before she remembered this place had weird food. Thankfully, the eggs tasted normal. "You have chickens."

"Chickens, General?"

"You probably call them something else. I meant the animals that laid these things." She pointed her fork at the eggs.

The mel-yew servant curtsied. "We call them harriks, good General."

They scrambled snake eggs? Winnie stifled a gag and pushed the tray aside.

"Are they not prepared to your liking, General?"

"They're fine. I'm more of a fruit lover. This is fruit, right?"

"Yes, General."

Winnie speared an orange melon ball and took a careful bite. Sugary juices touched her tongue, erasing the eggy taste. "So how do you guys collect harrik eggs?"

"The court jester, Polo, hides in the bushes below a nesting harrik. He mimics the cry of a wounded palum colt. When the harrik leaves its nest, hoping to make a meal of the prey, a collector climbs the tree and gathers the eggs."

Winnie nodded. "Inventive."

A honking noise sounded from above. A gray bird, bigger than a falcon, glided by. Its long talons gripped a mel-yew by the shoulders.

Winnie leaped up in alarm. "That bird's stealing

one of your people!"

"Begging the general's pardon, that was one of the royal guards on duty."

"You mean that bird can do that without dropping him?"

"Wiggets are trained to hold the guards well, General. These birds are educated and housed at the east end of the courtyard."

Winnie had just opened her mouth to ask if their sun rose in the east or the west, when a decisive rap sounded at her door.

"Excuse me, General." Nita hurried to answer it. She returned, looking grim. "The queen requests your attendance at breakfast, General."

"Perfect."

Nita's red-rimmed eyes watered. "But, General, I've already served you. Now you shan't be hungry for the queen's breakfast."

One bite of melon had only woken her appetite. Winnie patted her empty stomach. "I'm sure I'll find room."

A young toad person, dressed in a royal-blue tunic, met her in the hallway. "I am humbly at your service, General. May I escort you to Queen Bogen's private dining hall?"

"You may." She tried not to grin over her elevated status.

Her guide led her to an immense dining hall. He pulled out a high-backed chair on the right side of the long, mahogany table. Winnie thanked him. He bowed and departed. She draped her white linen napkin across her knees. She waited. And waited.

If she'd known it would take this long, she could

have jogged around the castle to keep up her training schedule.

Finally, just when she felt hungry enough to eat the tablecloth, a trumpet fanfare blasted from the open door. "All rise for Her Royal Majesty, Queen Bogen!"

Winnie jumped to her feet, napkin in hand.

"Good morning, General." The queen squatted in the royal chair at the head of the table. "It's just the two of us for breakfast."

Winnie returned to her seat. The queen rang a small bell. A procession of mel-yew servants, dressed in white, entered. The two in front carried plates of that deliciously moist bread, followed by a steward who poured bubbly red juice into the queen's and Winnie's goblets. Other servants brought thick yellow soup, scrambled harrik eggs, various meat dishes, and fruit.

Winnie sampled a little of everything, except the eggs and the grapes. She also passed on a plate of minced meat that looked like mashed beetles.

"We trust you slept well. Your rooms are satisfactory." It was a statement, not a question.

"Yes, Your Highness, very satisfactory. Thank you."

"We expect you'll require an office of sorts to plan your strategy and whatnot."

Winnie nodded. "Plus, I'll need some advisors."

"You are quite welcome to make use of our councilmen. When they're not meeting with us, of course."

The idea of sitting in the same room with all those grumpy toads made Winnie's insides twist. "No offense or anything, but your staff is a little too regal for me. My questions need to be answered by regular people."

"Though at times our advisors may act a bit above themselves, they are quite well equipped to answer any questions you might have."

Winnie picked at a crumb on the white tablecloth. "The truth is, Your Majesty, I need different opinions from different people. You know, vogan, mel-yew, palum."

Queen Bogen put down her fork. She focused her bulging pink eyes on Winnie. "Palum? That seems a rather odd request. They're not very bright, you know."

"I met their leader yesterday. Pall? He seemed smart." Winnie hoped he was smart enough to forgive her for her spring-water faux pas.

Queen Bogen steepled her knobby fingers, looking thoughtful. "Because you are Takka's champion, your unusual request shall be granted. Although it is well known throughout the realm that vogan do not sit in conference with palum."

"That's okay. I can probably get along without any vogan."

The queen took a deep breath. "Though it pains us, we believe it is only right and proper that a voga be present at your meetings. If you have no success finding one who is agreeable, we shall command one to join you."

"Excellent. Thanks. Also, I'd like a Brothers Ky and definitely Polo."

The queen puffed up like a white bullfrog. "Polo? Were you hoping to build morale by having him tell jokes to our army?"

"I thought since he can fool harriks long enough to steal their eggs, he might be smart enough to fool the lurkin."

The queen let out a melodramatic breath of air. "We don't see how he can help you, but he shall be informed of his new advisory position. Have you any other requests?"

Winnie nodded, enthusiastic again. "I promised I'd hire that little mel-yew I met at the snaps hunt yesterday. Cubby?"

"Now you wish to retain a mel-yew child as an advisor?"

"Yes, please."

Queen Bogen sighed again. "As you wish."

"Thanks, Your Majesty. I'd like to meet with them as soon as possible. You know, so I can get started on my strategy."

"They shall be summoned to your designated office after you've inspected the troops. But first you must be fitted with a uniform."

Winnie peered down at her dirty, rumpled T-shirt. "Good idea."

"Our seamstress, Gabelle, shall make you a fine military frock."

Movement in the open doorway caught Winnie's attention. Kip, dressed in a deep purple robe decorated with yellow half-moons and stars, hovered just outside. He even wore a pointed wizard's cap. He reminded Winnie of a young Merlin. And as much as she hated to admit it, he almost looked cute.

"A fine good morning to you, Your Majesty!" He dipped into a bow. "And to you, good General. Might I interrupt Your Royal Eminence for a brief demonstration?"

The queen raised a welcoming hand. "Enter, good Master Wizard."

He practically skipped inside, eyes aglow. "I've been practicing this all night!" He slid into the seat across from Winnie and wrapped a fresh linen napkin around the saltshaker. He murmured something she couldn't hear. The air crackled. Her ears popped just as the napkin vanished.

He beamed.

Queen Bogen stared at him for a long moment. "Is there some point to misplacing our linens?"

He grinned like an idiot. "Your Majesty, I thought we could embarrass the enemy by vanishing their clothes."

Winnie smirked, unimpressed. Any birthday party magician could make things look like they disappeared.

The queen looked equally unmoved. "We'd much rather you vanished the enemy and left their clothing, Master Wizard."

He rubbed his chin. "Before I can do that, I'll need an incantation that doesn't require the wand, Your Majesty."

"Carry on, then."

"Thank you, Your Majesty. I see Your Grand Majesty has invited the general to breakfast." He playfully shifted his eyebrows up and down at Winnie from across the table.

Winnie looked away, pretending not to notice.

"As you know, Majesty," he continued, "a good breakfast helps wizards perform at their best."

"Would you care to join us, Master Wizard?"

"Why thank you, Your Majesty, don't mind if I do."

Winnie had to hand it to him. He knew how to get his way. Was it his smile or the accent? Both were slowly growing on her until he lifted the dish of mashed beetles and started scooping them onto his plate. Nobody needed to see that.

She pushed back her chair. "I probably should get started, Your Majesty. I have a lot to do. I'd also like to see how the palum are making out at the lookout post."

"No need, General. Commander Fynn is already seeing to the palum."

"Could he teach them how to use my binoculars?"

"Fynn is on the way to the castle with his report as we speak. Traveling across our realm takes up a great deal of time, General, which is limited."

At the mention of time, Winnie instinctively checked her watch. The face was blank. She unfastened the wristband and tapped her watch on the tabletop.

"Me cell phone went too," Kip said. "I go by sundial now."

The queen leaned toward the watch. "Ooh, what is that?"

"Broken, Your Majesty." Winnie pressed a side button. Several notes peeped weakly from the watch's tiny speaker.

"How extraordinary. It sings."

"It's also supposed to tell time." Winnie laid it on the table.

Queen Bogen lifted the watch. "Our technical staff could look into the trouble."

Winnie snorted skeptically.

"We are far more advanced than we appear. We happen to prefer simplicity."

"Oh. Um, sure. I'll leave it here if they want to try to fix it."

"Be on your way, then, General." The queen's

focus remained on the watch. "A page will show you to Gabelle's fitting rooms."

The same page from before led Winnie down a long hall. "What's your name, good page?"

"I am called Loy, General."

He looked efficient enough for her staff. "Loy, how would you like to join the team I'm putting together to discuss battle strategies?"

The page bowed. "I'd be honored, General. I've heard stories of Your Eminence."

"Really? I guess I am kind of important. I'm here to"—she shrugged, hoping to appear humble—"save your world."

"A task you are most capable of, General."

"I'm looking for a voga adviser. Do you mind working with palum?"

"A small sacrifice if I may serve one so grand as yourself, good General."

"Then you've got the job," Winnie said, dazzled by her own self-importance.

Chapter 14

Gabelle's cluttered fitting room reeked of leather. Bolts of it lay in so many heaps Winnie barely fit inside. The mel-yew seamstress didn't seem to mind the closeness of the room. She hummed to herself as she snipped and clipped, tucked and pinned the soft, reddish material around Winnie's waist.

Within minutes Gabelle turned her toward a cheval glass so she could appraise her new formfitting battle tunic. It not only made her feel like a warrior princess, but it resembled the outfit she'd worn in her nightmare. The straps on her leather sandals crisscrossed up her calves the same way they had in her dream. She'd barely formed a thought about her missing knife when Gabelle handed her a leather belt. A sheathed dagger hung from the side.

Icy panic shot through her. What if Mikey got the timeline wrong? What if giant spiders had already landed on the beach? She had to see for herself.

"Thanks. See ya." Winnie sprinted out the door.

Loy marched beside her. "Sir, you look very much the general now."

She ignored the compliment. "Which way to the nearest exit?"

He led the way. "What is the alarm, General?"

She pointed at her uniform. "This. I have to check something."

Reaching the main hall involved one left turn, two rights, and another left through the corridors. Thankfully, Loy guided her, or she never would've found the pair of heavy doors. Two mel-yew doormen swung them open, allowing her to scurry out and down the outer steps. She glanced left to right for a carriage to take her to the beach. Only one cart heaped with straw stood in the courtyard. A loud honking sound from above gave her a better idea.

She turned to the page. "I need the wiggets."

"If you'll pardon me, General, there's no time to tour the grounds. The army is already assembled for your inspection."

"They'll have to wait." She strode from him in what she hoped was an easterly direction.

"General," Loy called, "Queen Bogen specifically stated—"

"It's an emergency." She ran to a fenced-in area where a dozen gray birds, similar to the one she'd seen earlier, perched on a row of tall posts. They faced a wizened mel-yew woman.

"Yes-yes," the trainer said in a high-pitched voice.

"Wigget-wigget," chirped the birds. "Yes-yes."

"No-no," one squawked. The others joined in, saying no.

"Harken," the trainer said. "We are learning yes-yes."

"Harken-wigget," the bird said. "No-no."

"No-no, wigget-wigget," the other birds said in unison.

The trainer sighed and shook her head.

"Excuse me," Winnie called from outside the fence.

The trainer's eyes glowed in recognition. "Why, you're the new general! How may I be of service?" The trainer bent into a deep bow.

Too anxious to find a gate, Winnie climbed the fence. "I wondered if you could spare one of your students to fly me to the beach. I need to inspect the lookout post."

"Right away, General. Please come this way."

Winnie followed the trainer to a shed. A wooden bin, filled with belts, straps, and leather vests in assorted sizes, stood just inside.

"We'd never been asked to transport a general." She rooted through the collection. "This should do."

The trainer handed Winnie a vest made of material so thick it reminded her of the kind she wore when she water-skied.

"This will protect your shoulders from the talons."

Winnie slid her arms into the vest. "I really appreciate you doing this on such short notice." The material fit tightly, but she could fasten the laces in front.

"We're pleased to do what we can, General."

Outside, the woman blew on a gold whistle she wore on a chain around her neck. Though Winnie heard nothing, all the birds straightened to attention.

"Harken to fly," the trainer said.

A huge wigget glided from its post and landed on the thick leather covering Winnie's shoulders. The large bird felt surprisingly light.

"Harken is an excellent flier," the trainer said, "but his speech isn't what it should be."

Winnie cringed. "This is safe, right? I mean, he won't let go once we're in the air, will he?"

"No, no, General," the trainer said with a smile. "My wiggets are very well trained. They would risk their own lives to protect a rider."

Winnie didn't want anybody risking lives, especially her own. Still, if she hoped to see what was happening on that beach, she had to trust the large gray bird. She took a deep breath. "Guess I'm ready."

"I have something for you." The mel-yew trainer toddled back to the shed. She returned with a gold whistle on a chain. She hung it around Winnie's neck. "Whenever you need their assistance, just blow twice on the whistle, and a wigget will come to you."

Winnie tucked the chain inside her tunic beside her mother's locket. "Thanks."

"Wigget, beach," the trainer said. "Wigget, big beach."

The bird clamped onto the material on Winnie's shoulders. "Wigget-wigget, big-beach." He flapped his huge wings.

Her muscles tensed. The material under her arms pinched as the bird lifted her. She rose only two inches above the ground when Harken squawked. "Wigget-wigget, too-big, too-big."

He gently returned her to the ground.

The trainer rushed to her. "I'm terribly sorry, General. Forgive me for saying so, but mel-yew guards are much smaller and lighter than yourself."

"Can we try another wigget? This is important."

"We've never done that before." The trainer tapped her pointy chin, considering it.

Winnie shifted from one foot to the other. Her insides jangled. She had to reach the ocean.

"Since this is an emergency," said the trainer, "let's

see if we can make this work." She took a leather belt from the bin and fastened it around Winnie's waist. She puffed into her silent whistle. "Sender to fly."

A second bird gripped the belt at her lower back. The wigget at her shoulders honked, and the other flapped his wings, pulling her upward in a prone position. This time she hovered a foot in the air before the one at her back said, "Too-big," and let go. The bird at her shoulders gently lowered her to her feet.

Her quivering body demanded that she give up. She took a deep breath. "I can't believe I'm saying this, but can we try one more?"

A moment later, the trainer attached leather bands to Winnie's ankles and called a third wigget. Upon the command to fly, the one at Winnie's shoulders pulled her up. The second again clasped the belt at her lower back. Finally, the third wigget's talons gripped her covered ankles. This time the birds lifted her and kept rising, inch by inch. Higher and higher.

The birds honked like Canada geese except words came out. "Big-beach," said the one at her shoulders. "Follow-follow," called the other two. As they flew upward, Winnie's muscles clenched. *Please don't let go.*

The birds cleared the treetops and leveled off. She peeked down and shuddered at the thought of falling from such a great height. She closed her eyes. The trio flew so smoothly that in time she opened them again. She stretched out her arms, enjoying the exhilarating sensation of gliding through the warm air.

The scenery quickly changed from valley to forest. They flew so high she spotted the beach and the smelly ocean long before they reached it. From her vantage point she found no signs of the enemy. She let out a breath of relief. At the beach, the bird at her ankles released first. The one at her back let go next, returning her to an upright position. The one at her shoulders safely lowered her onto the gray sand. She puffed so hard from relief over the safe landing she had to breathe into her shirtsleeve to filter out the smelly air.

Her heart rate finally returned to normal. "Thanks, guys."

The wiggets waddled beside her, murmuring, "Thanks-guys, thanks-guys."

Pall, the palum leader, trotted up to Winnie. He bowed his head. "Greetings, General! So good to find you well."

Relief that he hadn't held a grudge over the water incident relaxed her even more.

"Commander Fynn was just here seeing to everything, good General."

She turned toward the ocean. "I wanted to see a few things myself." A palum scout stood on the solidified water, facing the horizon, per her instructions. His arms, though, hung loosely at his sides.

"Why isn't your scout using the binoculars?"

"Binoculars, General?"

"You know. The black things you look through?"

He rubbed his muzzle thoughtfully. "Black things…"

"Mine," cried a shrill voice behind Winnie. She turned. Two palum colts yanked on opposite sides of the binoculars strap.

"Hey!" She stomped toward them. "That's not a toy."

The colts dropped the binoculars in the sand and

scampered away.

She picked them up. "This is what your scout is supposed to be using."

"It is indeed a black thing, General."

Winnie snorted. She wobbled across the jellied ocean to the scout on lookout duty.

"Good day, General." The scout gave her a polite bow.

"Yeah, yeah," she said absently. As soon as the ground stopped bobbing, she scanned the horizon through her binoculars. All remained clear. For now.

She faced the scout. "Your job is very important."

He bobbed his head. "Very important, General."

"You'll be the first one to know if anything is coming this way."

"Is something coming this way, General?"

She clapped a hand over her forehead. "What did you think you were doing out here all this time?"

"Standing."

She sucked in a breath of air to control her temper. The stench, full strength, started a coughing fit. She hacked a few more times, then said slowly, "The lurkin are on the way."

"The lurkin are?"

"You know the prophecy, right? Lurkin invasion? General Takka couldn't make it, so I'm here? Any of that sound familiar?"

"The lurkin are coming, General."

"You're looking for spiders. Huge, hairy-legged spiders. Got it?" She slapped her binoculars into the scout's human-like hand. "You need to watch the horizon."

The horse hybrid stared at the binoculars.

"What's the matter? Don't you understand?"

The scout nodded, then shook his horse head from side to side.

"First of all, since your eyes are on opposite sides of your head, just use half." She raised the binoculars so that one lens was level with his left eye.

"I see!" The scout aimed the binoculars at the beach. "My friends grow!"

She tugged his arm. "Look at the horizon!"

The scout aimed the binoculars at his feet.

"No. That way." She pointed. "Where the sky and the ocean meet."

"Ah. The much-far."

"I don't care if you call it your Aunt Sally. Just keep watching it. Now," she said with another strained breath, "are we clear on what spiders are?"

"I fear not, good General."

"Maybe you call them leggy things? Or crawly things. They make webs."

"I have never heard tell of leggy-crawly things, General."

She rubbed her throbbing temples. "Just look out there and watch for very large creatures with eight legs."

The scout gasped. "Eight legs, General?"

"Can you count that high?"

"One, two, five, eight," he said proudly.

She clenched her teeth and silently counted to ten. "Think of it this way. You're looking for creatures with many more legs than you have. Understand?"

The scout beamed at her. "I do, General!"

Winnie wobble-marched back to firm ground.

"Wigget-wigget, where-to, where-to?"

In a burst of inspiration, she pointed out to sea. "Take me that way!"

The wiggets waddled around her, chirping, "No-go, no-go."

She stomped her foot. "You have to. I'm the general."

"They never follow instructions that might lead their rider into danger," Pall said.

She looked from Pall to the nearest wigget. "What's out there?"

"No-go, no-go."

"How close is the danger?"

"Where-to, where-to?"

She huffed. "Can't you just tell me?"

"Wiggets have large thoughts but small words," said Pall. "Often what they know they cannot say."

She kicked at the sand. "That's just great."

"Where-to, where-to?"

"Back to the castle, I guess. Pall, let me know if you see anything out there. Even if it looks like a little speck."

He bowed. "Indeed, indeed. I shall report all little specks to you, General."

Just to be clear she added in a slow voice so it would sink in, "The specks will be coming from that way." She pointed out to sea.

The wiggets honked and, once again, lifted her into the air. They swiftly flew back to the castle. On their approach from above, solar panels gleamed from the castle roof. *Solar power* and *candles, what a crazy place*. Turning her attention to the ground, she counted eleven rows of mel-yew knights. They stood in formation in the courtyard. Guessing she'd found the army she was supposed to inspect, Winnie commanded the wiggets to land near them. They set her down, chirped a farewell, and flew away.

Fynn, the gray military toad, strutted to her. "Good of you to drop in, General. As you can see, the troops await your inspection."

Winnie ignored his sarcasm and marched up and down the ranks. The soldiers wore metal armor. The fishbowl-shaped helmets that covered their round heads had a single narrow slit cut out for their eyes.

"Can they breathe all right in there?"

"They are warriors, General."

She glared at him. "What's that supposed to mean? Warriors don't breathe? And what about hearing? Can they hear?"

"Most certainly they can hear." He marched to the front of the ranks and shouted, "Hup, hup!"

The knights clicked their heels together in unison.

"Porta-porta, tia-tia," commanded Fynn.

"Hut ho!" came the knights' muffled reply. They all pivoted to the left.

"There." Fynn's eyes flashed haughtily. "They can hear quite well."

"What's a tia-tia?"

"A command. What else would it be?"

"Sounds like something the wiggets might say. Where I come from, we say, 'left face.' It works just as well but doesn't sound so funny."

The voga's eyes bulged. "I beg your pardon?"

"I carry the banner in our marching band. I know all about this."

Winnie faced her army and explained the commands her marching band used at home.

"Begging the general's pardon," Fynn croaked. "Are you changing the words I use?"

"Just improving them." She faced the troops. "Okay, guys, ready? Attention!" She imitated her school drum major's commanding voice.

Simultaneously, the knights clacked their heels together.

"Please remove your helmets."

The mel-yew knights didn't move.

She turned to Fynn. "Are you sure they can hear?"

"That was an unusual order, General. Even for you."

"But it was an order," she said in a loud voice. "It's supposed to be obeyed no matter how unusual it sounds."

The knights' heads turned from side to side, looking from one neighbor to the other. Slowly, they removed their helmets.

"Thank you."

"General, they are accustomed to training in full battle gear."

"And I'm accustomed to looking at people's faces when I talk to them," she said so only Fynn heard. "Guards," she said, projecting her voice to the back of the ranks. "Do you understand my commands?"

All the little bald heads bobbed up and down. She ordered a left turn. They turned left. She ordered them to the right, and they complied. Just as she was silently congratulating herself on her leadership skills, she said, "About face."

Their heavy armor wobbled. Metal clanked against metal. The knights toppled over.

She covered her eyes but still heard their

floundering.

"You're quite the military expert."

She pulled her hands away, suddenly inspired. "Do you know what this means?"

"It means they've no need to turn all the way round. The royal army never retreats."

"Get the queen. I have something important to show her."

"Ordering me about now, is it?" he muttered under his breath as he strode away.

Winnie helped return the helmetless knights to their feet. She'd just finished lining them up in the shape of a large circle when Queen Bogen stepped onto the second-floor balcony. Commander Fynn stood at her side, glaring down.

Winnie faced the closest knight. "You're at attention. Don't move no matter what."

The knight blinked up, then stared straight ahead.

"You probably won't get this," she said, "but trust me. It'll make sense in time. Sorry." She shoved the first knight. The weight of his armor sent him reeling backward. His shiny metal back thumped into the metal chest of the knight behind him. The second fell neatly into the third. One by one, Winnie's silver domino army tipped over.

She spread her arms in triumph. "There! See?"

Queen Bogen spun on her heel and strode back inside the castle.

"Wait! I just made a huge point down here!"

A moment later, a voga page appeared at her side. "General, Her Royal Majesty commands an audience in her private chamber. She is in a state of fury."

Chapter 15

"You are still visible," Queen Bogen said.

Kip's hiding place behind a heavy blue curtain made him crave fresh air with mind-screaming urgency. Until now, he'd never thought of himself as a claustrophobe. Never thought of himself as a spy either, yet there he stood, squished between wall and curtain, waiting to eavesdrop for the queen. To add to his troubles, the curtain smelled of dust. If he sneezed and gave himself away, the queen might send him to the dungeon. When a door creaked open, he pressed his back tighter against the wall.

"What sort of military exercise was that just now?" Queen Bogen's voice boomed. "Knocking the royal guard on their bums!"

"That was epic out there!" Winnie's excited voice easily reached Kip's ears. "I just showed you the—"

"Anyone else would have been executed for such an effrontery."

He almost choked on his breath. Could she do that?

"I just showed you how weak your army is. You're welcome."

"They are mel-yew." Next came the slapping sound of webbed feet on the marble floor. Kip assumed she was pacing.

"Your Highness."

Winnie paused. He guessed to take a calming

133

breath.

"If they can't keep their own balance, how can they fight the lurkin?"

"The mel-yew have defended this realm since the Bogen reign began," said the queen. "Before you came here and tossed them willy-nilly, they were doing rather well."

Kip wondered if her faith in her army might be misplaced. According to the history book he'd perused, the Bogens had reigned only during peaceful times.

"They are our royal guard. If we command it of them, they will fight and succeed."

No response from Winnie.

"Do you disagree with us?" Queen Bogen said sharply.

What had Winnie done now? Had she rolled her eyes? Grimaced?

"No, Your Majesty." She almost sounded contrite. "Obviously, they're trained to fight to the death. All I'm saying is they wouldn't have to die if they got help from stronger fighters."

"We have discussed this matter with you before. Vogan are royalty and do not fight. The palum are simple beings incapable of defense. We have no other subjects."

Kip contorted his face to prevent the dust from tickling a sneeze out of him. Why couldn't Winnie say she was sorry and leave so he could breathe again?

"Your Majesty, if you think you can win a war with the army you have, you're making a huge mistake."

He groaned inwardly. Why did the ruddy girl always need the last word?

"We do not make mistakes of any size. And one more thing. Did we or did we not order you to remain on castle grounds this morning?"

"I don't think so." Now Winnie sounded huffy.

"We distinctly recall informing you that Commander Fynn went to the watch post to look into things. You disregarded our order and went there all the same. Why?"

"I flew with the wigget birds."

The announcement surprised him. They didn't seem strong enough to carry anything heavier than a mel-yew.

"I thought the only reason you didn't want me to go was because it took too long."

"Your thoughts on why we give an order are of no consequence," Queen Bogen said. "You'll do as you're told with no arguments. The rank of general does not give you the authority to go about doing as you jolly well please, flying off in all directions, tipping over the royal guard. If everyone did that, we'd have utter chaos."

"Sorry," Winnie muttered.

A wave of relief rippled through Kip's insides. Finally, an apology.

"Sorry?" the queen bellowed.

His muscles tightened again.

"You are the most impertinent general we have ever encountered. Leave our sight before we have you thrown back into the dungeon!"

Stomping feet, then a door slam.

"She's left, Master Wizard."

He stepped from behind the curtain and took a deep savoring breath of cool air.

"You and the general are of the same world?"

He nodded.

"You don't sound alike."

"Same world, just different accents, Your Majesty."

She gazed out the window. "Do you have feelings for her?"

"She's a bit arrogant," he said with a shrug, "but she's all right. Mostly."

"Then your job, Master Wizard, is to keep close watch over her. Protect her from herself. We cannot allow her to continue to undermine our authority. If she defies us one more time…"

He straightened to attention. "You can count on me, Your Majesty."

"Good. And as a precaution, keep practicing your vanishing spells in case we need to make the general disappear."

He tried to look indifferent, but his face must have betrayed him.

The queen's eyes blazed. "If you haven't the courage to obey our will—"

"I'm at your command. In the meantime, why don't I keep her out of trouble for you?"

Queen Bogen nodded. "She should be meeting with her little band of councilmen now, Master Wizard. You may 'keep her from trouble' by attending that meeting. She's been given Conference Room Seven."

He bowed. "Yes, Your Majesty."

"We're on our way to Meeting Chamber Four ourselves, making banquet plans for the pre-hunt. You may report to us there."

"As you command." He bowed again and strode

out.

Winnie's conference room barely held one table and the seven plush chairs that surrounded it. Her little band, as the queen called them, occupied every seat except for the one at the far end of the table.

Kip flashed what he hoped looked like a winning smile. "Don't mind if I sit in, do you?"

Winnie merely shrugged.

He eased along the right side of the table, past a voga page and a mel-yew monk, to the vacant chair opposite Winnie. "If you need any advice, I've got it in spades." With a whoosh, the ace of spades appeared between his thumb and forefinger.

She groaned and looked away. A few of her "councilmen" clapped until the voga page, seated at Winnie's right, glowered.

Once the room fell into silence, the page turned to Winnie. "General, with your permission I shall introduce your staff."

She smiled. "Go for it, Loy."

"Seated directly across from myself is Freeden." He waved toward a mel-yew child on Winnie's left. Kip had never seen him before.

"He likes to be called Cubby," Winnie said.

Loy hesitated. "As you wish, General. Beside, er, Cubby is—" He grimaced. "—Polo, the court's jester."

The little comic, dressed today in bright green, stood and bowed.

Ignoring the palum seated on Polo's other side, Loy continued, "On my right, we have Brother Mapes of the Brothers Ky. At the far end of the table is our Master Wizard."

Taking that as a cue to perform, Kip pulled a red

silk scarf from his fist.

"No magic."

With a shrug he returned the silk to the inside pocket of his robe.

"And lastly, as it should be," Loy said, "I introduce Pall, the lowly palum."

Winnie leaned forward to examine the creature's horsey face. "That's not Pall." She sat back. "The stripe down his nose is too wide."

Loy spoke in a stage whisper loud enough for Kip to hear. "If you please, General, they are all named Pall. Makes it easier for them to remember."

"They all have the same name?"

"Yes, General," said Loy. "You've caught the gist of it straight away."

"Doesn't that get confusing? I mean, what happens if there's a whole herd of them and one of them wants somebody's attention?"

"They were born confused, General," he said. "Besides, what does it matter what happens when palum are amongst themselves?"

"Just curious."

Kip pressed his lips together to keep from smiling. As annoying as she could be at times, he found her curiosity appealing. And he rather liked the way her uniform showed off her figure.

"Pall, what do you do if somebody calls your name when you're with your people?"

"If called, good General, I should come forward."

"But you all have the same name."

"Excuse me, General?" Kip said. "I expect it's a bit like shouting fire in a crowded theater? They would—" He cleared his throat. "—stampede."

"Oh. I guess we won't do that."

"A wise choice, General," said Loy. "Shall we get on with the meeting?"

"Exactly, I just talked to your queen." She made a sour face.

Loy's frog face wrinkled into a haughty sneer. Had the queen ordered the page to report on Winnie's meeting? If that was the case, he'd better step in and save the situation.

"What the general clearly meant to say," Kip said, "was she just spoke with our illustrious queen."

She glared at him. "Is she your girlfriend now?"

He bristled.

"As I was saying, the queen doesn't think her royal army needs help fighting the lurkin."

Loy's shoulders stiffened. "Our queen is never wrong."

"She doesn't know the enemy the way I do."

Loy's eyes narrowed. "Forgive my contradiction, General, but no one has seen the enemy. Not even our oracle."

"I have, and they look like fifties sci-fi spiders. I saw them in a dream."

"Are you barking mad?" Kip cried out. "Dreams don't count."

"They do here. See what I'm wearing?"

He did and appreciated it, but she clearly was not in the mood for appreciation.

She tugged at her tunic. "I dreamed I wore this. It looked exactly like this. Polo sang a ballad about Bogen of the vogan in the same dream. Almost everything I dreamed came true. If I say I saw man-sized spiders attacking the castle, then that's what's going to happen."

"You said almost everything. Which bit wasn't true?"

"When the lurkin attacked, they kind of marched to…" Her voice faded to an inaudible mumble.

He held a hand to his ear. "Sorry?"

Only slightly louder, she said, " 'Ride of the Valkyries.' "

"There we are, then." Kip slapped the table in triumph. "That can't happen. Nobody in this world knows our music."

She stared hard at him. "The dream was right. I know it."

He fell against the back of his chair and shook his head.

"Master Wizard," Loy said, "perhaps you know a spell that could restore the good General to sanity."

Kip let out an amused snort. He had to admit she sounded a bit bonkers.

"What would anybody here know about sanity?"

Loy gasped. "General. How can you—" The rest of his words were drowned out by boisterous music, blasting from a speaker near the ceiling.

Kip recognized the tune. He hadn't known it by title, but it definitely originated in his world.

Winnie shot from her chair. "Battle stations. We're under attack!"

Her staff responded with wide-eyed stares. Kip didn't care about them now. He hurried after Winnie. After all, he'd promised Mikey he'd help her. If monsters were truly attacking, she needed his magic.

Chapter 16

Ever since Winnie got the smart watch for her fourteenth birthday, each morning, Wagner's rousing classic woke her. The tune inspired her to seize the day. Now hearing it blasting from the castle speakers meant a call to war. She bolted into the corridor, snapping her head left to right. *Which way?*

Kip burst from the room, right behind her. "Looking for the queen?" he shouted over the music. "I know where she is."

"Show me."

He clasped her hand. They raced through a maze of corridors. The song's final note vibrated off the walls just as they skidded to a stop in front of a closed door with a large number four painted on it. Two mel-yew knights stood guard outside the room.

"This is it," Kip said, still panting. "Meeting Chamber Four."

Why not the throne room? That's where the spiders attacked. Although, if Queen Bogen was here, maybe Winnie had time to warn everyone to prepare for the attack. She dropped Kip's hand and rushed to the closed door.

He grabbed the back of her tunic, stopping her. "Let's sort out what we're saying first."

"What's to sort out?" She struggled in his grip. "We're under attack."

"We don't know that. The music's stopped. You said the spiders marched to the music."

She puffed in exasperation, unwilling to admit he might be right. "The music could start again at any minute."

"We can't just rush in. They've got protocols."

She finally yanked free. "You think they want us bowing and curtsying when the whole castle is under siege?" She stomped to the chamber door.

A pair of mel-yew knights clanked their metal heels in unison. They stepped toward each other, blocking the entrance.

"Stand down, men," Winnie ordered. She remembered hearing that line in a movie.

"Begging the general's pardon," spoke a muted voice from inside the helmet of the guard on the right. "Queen Bogen is meeting privately with her councilmen."

Kip hovered behind her, breathing down the back of her neck.

"Probably discussing national security. Play by their rules."

She elbowed him in the stomach. "I gotta get in there."

"My apologies again, General," said the knight, "but our instructions were made explicitly clear. Only the Master Wizard may enter."

"What?"

"Ha!" Kip said.

The knights separated for him. He strutted forward and opened the door. When he looked back to sneer at Winnie—and she knew he would—she slipped between the knights and pushed into the room ahead of him.

The temperature difference between the cool halls and this humid room blasted her in the face. Parted curtains revealed an open floor-to-ceiling window letting in the sultry air. Her stare shifted from the brilliant sunlight streaming inside to the queen. She sat at the head of an oval table with her advisors along both sides. Each pair of hands held playing cards from her world. That infuriating Kip must have brought them through the time tear.

"What is going on in here?" Winnie demanded.

Queen Bogen placidly looked up but not at her. "Master Wizard, we expected you to arrive alone."

He stepped forward, but Winnie shoved him aside. "We're under attack!"

Commander Fynn sprang from his seat. He punched a button behind the nearest curtain, setting off an alarm. Its deep buzz pulsed so loud Winnie felt it in her throat. At least that body-shaking sound proved the commander took her seriously. Rushing footsteps clattered down the corridor outside the chamber.

The queen threw down her cards. "To war!"

"By your command." Fynn dashed out.

The rest of the queen's council scrambled to their feet. A different battle raged inside Winnie's head. Her inner warrior wanted to join the charge, but her thudding heart and frozen legs fought for self-preservation.

The councilmen didn't join the fight either. They argued whether they should evacuate the queen to the north tower or the south.

"Enough," the queen commanded. "We intend to observe the battle from this very spot." She strode to the center window.

Zyke jumped to her side. "At least let me protect you, Your Majesty."

Since Winnie's legs refused to leave, she let her controlling side take over. "Call for palum reinforcements."

"For the umpteenth time, General, no. What manner of monarch would we be if we sent peaceful creatures to war?" Queen Bogen glared out the window. She punched the button behind the curtain, silencing the alarm. A decisive clack of metal boots sounded from the courtyard below. "Well, well, well."

Zyke harrumphed.

Winnie's legs finally came unstuck. She tore around the table to the window. Far below, Commander Fynn and the mel-yew troops waited in formation. Alone. Relief flowed through her. They were safe for now.

Kip remained by the closed door as if braced for action. "What's coming?"

"Unless they're invisible," Zyke said, "nothing."

Winnie refused to believe him. "Then they're still at the beach."

"I'll call me familiar, shall I?" said Kip. "He can fly round the area and see if anything's on the way."

The queen waved her hand. "Have it done."

He bounded to the window and whistled through his teeth. A black bird with a bright orange beak glided inside and lit on his shoulder. Kip mumbled to the bird, and it flew away.

"This should only take a tick."

The bird gave Winnie a new idea. "Your Majesty, we need your flying guards. If they carried heavy rocks, they could bomb the enemy."

"And what enemy would that be?" Zyke said in a superior tone.

Now it was Winnie's turn to harrumph. "Look. I'm telling you they charge to that music."

Queen Bogen blinked back. "Music? Are you hearing music, General?"

"Your Majesty," Jebb, the green toad, said, "vill wine can make people hear things that aren't there. Perhaps the general had too much with breakfast."

Winnie spun toward him. "I didn't drink any wine! I'm talking about the music that played in the hall a minute ago. It's an omen."

"Oh, that music." Queen Bogen smiled. "We told you our technicians were up to the task. They've recorded the music. They even put your timepiece right."

Now her dream made sense. Frama-12 got Wagner's music from Winnie's watch. Since nobody seemed to be in any hurry to head to the throne room, maybe the lurkin hadn't reached the watch post after all.

Queen Bogen gently stroked Winnie's watch, now strapped to her white wrist. "Such a handy adornment. We suppose you'd like it back."

Winnie definitely wanted it back but not right now with warts touching it. "Uh, you can borrow it a little longer."

"How wonderfully kind of you, General."

While Winnie debated whether to nod or curtsey, Kip's pet bird flapped back into the room. It carried a dazed, little, floppy-eared rodent in its beak. The bird dropped it at Kip's feet. "This was the only threat. The grounds are now safe," the bird said. "Baubles for me trouble?"

Kip pulled a gold button from his wizard's robe. He tossed it into the air. The black bird caught the button in its beak and flew away. Kip waved his hand over the dazed animal while mumbling under his breath. The air crackled and sizzled. Winnie's ears popped just as the animal vanished.

"What a relief, eh?" Kip said, "We're not under attack."

She blinked at him in disbelief. Had he really made that fuzzy little creature disappear, or was it just another trick? Her ears still hurt, though. What about that?

"We never were under attack." The queen's bulging eyes shot a heated stare at Winnie. "Don't believe for a moment the loan of this trinket will change our opinion on what transpired today. You had us put the royal guard on alert for nothing."

Winnie looked from the queen to the empty spot at Kip's feet. Why didn't anybody demand to know how he'd made that furry rat with bunny ears go away?

"What you just observed, Your Majesty," Kip said, "was a test of your guards' emergency response time. Admit it. They could've assembled a bit faster. That's the whole point of practice drills, wouldn't you say? To improve efficiency?"

Queen Bogen dipped her head in a half nod. "Our own father used to say something very similar. We believe the expression was 'practice drills bring many kills.' At the time he was referring to the hunt, but the phrase is still apt."

She and her advisors returned to their card game.

"Good work, General." The queen collected the cards and began to shuffle.

Winnie had to give the nutty wizard props for making her look good. Maybe he wasn't so bad after all.

"In the future, please inform us of all practice drills. May we deal you in, Master Wizard?"

Kip rubbed his hands together. "Don't mind if I do." He slid into Commander Fynn's vacated seat.

Winnie shifted her weight. "Uh, is everybody just going to play cards now? We probably should talk about this war thing. That music really was an omen. I had a..." She caught herself. Not everybody believed in dreams. "I had a premonition."

"Did you really?" the queen said absently as she dealt the cards.

Winnie pulled up a stool between Kip and Zyke. Maybe she could steer the conversation back to the upcoming conflict. Before she could bring up battle plans, Jebb spoke first. "Might we return to our original discussion, Your Highness? As the hunt is at hand, you still must choose the main dish for the banquet. Would Your Highness prefer skitter stew or scrambled wiggies?"

"Dear sir," the queen said. "Of those choices there is no contest."

Food? Were these people insane? "Excuse me, but weren't we just talking about the war? That's a little more important than what you'll serve at a banquet, don't you think?"

Kip cleared his throat and gave Winnie a stern look.

Jebb rearranged the cards in his hand. "Obviously, you have never treated your palate to the delicacy we call scrambled wiggies."

"Our seneschal makes a good point," the queen said. "Scrambled wiggies stand alone."

Winnie curled her lip in annoyance. "I'm glad they're standing by themselves, because we have more important things to discuss. Like my premonition. It says the lurkin will crash through the castle gates."

Kip cleared his throat louder.

"Nothing will reach our gates," the queen said. "Unless you tip over the army again."

Her councilmen chortled along with her.

Winnie took a deep, calming breath and tried again. "All I'm saying is you have to recruit stronger fighters to help the mel-yew."

"Shall it be scrambled wiggies, then, Your Highness?" Jebb asked as if Winnie hadn't even spoken.

"Look," Winnie said through clenched teeth, "if we don't build up the army now, you'll lose everything. Not just wiggies. Whatever they are."

"We will be celebrating the hunt quite soon. We decree there shall be no more talk of this boorish war of yours until after the hunt."

"It's everybody's war!"

"We do hope you're not raising your voice to us, General. As you are aware, such conduct is unforgivable."

Kip jumped up. "Your Majesty, the general is so overtired she doesn't even realize she's speaking so loudly."

"I'm wide awake. Make them listen, Kip. They'll believe you. You're the wizard."

"Even when she's tired, she's the most insolent general we have ever had the misfortune to encounter."

"She might be talking in her sleep, Your Majesty," said Kip. "That's how tired she is."

He mumbled a few incomprehensible syllables. Instantly, her eyelids drooped closed. The queen's voice faded.

Winnie fell into a dream where she sat in a swaying Ferris wheel car. It reached the bottom, then whooshed upward so fast she laughed. She gripped the bar with both hands. At the top it eased to a halt. An unmoving dark sea lay in the distance. Frama-12's odorous ocean didn't just assault her nose during the day. It even haunted her dreams.

A second smell, sweeter and familiar, blew in from her right. Her dad's cologne. She turned. Dad sat next to her. His hair looked sleep tousled, and he wasn't wearing his glasses as if he'd just woken.

She let out a delighted squeal and gave him a hug.

After they pulled apart, he wrinkled his nose. "What stinks?"

She grinned, feeling silly, feeling relieved. It felt like visiting day at summer camp all over again. "It's the ocean."

"Smells like rotten eggs and three-day-old roadkill."

She laughed. "Believe it or not, you get used to it."

He chuckled along with her. "I don't believe it."

"How'd you get here?"

"I'm not sure. One minute I was dreaming about deep-sea fishing when Mikey showed up and asked me to visit you. He wanted us to talk about a gherkin takeover. The kid's imaginative, but rogue pickles?"

"I think he must've said lurkin."

Dad nodded. "He said you'd understand. His

message to you is they're still a few weeks away."

"Is he one hundred percent positive about that?" She squinted toward the horizon.

He lifted a pair of binoculars and focused them on the ocean.

"See any lurkin out there?"

"What do they look like?"

"Giant spiders, but nobody wants to believe me."

Still looking through the binoculars, he said softly, "Are you being diplomatic?"

"Maybe."

He lowered the binoculars, but when she tried to take them, he wouldn't let go. She stared into his eyes. Without his glasses, she easily saw his loving concern.

"You have to make an effort to get along with the people here," he said gently.

"Dad, I am." She tugged at the binoculars.

He still wouldn't let go.

"Your teachers always say you have leadership qualities," he remarked, "which is good. They also say you have a tendency to get pushy. Not so good. Mikey claims you're provoking a queen this time. Queens don't give their subjects detention; they put them in jail."

Queens put their subjects in dungeons, but Winnie kept that to herself. "Dad, she's almost as bad as having another stepmother. I don't like ladies who aren't my mom bossing me around."

"I've got news, Win. You didn't always like it when your mom told you what to do either." He finally let go of the binoculars. "Seriously, you need to be a team player."

"I'm not on a team. I'm at war." She focused the

lenses on the jellied ocean.

"Sweetheart, warriors need allies. Don't try to do this on your own."

When Mom's medicine stopped working, she'd fought alone. If Winnie hoped to stay true to her mom's bravery, she had to do the same.

"Did you hear me, Win?"

She lowered the binoculars. "I wish you were really here instead of in a dream."

"What I'm telling you is still true. The only difference is I won't remember this conversation. You will." He thumped her lightly under the chin. "Get some allies."

His image faded, leaving Winnie alone on the Ferris wheel until it faded too.

Chapter 17

Thanks to extra practice, Kip finally possessed the skill to make living beings disappear. Now, if ordered, he could make Winnie vanish. Not that he'd do it. The girl might be trouble, but she was all he had from his world. As she lay sleeping on his laboratory cot, ten feet away, she looked so peaceful and, dare he add, gentle?

Surely, the magic to change her attitude existed within the obedience spells book. Cool damp air rustled his candle flame, making the words on the browned pages appear to dance. The symbols looked more complicated than he'd expected.

He sighed. If Winnie only tried harder to get on with the queen, he wouldn't have to resort to enchantments. Although he had to admit he admired how she stood up to authority. If he dared do the same with his own parents, a bag-boy job might not be waiting for him when he and Winnie returned home. If they returned.

"What are you doing?" Willum said from the window sill.

Kip jumped at getting caught looking at his sleeping damsel. He returned his attention to the incantation book. "Research."

Willum toddled across the open pages. He cocked his head at the printing. "You've got the wrong book."

Thunder grumbled in the distance, echoing Kip's own irritation. He knew he had the right ruddy book. It promised spells of obedience.

"Love potions are in that one." Willum pointed his beak toward a red volume, resting on the floor beside the desk.

"What are you on about? I don't want that."

The bird cackled. "Yes, you do."

Kip shook his head in firm denial. He didn't see Winnie in that way. At least he didn't believe he did. Still, Willum's suggestion sent a flutter tickling across his chest.

He laid the red book on top of the one on obedience and flipped through it. For research purposes only. The idea that Winnie might find him attractive held a certain appeal. If she fell in love with him, she might not act so prickly toward the queen. But a potion wasn't true love, and what was the point of love if it wasn't true? Then again, did he even want love? Especially when Winnie could be so contrary. Kip drummed his long fingers over the printing, trying to decide.

Willum hopped onto Kip's shoulder. "What are you waiting for?"

Kip hissed for silence. "She's sleeping."

"I'll bite her nose. That'll wake her. Then we can make all the noise we want."

"Leave her be. She needs rest."

"She can hear you," Winnie said in a drowsy voice.

He slapped the love-potion book closed. "Nothing," he blurted. A surge of hot guilt shot through him. He shoved the book under his desk.

She propped herself on her elbows. "Where am I?"

"Me lab," he said, glad for the change in topic. "Like it?"

He watched her scan the room. Her gaze paused at the room's highlights. The skull, used as a candle holder—what self-respecting wizard didn't own one of those? Her attention moved to the shelving filled with ancient tomes—real wizards never called them books. Finally, she stared at the Bunsen burner where rainwater heated for tea.

Her stare moved full circle, landing on him. "Why do you need a lab?"

Willum flapped his wings. "She isn't very bright, is she? In fact, she's quite dim. Are you sure you want—"

Kip clamped his fingers around Willum's beak before the bird mentioned the word love. "I heard the cook's making your favorite meat pies tonight."

He let his familiar struggle for a bit before he let go of his beak and shooed him out the window.

"Did you teach that bird to say I'm stupid?"

He forced a laugh. "Don't mind Willum. If it's not a shiny coin, it's dim. That's just the way birds think."

"Har har." Winnie stood and combed her fingers through her ruffled hair. "How'd I get here?"

"The guards carried you up after you fell asleep."

She put her hands on her hips. "Did you hypnotize me?"

"It was a sleep incantation, actually. I needed to stop you from offending the queen. You're welcome."

"There's no such thing as sleep incantations."

"If you don't dial it back a bit, Queen Bogen might order your execution."

Her eyes widened but only briefly. "You're kidding, right?"

"Her threat is just as real as me magic. Now, I could put a convincement spell on you to make you believe me, but I'd rather you believed me because I'm right."

"You'll have to show me something that doesn't look like a trick if you want me to believe." Before he could conjure a spell to sway her, she marched to the door.

"Wait, don't go yet." He raised his hand and muttered a hold spell.

Her body went stiff. "Why can't I move?" Since her mouth still worked, he hadn't completely mastered the spell.

"Please, don't go." He murmured the words to release her. Louder, he said, "I'm serious about the queen. She is not pleased with you."

She stumbled forward, caught her balance, and slowly faced him. Her eyes looked rounder than he'd ever seen them. "You really can do spells."

Had he finally convinced her? "Um, well, you know." He shrugged. "Probably something in the air, but yeah, I can cast the odd one or two."

Her deer-in-the-headlights expression immediately morphed into full-on confidence. "Excellent! Then your magic can make the queen agree to let the palum fight this war."

"That particular spell won't work on subjects who believe strongly. And Queen Bogen feels passionately about protecting the palum."

"I want to protect them too, but they're part horse. A horse's hoof can knock a person out. And if you've ever been bitten by one, they can leave a scar. I have one to prove it."

"We'll never convince the queen to use palum in a war. Sorry."

"Can you at least cast a spell to see how far away the lurkin are? Oh! And while you're at it, find out what they look like."

"I don't know the spell for distance yet, but maybe we can see them. I've got a crystal ball." Kip retrieved it from the cabinet under the window. "It's got a crack. Hopefully, that won't affect what we see."

A thunderclap made them both jump.

"So it might work?"

"We'll give it a go, shall we?" He carried the palm-sized ball to the table by his unlit fireplace. Droplets began to ping off the metal roof. Soon a wall of water gushed past the tower window.

"The storm won't last," he shouted over the noise. "They never do. Sit there." He nodded at the overstuffed chair beside the table.

Winnie bounced onto it as he pulled up a dusty ottoman for himself. He laid the clear ball on the table, the cracked side facing down. "Right. Here goes."

He gently clasped the crystal orb in his fingertips and peered into it.

"Shouldn't it sit on a base or something?"

"No."

"Aren't you at least supposed to wave your arms around?"

He scowled. "Shh. Just look into it."

"I'm not magical. How am I supposed to see anything?"

He let out a sigh and looked up. "If you'd give me a second to concentrate, I might be able to bring up something we both can see."

"Oh. Sorry. Okay."

He lowered his head again. The pattering rain relaxed his mind. He peered deeply into the glass, allowing his eyes to fall out of focus. *Please show us what needs to be seen.* The silent chant played in his mind. After multiple repetitions the crystal clouded into a gray mist that slowly swirled. Winnie gasped, but the sound didn't break his concentration. *Please show us what needs to be seen.*

The churning mist spun faster, condensing into an image of a creature with an oval-shaped body that stood on eight spindly legs. Kip's mouth dropped open. *Blimey, can't believe that worked.*

Chapter 18

The ball went clear again. "Did you see that?"

"A daddy longlegs?" Winnie said in awe.

"Is that how they looked in your dream?"

"Nope. More like giant tarantulas. Do you think the crack in the crystal ball did that?"

"Not sure." He rose and returned the ball to the cabinet. All he knew for certain was his focus on the crystal ball had given him a headache, and he wanted to relieve it. "Fancy some tea?"

Her eyebrows lifted in surprise. "You have tea?"

He removed the boiling water from his Bunsen burner and spooned ground bark into two mismatched teacups. "I probably should warn you it's not typical tea."

"Not a problem. If it's warm, I'll take it. It's chilly in here. Oh, by the way, after you put me to sleep, I had another dream message. We should have a couple weeks before the lurkin get here. Hopefully, that'll give us time to figure out how to stop giant spiders."

Kip poured the steaming water. "Wouldn't it be a lark if they were normal-sized and we're getting worked up over nothing?"

"I wish, but I doubt this world works that way."

"Haven't you ever agonized over a test at school, and when you got to the classroom, it was open book and stupid easy?"

"This is war, Kip, not a pop quiz. We better 'study' just in case. I think it's weird, though, that the lurkin in your crystal ball and the ones in my dreams look so different. And while we're on the subject, how come we've seen two kinds of spiders and the oracle hasn't seen anything?"

"Maybe you've got special powers that helped us see a future the oracle couldn't."

She laughed. "Me? Special powers?"

He stirred the tea. "Why not? I've got some. We needn't grapple with it now. A banquet and the hunt are coming up. The queen won't discuss the war now anyway."

"What is the hunt?"

"No idea." He held up a bowl of beige granules. "Sugar?"

She perked up. "You have sugar?"

"It's something of a substitute that tastes sweet."

She nodded. "Sure, why not?"

He tipped a spoonful into each mug and brought them to the table. He sat on the ottoman, knee to knee with his guest.

She sipped his version of herbal tea and nodded. "Not bad. What's in it?"

He grinned. "Probably best if you didn't know."

She smiled back. "Powdered eye of newt?"

"With a touch of dried bat dung," he teased.

She didn't just laugh; she gave him a captivating smile. His cheeks blazed with heat. He took a quick sip of tea to hide his blush behind his teacup.

The storm ended as abruptly as it started. Sunlight streamed through the window, brightening the room.

"We should keep clear of the queen while she's

planning her banquet," he said.

"Fine with me. She gets on my nerves anyway."

He laughed. "She gets on everybody's nerves. Why do you think I taught her to play cards? To stop her pestering me about making the lurkin disappear."

She hunched forward, suddenly intent. "You could, right? That wasn't a trick when you made the rat-bunny disappear. It really vanished, didn't it?"

"It really vanished. And they call them hoppers."

She smirked. "They would, wouldn't they? Where did it go?"

"I might've accidentally sent it to an adjacent world."

"Like ours?"

"I honestly don't know. That's why I'm not too keen on making big things disappear, especially enemies."

She groaned. "We're in serious trouble."

"Not necessarily. We've got Takka on our side. I took your advice and met with him in that dream place. He believes in us. So do I. We can win this. Spiders are just insects, right? They won't have bombs or guns."

"Ooh, I know. We'll build a giant catapult that sends enormous boots at the spiders to step on them."

He laughed, enjoying this side of her personality. "I'll bet the queen's technicians could do that. They made your tune play through the speakers."

Her playfulness changed to concern. "In my dream those insects broke down the castle door to that tune."

"Let's not think of that just now. We'll let things simmer at the backs of our minds. Something cunning is bound to pop up, right? For now, why don't I show you the sights?"

"Are there any sights?"

He beamed. "Surprisingly, yes. I know a perfect place."

He had hoped to take her there right then, but she wanted to jog. She claimed to be in training for a foot race. Unexpected visits to alternate worlds wouldn't interfere with her workouts. In her defense, she invited him to jog along. He declined, remembering how fast she'd run the day he accidentally nicked her favorite locket back home. While Winnie jogged, Kip stopped at the kitchens to order a picnic lunch for the next day.

****

On their first outing, Kip proposed a hike to the top of Mount Kee. Winnie, who'd already run for the day, suggested they travel by wiggets. He agreed, eager to give it a go. At the wigget sanctuary, the trainer fitted them both with vests and straps.

"This is brill!" he called as they glided through the air.

Winnie laughed. "I know, right?"

The birds set them down at the highest point where they ate cold meat pies. Over the treetops, past the castle, lay farmland and several mel-yew villages far beyond.

"We could set up another lookout post here," Winnie said between bites. "You can see for miles. So far, no spiders, which is awesome. Plus, it's so peaceful."

"Agreed," Kip said. The pastoral scene, however, couldn't compare to his newfound fascination with Winnie. Not that he'd admit it to her just yet. He couldn't tell if she had changed or if he had.

"So," she said, drawing out the word.

His heart pounded to an eager beat. Was she feeling the same interest in him? "Yes?"

"Do you think we're speaking Framan or English?"

His shoulders sagged. Okay, maybe not. Fortunately, he too had considered the language topic. "Framan. I believe something in the time tear adjusted our brain, allowing us to communicate easily. Anyway, that's how I explain the headache I had when I first came here."

"I got a headache too. You're right. That could be a side effect of being able to communicate."

"Verbally, anyway. Their written language looks like nothing I'd ever seen before. The only way I can read their books is with an enlightenment potion."

"Mikey never explained language. They have a few weird words though, like 'tia-tia' to make the army turn. What's that all about?"

"Dialect?" he guessed.

"Weird stuff in a weird place shouldn't surprise me, but I still want to understand, ya know? Like, what made some people look like horses and others look like toads?"

They actually looked like frogs, but he kept that to himself. They were getting on too well to ruin it by correcting her. "Genetic experiment gone awry."

Her eyes widened. "Agree. Look at their ocean. Only an advanced civilization could make a mess like that."

He grinned back. "Exactly."

She laughed and nudged him. "Did we just agree on something?"

Their new camaraderie led to a second date, a palum-cart ride to the west forest. Kip ordered the palum to stop quite a distance from their destination. He had discovered it alone and wanted to keep it private.

He guided Winnie along a narrow path cut through the forest. At the palum cart, he'd taken charge of the cumbersome picnic basket and instantly regretted it. When he offered her the much lighter ground cloth as a chivalrous gesture, he'd forgotten how swiftly the blasted girl walked. The rolled-up cloth tucked under her arm allowed her to move at a speed he could barely match. Thankfully, she ambled along in silence. It took all his effort to hide his panting breath from her.

Finally, a quarter of a mile later, she pointed at a gray shimmer between the leaves. "Is that water?"

He grinned, encouraged by the excitement in her voice. "It's a lake. Well, a really big pond if I'm honest."

She let out a gleeful hoot and raced toward it.

Kip, weighted by the picnic basket, moved at a slower pace. By the time he reached the lake, she had already dropped the ground cloth and unlaced her Framan sandals. She scuffed her bare feet through black sand at the edge of the oval, half-acre expanse of blue-gray water.

"Look how clear this is."

"I think it's fed by an uncontaminated spring."

"I'm surprised the queen lets you come out here. This place is awesome."

He silently agreed. "I don't believe anybody knows about it. It's too far off the path for palum to come this way. And there aren't any mel-yew settlements nearby."

She looked back. "How'd you find it?"

He shrugged. "I get around." He chose not to admit

that he first visited the area after Willum had bragged about succulent worms that lived at the water's edge. He'd never seen any, but the swimming was bliss.

She hesitated at the water's edge. "You said uncontaminated spring. Are you sure?"

"I've swallowed a bit whilst swimming with no ill effects. So far."

Except for the sandals, Winnie wore her Earth clothes today. She waded to her knees and splashed water on her face. "It tastes just like spring water!"

He unrolled the ground cloth. "Don't know if we can trust it too much, though."

"Too bad Mikey didn't remind me to pack my suit."

Kip, dressed in shorts and a Manchester United T-shirt, didn't let the lack of swim trunks dissuade him. He kicked off his sneakers. "Pretend you're already wearing one. Race you to the other side."

He plunged into the water.

She quickly overtook him and reached the opposite bank five strokes ahead. They swam back to the deepest part of the lake and treaded water, facing each other.

"What are you," he teased, "part fish?"

She grinned. "I'm surprised you didn't put a spell on yourself to swim faster."

"Me wand doesn't work outside, remember?"

She giggled. "You're the nuttiest wizard I've ever met."

He gave her a flirtatious smile. "How many wizards do you know?"

She laughed and dove underwater. He tried to grab her foot, but she was still too fast.

Back on the beach, they dried in the sun and ate

lunch. Trilling birds and chattering insects in the trees serenaded them.

Winnie broke the silence. "My mom loved the lake."

Kip opened his mouth to agree. Her solemn tone stopped him. Even the leaves, shushing in a soft breeze, joined the respectful silence. He hadn't forgotten that she'd lost her mother.

She stared out across the water. He waited. The stillness stretched on.

"Dad sold our lake house last year. We just couldn't go back without her."

"I'm so, so sorry."

She sprang to her feet. "Gotta swim now." At the deepest part she dove under.

He sat up, watching and waiting. He held his own breath until his pulse pounded in his head from a lack of air. She didn't resurface. He gasped for breath and leaped up, scanning the still water for her.

He charged into the lake just as her head popped up. Now that he knew she was all right, he pretended he'd only come in to cool off. They swam for a bit, but the comfortable atmosphere had changed. He wanted to make it right again but didn't know how.

On the ride home, he wanted to offer comfort by draping an arm around her shoulders. Winnie, in her usual fashion, had other plans. Due to her strict exercise regimen, she chose to race ahead of the palum cart. Kip rode alone, silently hating her marathon training.

At the castle she wasn't even winded. "Thanks, it was fun, see you tomorrow," she said in one breath and turned away.

"Wait. Do you want to see the queen's gardens? I

could show you."

"Maybe tomorrow." She sprinted off without looking back.

Willum lit on his shoulder. "Kiss her yet?"

Kip shrugged the bird away. If he couldn't be with Winnie, he'd rather be alone.

Chapter 19

The tiny Frama-12 lake had reminded Winnie of the one at her family's vacation home. Lake reminders always brought up thoughts of her mom. As she jogged ahead of the palum cart, her mind fell into a memory from the summer Mom died. After friends and relatives returned to their own lives, Winnie and Dad had withdrawn deeper into their grief. They spent days just staring vacantly at the TV. Then Uncle Ned, Dad's older brother, showed up.

"Clive, Winnie," her uncle said in a stern tone. "Put on your running shoes. You're coming with me. Now."

Neither had the energy to protest. Uncle Ned drove them to an unused high school track.

"Follow me," he said. "We'll start slow."

For the first fifty yards, Winnie's legs felt zombie stiff. Eventually, her muscles warmed. The *skiff, skiff* of her sneakers on the track almost sounded joyful. Almost. At the straightaway Uncle Ned was only half a dozen steps in the lead. Daddy lagged far behind.

"Keep up, Clive," he said over his shoulder. "Hey, Win, I bet you can't catch me."

Her uncle's taunt brought out her inner warrior. A sudden will to win surged through her. She burst ahead, easily passing him. With each stride she felt fierce, strong, and powerful. The faster she ran, the better she felt. She flew around the first curve so far ahead of the grown-ups she saw them across the grassy center of the track. She wanted to show Uncle Ned and Daddy she could beat either one in a race. Their cheers motivated her to run faster. For a full minute, she forgot about missing her mom. Face hot, puffing for breath, she slowed to a walk. Then her grief flooded back. She crumpled to her knees, sobbing.

Daddy reached her first and hugged her tight. "Let it all out."

The permission to cry seemed wrong. Mom never cried. If Winnie wanted to be a warrior just like her mom, she had to stop. She stood with one final sniff. "I'm okay," she'd lied.

Even on Frama-12, running lifted her spirits. So did spending time with Kip. Now, though, she worried she'd made a huge mistake bringing up her mom. She reached the castle gate ahead of Kip and the palum cart, which gave her time for more uneasiness to set in. What if she'd said too much? Would he think her weak for missing her mom? She'd had people tell her to "get over it" more than once.

She frowned, annoyed with herself. Warriors lived private lives. At least she thought so. Until Mom couldn't hide it anymore, she'd kept her illness a secret. Maybe Winnie was supposed to keep secrets too.

The cart rolled through the gates. Before Kip hopped out, Winnie knew she couldn't face him. Not right now at least.

"Thanks, it was fun, see you tomorrow," she said in one breath and dashed away. If he tried to follow, she could outrun him. She sprinted up the staircase but slowed to a walk in the hallway to her rooms. Soft laughter from inside drew her to the balcony. Nita and another mel-yew woman sat at the balcony table.

Winnie considered asking them to move the party, but a plate of cookies lay between them. "Hi, guys." Maybe they'd invite her to join them.

The women threw themselves at Winnie's feet, wailing and talking over each other. She stared down at them, baffled. Had they broken something of hers? With the exception of her watch, which the queen still borrowed, she hadn't brought much to Frama-12. Her locket! She gasped and reached for it. Thankfully, it still lay safely inside her T-shirt, along with the whistle to call wiggets.

"What did you guys do?"

Nita looked up. She swiped at the tears on her cheeks. "My sister and I…" She waved at the snacks on the balcony table. "We paused in our duties."

"That's it? In my world everybody takes a break. It's so you don't work yourself to death. This is your sister?" She smiled at the other tiny mel-yew woman. The two looked identical, except Nita wore a red chemise, and the other woman wore a plain gray tunic.

"Her name is Nola, good General. She toils in the royal laundry."

"You definitely need a rest from that. Come on, ladies."

The women rose.

"Sit back down before your tea gets cold."

They stood woodenly in place.

"No, really. Sit. Sit."

Nita curtseyed. "May I get you some tea, General?"

Winnie pulled a third chair to the table. "That

would be great, thanks. I wouldn't say no to one of those either." She nodded toward the cookies.

Nita scurried away and quickly returned with an extra teacup and a silver tray filled with more cookies. These had cinnamon sprinkled on top. At least it looked like cinnamon to Winnie.

"What do you guys call these? Cookies?"

"We call them sweet-treats, General."

They were sweet and definitely a treat. In fact, they tasted like snickerdoodles. Winnie sighed. "These are amazing. Did you make them?"

"The cook bakes all treats," said Nita. "He made these from a new recipe he received from the wizard."

Kip had done that? He possessed more good qualities than she realized. Winnie bit into another scrumptious cookie. She could learn to like a guy who knew how to make snickerdoodles.

****

After that two-day break, Winnie returned to warrior mode. She didn't care if the attack was weeks away. She still wanted to check the ocean for any signs of lurkin. Just in case.

No one passed her on the staircase. The castle, usually bustling with official-looking vogan hopping through the corridors and servants scurrying back and forth, was strangely vacant. Even the royal doormen had abandoned their posts. She was so used to having it immediately swung open for her that she almost walked into the door.

Outside, the courtyard buzzed with activity. Vogan shouted orders. Mel-yew servants rushed to do their bidding. Palum trotted through the open spaces, setting up long tables and chairs. Mel-yew cooks, wearing chef hats, tossed ingredients into bubbling cauldrons. A team of apron-clad toad men fired up a row of barbecue grills. It looked like all the queen's subjects were prepping for a party.

The hunt, Winnie guessed. If it kept the queen occupied, Winnie liked it. She eased past the hubbub to the wigget sanctuary. The large gray birds dozed from their perches.

"Hi!" she called out. "I need to take another trip to the beach."

The trainer didn't appear.

"Won't be long," she said, even though the birds seemed to be alone. She slipped into the shed and helped herself to a vest, belt, and ankle protectors. Back outside, she blew into her golden whistle. No sound came out, but all the birds jumped awake. She puffed into it until three wiggets swooped from their perches.

"Wigget-wigget, where-to, where-to?" they squawked.

"Big beach."

They honked and flapped, lifting her into the air. The wiggets caught a warm current and flew higher. Now that flying had become familiar, Winnie laughed at the speed and the wind whipping through her hair. She enjoyed the ride until the odor of dead fish and rancid oil brought back old worries. She never should have let Kip and his picnics keep her from her mission.

The gray beach loomed in the distance. Far below the only movement came from a herd of palum picking berries. After landing on the sand, she wobbled over the rubbery sea to the palum on guard duty.

He held the binoculars and even pointed them at the horizon but looked through the objective lenses.

"Pall, you're holding it backward."

The palum snorted in surprise. He lowered the binoculars to bow. "What a great general you are to remember the names of all your lowly scouts."

"May I?" She eased the binoculars out of his hands. Clear, all the way to the horizon. *Still safe.* That comforting thought gave her the patience to teach the scout which end of the binoculars to look through. She didn't even mind that it took three tries.

Confident the enemy hadn't begun their march, Winnie flew back to the castle grounds and the queen's banquet. She stepped to the end of a long queue of vogan and mel-yew. As she moved closer with the line to the first steaming cauldron, the smell of rotten eggs and moldy cheese filled the air. She breathed through her mouth to keep from gagging.

A female server, stirring the cauldron, smiled up at her. "Greetings, General."

"Um, what is that?"

The server beamed. "Scrambled wiggies, dear General. Made fresh this morning." She lifted her ladle full of weird brown blobs in yellow goo. "It's a delicacy."

"What exactly is a wiggie?"

"Wigget hatchlings." The server grinned. "They can't all fly for the royal guard, can they?"

Winnie's insides clenched. "Maybe later." She reached for a crystal goblet. The reddish-brown liquid inside looked like a syrupy version of the raspberry tea she drank at home. "What kind of berries are in this?" She lifted the glass to her lips.

"Vill wine comes from no berries, good General."

Winnie took a sip. Thick spicy fluid burned her

tongue.

"It's made from the fermented blood of the snaps."

Her eyes bulged. The back of her throat constricted. She returned the glass to the table and bowed out of line. Thick, peppery liquid rolled around in her mouth. She ducked behind a bush to spit it out. Smoke rose from the ground where it landed.

She returned to the buffet line and grabbed an orange wedge. At least her eyes told her it was an orange. Her taste buds shouted, *rotten lemons soaked in brine!* Winnie darted to another bush to spit out her second mistake. Where was Kip? He knew what was edible. On her third pass through the food line, she found the yummy bread. She stacked ten slices onto her plate.

"There you are," Kip's British accent spoke from behind her.

"Hey!" She smiled, glad to see him. "I had some of your cookies yesterday. Why didn't you tell the chef about grilled hamburgers? I've been eating poison out here."

He chuckled. "Baby steps. Desserts are easier than changing a whole diet." He turned serious. "For what it's worth, the mel-yew are on your side."

She cocked her head. "Huh?"

"They appreciated your kindness to the servants. In return, they're keeping their ears open for you. Listening and whatnot. Unfortunately, it's bad news. Polo's got a song for you. I've enchanted the lyrics so only we can hear the true message."

"Wait, what?"

Polo bounced onto the outdoor stage to the crowd's applause.

Kip nudged her. "Listen."

Polo strummed a mysterious tune on his lute. "Beware," he sang, "beware! The hunted must beware. If you are here but come from there, beware, beware!" His little black eyes bored into Winnie's. "Hunters have blood in their eyes. They'll harm you; it's you they despise. It will seem a mistake, but your life they shall take. Be alert, be aware, stay alive!"

The audience laughed harder with each worrisome line. Winnie shivered.

Kip wrapped his arm around her. "The oracle would never allow it. Still, there it is."

"Death to the different, the hoppers, the glunt," Polo sang. "If you cannot be changed, you'll be lost to the hunt."

Her plate, forgotten, slid out of her hand, shattering on the hard ground.

Kip hugged her tighter. "Don't worry. I'll keep you safe."

Loy, her page advisor, joined them. "General Windemere, Queen Bogen has asked me to convey an invitation for you to join her party on the hunt today."

She gulped. "Me?"

He bowed. "This is quite an honor. As a rule, only vogan go out."

And only vogan come back. She tried to swallow with a dry throat.

"Please send the general's apologies," said Kip. "She doesn't feel well today."

Thankful for his excuse, she played along, pressing a palm to her forehead. "I might have a fever."

"Dear General," the voga said, "to refuse Her Majesty's request would be a grave insult. Surely, you don't wish to insult your queen."

She had insulted the queen a dozen times already. "Tell Her Majesty I thank her for the honor. I'll join the hunt even though I don't feel well."

"Splendid! The queen will be pleased." Loy bounced away.

She shivered in the warm air.

"Nobody'll tell me what they do out there," Kip said in a low voice. "But when you get right to it, they're just amphibians. I mean, without teeth, they can't tear you apart."

"What?" She stumbled back a step.

"I meant it as a good thing. Not getting eaten alive, I mean. I'll follow you, shall I? On the wiggets. To make sure you're safe."

Technically, warriors took care of themselves, but she was willing to make an exception. The more people looking out for her the better. "Thanks."

He leaned so close his lips bumped against her cheek. "Cheers." He hurried away.

Winnie lifted her hand to her cheek. A herd of toads was about to maul her, but one question jumped ahead of all the others. *Did he just kiss me?*

Chapter 20

Kip sprinted through the crowd, veering around revelers and serving tables. At the bird sanctuary a gaggle of wiggets preened on their perches. When he hastened past, several ruffled their feathers.

"Minah, are you free?"

She toddled into view. "Master Wizard, why aren't you enjoying the festivities?"

"May I borrow your fastest wiggets?"

"I'm sorry, Master Wizard. None are available."

"But…" He twisted around. At least ten roosted on their posts. Two more birds landed and pecked at the ground by his feet. "What about these fellows?"

"They've just come off guard duty and need their rest. It pains me to deny you, but I must think of my charges, mustn't I?"

"I could cast an invigorating spell on them." He could if he remembered how it went. Was it *ka-mee-ka-mah* or *ka-mah-ka-mee*? The wrong way put the subject to sleep.

Minah's shoulders stiffened. "I never allow spells here, Master Wizard. You know as well as I they are often unreliable and rarely last. What if my wiggets lost their strength mid-flight while they transported you?"

"What if we had four instead of three carry me?"

"I'm sorry."

"You can't spare four?"

"I've raised these darlings from hatchlings, Master Wizard. They're like children to me. It's my job to see they don't overextend themselves, for their protection as well as their riders'."

His heart pounded in his ears. Polo's song had foretold danger, and Kip had promised to keep Winnie safe. She needed him. "Minah, please. The general's life is in jeopardy."

"Things can't be as critical as that."

He took a deep breath to calm his jangled nerves. "Queen Bogen took the general on the hunt. She plans to lose her."

Minah's pinched face broke into a smile. "I've heard that rumor as well, Master Wizard, but have no concerns. The oracle would never permit that. Besides, it's my understanding that the queen's council merely wish to frighten her."

How could he believe a bird trainer? She spent all her time with wiggets. She couldn't possibly know what went on in the castle.

"I need to see that she's all right. Is there any other way I can follow her? Perhaps by palum cart?"

"I doubt you'll find a palum hardy enough to pull a cart all the way up the mountain. The queen's party always hunts in the high country."

"Please, you've got to help. The wiggets can't all be tired."

She looked away, but not before he saw the guilt in her eyes.

He bent over her. "You're keeping them from me on purpose. Why?"

She bowed her head.

"Did Zyke put you up to this?"

Her head snapped up. "I never take orders from *him*."

"Then who do you take them from?"

She averted her eyes again.

He huffed. He paced away from her, then stomped back. "Minah, tell me."

Nothing.

"Please?"

She slowly raised her eyes to meet his. "Our oracle."

"Maggenta? That doesn't even make sense. She's supposed to be on our side."

"Please, Master Wizard, it's for your own safety."

"I've got magic to keep me safe. Winnie doesn't."

The mel-yew trainer stood thinking for a long moment. "There is one possibility."

"Anything."

"We have older flyers living in the west forest."

His muscles sizzled, anticipating the race to get there, but Minah wasn't ready to let him go.

"After they've been in service for three years, wiggets are returned to the wild. They aren't as strong as the young ones. Your cape should protect you from their talons. I recommend at least six to carry you."

"Brilliant! Let's call them!"

"You'll need a special whistle." The mel-yew trainer padded to her shed. He loped after her, hoping to speed things up. Inside, he followed her gaze to a silver whistle that hung from a high peg on the wall. He snatched it down before she raised her arm.

"This it?" He slipped the strap over his head. "I just give it a toot, and they'll come?" He raised the whistle to his lips.

"Not here, Master Wizard! Gracious me, we'd have utter chaos if you called them here. No, it's the west forest where you need to be."

"Thanks." Kip raced from the sanctuary. Despite the great distance to the west woods, he sprinted the whole way. Once his breathing slowed to normal, he blew into the whistle. No response. He tried three more times before one wigget with rumpled feathers landed at his feet.

"Where-to, where-to?"

He blew the whistle again. Two more elderly wiggets flew to him.

"How strong do you chaps feel today?"

"Where-to, where-to?" they chirped in unison.

"I appreciate your enthusiasm, but we need more."

"Need-more, need-more."

He puffed into the whistle eight more times. Only one other bird appeared. He looked grayer than the other three. "Is this it?"

"Where-to, where-to?"

"Looks like I'll be needing that invigorating spell after all. Sorry, Minah," he mumbled. He stretched his arms toward the birds. "*Ka-mah-ka-mee*."

All four dropped over in a deep sleep.

"No!" Kip wailed at the sky.

Chapter 21

Loy led Winnie past the spectators to a corner of the courtyard where a pack of toads gathered. She stood apart from them to give her a head start if they tried to attack her. The buzz from their eager voices reached her ears, but no specific words.

A trumpet fanfare ended their conversations. All the toads turned toward the music. Winnie did too. Spectators separated, allowing Queen Bogen and her councilors to strut through. Several mel-yew shouted, "Hail to the queen," prompting a roar of cheers.

Queen Bogen nodded to the crowd, then directed a piercing stare at Winnie. "General. We're pleased you'll be joining us today."

Winnie held her head high. "Wouldn't miss it," she lied.

"We'll be searching the high country for glunt."

Winnie still wasn't sure what the glunt were, but *high country*? She understood that part. If the queen wanted to lose her, abandoning her at the top of a mountain would do it. Her mind scrambled to find a loophole. Then she remembered Kip's excuse.

"I could never hike to the high country." She faked a wheeze. "Medical condition."

"Nonsense, General, the fresh air will do you good. Besides, we've no intention of making you walk. Note the leather contraption on Commander Fynn's back."

The commander stepped up to her, wearing a wide leather belt. When the massive toad squatted down, the belt looked like a saddle. It also had a pommel and stirrups.

When he crouched, Fynn's height made him no taller than a small pony. Still, goose bumps sprouted on Winnie's arms. As much as she loved horses, they scared her a little, even the short ones. Last year at summer camp, her horse had shied at a jump, and Winnie had sailed over his head. The fall had been more embarrassing than painful. Ever since, though, riding made her apprehensive.

She sidled away. "I wouldn't want to inconvenience the commander."

"You'll be no burden." Fynn's mouth curled into a hungry grin. He looked like a toad about to swallow a dragonfly. He couldn't swallow her, but he could buck her off. She didn't even have a helmet.

"Do climb onto Fynn's back," Queen Bogen said. "There's a good general."

Winnie clasped the pommel with a trembling hand. She slid her foot into the left stirrup and swung her right leg over Fynn's broad back. She tried to sit straight in the saddle on his slanting back.

"Are you quite comfortable, General?" Fynn's cheerful voice sounded fake.

She hoped Kip and his wiggets would hurry. "Think so."

"Right. We're off, then." The queen waved a royal hand to the other hunters. The royal bugler blasted one long note, and the other toads crouched onto their haunches. The spectators cheered and waved colored scarves.

The queen took the lead, and the toad people followed in single file. The hunting party crossed the main lawn and through the castle gates, leaving the cheering crowds far behind. They leaped through a short patch of woods, to a mountain where the dirt road steepened. Winnie clung to Fynn's saddle. Her "steed" followed the toads as they leaped onward and upward.

A mile into the ride, Winnie finally got the hang of it and relaxed into Fynn's stride. She only wished she trusted her balance enough to lift her head to look for Kip. Believing him nearby gave her the confidence to sway in time with Fynn's bouncy motion.

Fynn and the other hunters hopped along a narrow path dug into the side of the mountain. On her left lay a deep drop. Her heart thudded. "Uh, Fynn? Aren't we getting a little too close to the edge?"

He followed the others higher up the mountain. One by one, his fellow hunters cut into the brush until Commander Fynn hopped alone toward the mountain top.

An alarm bell went off in Winnie's head. "Where'd everybody go?"

"In pursuit of their prey."

"After glunt?"

"Obviously."

The swampy smell of his sweat made her nose twitch. She wanted to pinch it shut but didn't dare take her hands off the pommel. She gripped tighter and stole a peek overhead. Where was Kip?

She faced forward again. The path seemed to meet nothing but open sky.

"Wait a minute!"

Through the whistling air came the click of an

undone buckle.

"You'll mock us no longer." He jolted to a stop.

The same thing had happened in summer camp. This time Winnie and the saddle flew over Fynn. She plummeted toward the distant treetops.

"Kip!"

She shrieked and flapped her arms as she plunged through the top of the tallest tree. Pliable limbs bowed under her weight. The tree's rubbery, tennis-racket-shaped leaves volleyed her and the saddle downward, branch by branch. The saddle fell away moments before her stomach slammed against a bough, knocking the air out of her. She bumped her chin, biting her tongue. Instinctively, she clung to the wide branch and gasped for breath. The saddle kept falling until it landed across the jagged rocks far below.

That could've been me. Her heart revved at the thought. She'd practically died. Yet all around her, birds tweeted happily. A fragrant breeze drifted through the willowy leaves. The world kept going. Thankfully, so did Winnie. Her breathing slowed to normal. She sat up and, with knees braced around the branch, eased backward until she sat against the trunk. Only then did she feel safe enough to examine herself. She tasted a little blood from biting her tongue but not enough to worry about. Surprisingly, she only had a few scratches on her arms and legs. All her body parts seemed intact.

She breathed deeply. Yup, her lungs still worked. The dull pain in her stomach felt no worse than doing a belly flop into a swimming pool. The warrior had survived! All she had to do now was climb out of the tree. She reached for a lower branch but didn't dare stretch the extra inch to grab it. What if she missed or the branch snapped? She pulled back to safety.

Too bad they didn't have fire departments with ladders on Frama-12. On the off chance she might find a hermit with a rope, she called, "Hello?"

An eerie screech answered in the distance. Winnie clamped her mouth shut. If a snaps heard her, it might try to shake her out of the tree.

She slumped against the trunk. Where was a wigget when she needed one? Wiggets, of course. She laughed at herself for almost forgetting the whistle tucked inside her tunic. She gave it two quick blasts and waited. One minute. Two minutes.

She swung her legs impatiently. She blew into it over and over. Finally, one ragged-looking wigget lit at the end of her branch.

"Wigget-wigget. Where-to, where-to?"

"We need two more," she said and blew the whistle.

"No-more, no-more," the wigget said. "Where-to, where-to?"

"Just down. Can you manage?"

"Manage-manage. Wigget-wigget."

Its talons locked onto the leather vest she hadn't removed from her last flight to the beach. It lifted her from the branch. On the way down its wings flapped harder. "Too-big, too-big."

The ground rose up to meet them. Winnie didn't remember hitting it.

Chapter 22

Kip stood alone in the woods, fuming. Four wiggets lay unconscious at his feet even though he'd said the undo spell twice. *Bloody incantations.* He needed to look up flying spells in his lab. He started down the trail toward the castle when a commanding female voice shouted, "Halt! Do not leave them here."

He jolted to a stop and looked around. All he faced were trees. "Who's there?"

"One who respects all life," the disembodied voice replied. "Your magic has made these lives vulnerable."

He peered over his shoulder at the birds he'd accidentally put to sleep. Now that the voice had brought it up, she had a point. In their present condition, the wiggets were easy targets for any carnivore that might happen by.

Kip looked to the sky. "Can't you watch over them? The spell won't last long. I've got places to go."

"Your place is right here, Wizard. Events have been set into motion."

Only an oracle would talk like that. "Maggenta?"

"I answer to that name."

"Where are you?" Her voice seemed to come from everywhere at once. "Why won't you let me help Winnie?"

"You'll help by staying out of danger."

"What kind of wizard would I be if I only worried

about me own safety?"

"One who lives to see tomorrow. I am aware of circumstances you don't understand. Go back to the castle. Take your birds with you." Her final words drifted away on a sudden chilly wind.

"Go back to the castle and take the birds with you," he muttered in a falsetto. He snatched off his cape and laid it on the ground. "I'm aware of *circumstances*." He carefully lifted each limp bird onto his cape.

At least his levitation spell worked. The birds and cape floated behind him all the way to the castle.

The wiggets napped in front of the unlit fireplace. Kip paced and grumbled to himself. He circled the lab five times, then bellowed at the ceiling, "Where is a book with powerful spells?"

The floor shook under his feet. Bottles rattled. Three shattered. His bookshelves swayed and banged against the wall. A single book spewed from the top shelf. It crashed to the floor, and the room went still.

A satisfied smile played on his lips. He liked it when magic listened to him. He crunched over broken glass. A book as thick as a dictionary, its black leather cover cracked with age, lay at his feet. He carried it to his desk and tapped the faded title with his wand. The lettering glowed. *Open this book only if you dare release the power of Krell.*

That sounded promising. He whistled for his familiar.

After a short wait, Willum glided through the open window and landed on the hearth. He hopped among the sleeping wiggets on the floor. "What's all this, then? One familiar not enough for you?"

"Don't be daft. Once they wake up, they're me

transportation. What's Krell?"

Willum landed on the black book. "Krell is not a what but a who. If you'd studied your history properly, you'd know Thaddeus Krell was the most powerful wizard of the realm. He vanished three monarchs ago. You don't want the power he had. It comes from a dark place."

"Black magic, you mean?"

"Fury magic, I mean. It works when you're cross."

"That's all right, then, so long as it's not black magic."

Kip shooed the bird out of the way and opened the book. Instantly, it drew him into the text. It wasn't so much that he read the book as the book read him. Each succeeding page reached into his mind, probing every negative thought he had ever had. It didn't simply conjure past memories. It grabbed them in an angry fist and shook free every slight, every disappointment, every annoyance he had experienced since preschool.

With each memory, more hot fury welled inside him. It pummeled at the very fiber of his being, threatening to burst through his skin. When he could hold it no more, he snapped up his right arm. The book told him where that raw force must go. He aimed his hand toward his wand on the table. His rage turned to lightning that sparked through his fingertips and surged into it. Every snub, every insult increased the electrical arc's intensity.

Yes. Sparks crackled around it. *There lies a wand worthy of a wizard.*

Once the heated stream played out, the wand sailed across the room. It banged against the far wall. Kip fell backward and landed on his backside. The fall didn't hurt or even knock the wind out of him. He vaguely sensed anger but chortled instead.

Willum waddled beside him, muttering, "Now you've done it."

"Nah, I'm okay." Kip patted the stone floor. "Yo, this is, like, solid. Good thing I didn't crack my skull, bro."

Willum ruffled his feathers. "Your wizard voice is gone."

Kip cocked his head. "Huh?"

"You've gone and split yourself in two," Willum sputtered.

Kip could account for all his body parts. Still, hollowness gnawed at the pit of his stomach. He stood. "What just happened?"

Willum flapped his wings. "The book, that ruddy book."

Kip turned to the tattered book on his desk. He vaguely remembered putting a decipher spell on his wand last week so he could read the books. He stared into his empty hands. "Wasn't I holding my wand a second ago?"

He peeked under the desk. Only a dusty quill pen lay beneath.

Scratching noises from behind the wall beside the fireplace halted Kip's search.

"Sounds like you've got a visitor."

A brick wiggled loose and thumped into the room. Three more dropped out. Polo's bald head poked through the opening in the wall. Kip helped pull the rest of him into the room.

"I do beg your pardon, Master Wizard, for not using the door." Polo slapped the dust off his tunic. "I didn't want the queen's guards to know I'm here."

"Keeping it on the down low. Gotcha. What's up?"

Polo looked him up and down. "Are you well, Master Wizard?"

"Yeah, I'm cool. What about you, little dude? You look hyped."

He raised an eyebrow at Kip. "I have troubling news. The queen and her hunting party just returned. Without our dear general. I fear she's been lost to the hunt."

Kip's heart thudded. "Is she alive?"

"We believe so, Master Wizard, but you'll need your magic to find her."

All he needed was his wand. Where was it?

The air throbbed with energy. He raised his right arm, and the wand hissed through the air toward him. It slapped into his open palm. A raging force poured into him, filling him up. He felt whole again, only more so.

He also understood what Willum meant by his "wizard's voice." It had started the summer he'd turned ten. During a three-week trip to England with his parents, Kip began imitating a British accent. Mom and Dad laughed about it at first. They asked him to stop, but he couldn't. He enjoyed it too much. During a bus tour of London, they told him this would be their last vacation as a family. He hadn't even seen it coming. In desperation he tried extortion. *Call off the divorce, or I'll never speak Yank again.*

The adopted accent didn't change a thing, but at least it embarrassed his parents in front of company. He'd been talking like an Eastender ever since. It came so naturally now that even his friends forgot his American roots.

As the painful memory faded, he tightened his grip on his empowered wand. His body quivered with rage. The wand coaxed him to focus on the person responsible for putting Winnie at risk.

His wizard's voice returned. "Where's the queen?"

"Master Wizard, you're back." Polo sounded relieved.

Willum flitted through the room. "Not good, not good."

Polo bowed low. "Master, the queen is with her advisors, sharing hunting stories."

Kip stormed through the corridors. His right hand gripped his wand, his left clenched into a tight fist.

Two mel-yew knights guarded the queen's meeting-room door. With a flick of his wand, a blast of air sent them hurtling down the corridor. They landed with a clatter ten feet away. He aimed his fired-up wand at the door. A second blast tore it from its hinges. The door fell into the room with a crash. He stomped across it and into the chamber.

"Goodness gracious, Master Wizard," said Queen Bogen. "What an entrance."

"Where is General Windemere?"

"There seems to have been an unfortunate accident, we fear."

He aimed his wand at her. "What kind of accident? Choose your words carefully, or I'll cut you down from here."

The queen's councilmen leaped to shield her. Kip's wand reacted faster. All four froze where they stood. A second sweep of the wand silenced their voices.

"Master Wizard," she blustered. "Release our councilmen immediately."

Anger pulsed through him. "I'm giving orders now. Where is the general?"

"We don't know the exact location. Somewhere in the high country. The general rode on Commander Fynn's back. Through no fault of his own, a strap broke, and the general fell. It couldn't be helped."

"You'd better hope she survived." Kip spun on his heel and marched out.

"I said release our councilmen," Queen Bogen called after him. "If you disobey, we shall have you stripped of your wand and your cloak!"

He kept going, his cape billowing out behind him.

"Insolence! This is why our ancestors did away with wizards!"

Willum flew after him, landing on his right shoulder.

Kip didn't break his stride. "Are the wiggets awake yet?"

"Just beginning to stir, Master."

"Good. Have them meet me at the north side of the castle as soon as they're able." He shrugged Willum away.

Kip charged up the staircase to Winnie's rooms. A violent search for an article of her clothing ended at the closet. Her freshly laundered Earth clothes hung inside. He snorted in annoyance. For the enchantment spell to work, he needed her essence.

The wand vibrated. He turned toward her bed. Her running shoes lay beneath. He snatched the nearest one and tugged the shoelace free. He expertly pronounced the words that brought inanimate objects to life. The enchanted shoelace zinged into the air.

"Show me to your mistress," he commanded.

The lace wagged eagerly and shot out the window.

"Oi!" He zapped it with a slackening spell to slow it down. Outside, his awaiting wiggets gripped his cape with their talons.

"Arise."

The giant birds lifted him. To lighten their load, he concentrated on buoyant thoughts.

Willum flew beside him. "Where we off to, then?"

He pointed at the airborne shoelace. "We're following that."

The shoelace guided them up the mountain to a rising cliff. The flying string veered left and over the edge.

Kip's breath caught in his throat. No human could ever survive a fall from that height. His wand hummed to life. Vengeful thoughts banged against every corner of his mind, but he shoved them aside. Panic for Winnie's safety surpassed the wand's desire to destroy those responsible for harming her.

Gut-plunging fear clung so heavily on him that his power diminished. It affected his elderly wiggets. "Too-big, too-big." They dropped fifteen feet.

He focused on the mental image of leaves gliding on a soft current. The birds caught an updraft and stabilized. The lace zipped into a cave high up on the side of the mountain. The birds followed and landed in a large room cut into the stone. They waddled and preened.

"Ah, the wizard," a female voice spoke from deep inside the room. A gray voga woman, dressed in a plain brown cloak, stepped forward.

He blinked at her in surprise. He hadn't expected a voga this far from the castle. He'd never seen one with blue eyes before either.

The woman smiled a welcome. "My sister Maggenta said you'd be by. I'm Cyann."

He hesitated at the mention of the oracle. Would she strip his powers? The wand pulsated in his hand, putting him back on track.

"Where is the general?" he ordered.

Cyann let out a weary sigh. "What foolishness have you unleashed?"

"The power of Krell," Willum said.

Kip ignored them both and searched the large, open room. Past the hearth, around the overstuffed chairs and a table, stood a cot. Winnie, so still, so vulnerable, lay on it. In two long strides he reached her side. "Winnie, can you hear me?"

She didn't open her eyes. She didn't move.

He dropped to his knees. This was all his fault. He had promised to protect her. At the height of his despair, confident whispers seeped into his head. *She breathes.* It was the first offer of comfort his wand had given him since the Krell book had filled it with extra power.

He gently took her warm hand in his. He pressed his lips to it, silently willing her to open her eyes. He waited with breath held. No response.

The wand sent an angry spark up his arm. Now was not the time for regret. Its fury coursed into his body, filling him with one goal. *Kill the queen.*

Chapter 23

Gray-blue waves rolled toward shore. At first, Winnie didn't understand what it meant. Her head throbbed, and the sun burned too deeply into her scalp for logical thought. Finally, the meaning behind the moving water sank in. *I'm home!* Dorothy had needed ruby slippers. All Winnie had to do was fall out of a tree. *Or wake up.* She breathed in the fresh salty air.

Nearby, Mikey built a sandcastle and hummed to himself.

She sat next to him, happy to be back. "Hey, bud, you'll never believe the dream I just had. Your queen was a giant white toad!"

He blinked at her from under his long bangs.

"And her people tried to kill me. Some crazy dream, huh?"

"That was rude, but they won't try that again. You have my word and the oracle's." His little hands gently patted more sand into place.

"I don't think you can control my dreams. Can you? I mean, in my last one the lurkin never came."

"Good thing they're slow, huh? That'll give you time to recover before they reach the shore."

"Maybe in my next dream, I'll be able to fly. Ya know, like Superman? If I can see the lurkin from the air, I can soar back to the castle and warn everybody. The wiggets probably won't carry the mel-yew fighters over the ocean, but we can still fight from the air. We'll get the flying snakes to spit coconuts at them."

"Coconuts!" He fell over backward, laughing. "You're funny, Windy."

She pressed her palms to her temples. "I'm a laugh a minute. Come with me to the house. I need aspirin, and you can't be out here alone."

"Dream aspirin won't help you."

"Ha ha. Frama-12 was the dream, not this."

Or was it? Mikey hadn't created a typical formless little-kid sandcastle. He'd perfectly designed a replica of Queen Bogen's fortress in the sand. It even featured detailed arches and battlements.

Her mouth dropped open. "Wait. This part can't be the dream. I smell the ocean. I feel the sun burning down on me. And I have one killer of a headache."

"I'm not sure about the smells, but the heat is from your fever." He sat back on his heels. "The headache is from the fall you took."

She stared at the sand, desperately wishing to be home. Why couldn't the lurkin threat be the dream? Her head hurt too much to handle a battle, even with a delay. And, as much as she hated to admit it, she wanted her daddy.

Mikey stood and dusted the sand from the back of his bathing suit. "Your dad's dreaming about exploring the North Pole right now. But he'll come if you ask him to."

"Yeah, right. Abracadabra, Dad appear." She meant it as a joke.

A man Dad's size materialized on the beach. He wore a snow-covered parka, tinted goggles, and furry boots.

The Arctic man shoved his fur-lined hood off his head. Gobs of melting snow plopped onto the sand, sizzling in the heat. The winter clothes melted into tan shorts and a white T-shirt. Winnie's dad smiled. "Hey, Win. This is weird, huh? Weren't we just on a Ferris wheel?"

She grinned up at him. "For you, maybe. For me, it's been a couple days. Dreams are funny like that."

Now that she'd brought him here, she couldn't remember why she wanted him. The fact that he appeared gave her a new, intriguing thought. Did she have the power to make anyone appear? Anyone…like her mom?

Her wish emerged as a smoky whisper that rippled beside Dad. It grew into Mom's solid shape, so vibrantly alive and dressed in a white, one-piece bathing suit.

"Glynnis?" Dad said in an awed whisper.

Winnie jumped up and let out an excited squeal. "Mom!"

Dad cocked an eyebrow. "This isn't right. Glynnis, you can't be here."

Mom's smile dissolved along with the rest of her.

Angry tears blurred Winnie's vision. "We need to bring her back."

"Win." Worried lines appeared on his forehead. "That's not how it is now. We have Maria."

She sank to her knees on the sand. She didn't have to look up to know Dad had vanished. She felt the void in the air.

Mikey knelt beside her. "He just woke up. You have to leave too."

She squeezed her eyes shut. "I want Mom."

The desire brought her back. Winnie rested her head on Mom's soft shoulder. She hugged as hard as she could, but Mom dissolved again, leaving Winnie alone with Mikey.

Even with her eyes still closed, she sensed him at her side. Neither spoke. The waves splashed against the shore. The pounding headache worsened. Maybe if she slept, she'd escape the pain. Warriors had to sleep sometime.

"Rest is a good idea," he said. "To get your strength up."

She nodded. "I need another minute before I go." She opened her eyes. The ocean waves rolled in and out. She silently prayed for the strength to do what needed to be done.

"Windy?" He slid his hand back and forth in the sand. "Could you...could you tell my mom I love her?"

"You're asking the wrong person, buddy. I'm still in Frama-12, remember? Your mom's right here."

Mikey stared back with sad eyes. "I meant my Frama-12 mom."

"*Ohh.*" Takka would naturally miss his family. If her head wasn't killing her, she would have figured that one out sooner. "What's her name?"

Before he answered, Winnie fell away from the beach and into a black void.

Chapter 24

Kip watched over Winnie, lying so still. The longer he sat with her, the greater his need for revenge became. A vision replaced reality. *I storm through the castle corridor. One flick of my wand sends knights and servants hurtling from my path. I face the queen, her pink eyes wide with fear. I call on the power of Krell, and lightning shoots from my wand.*

A change in air pressure made Kip's ears pop, yanking him to the present. He recognized the pain and understood. Someone had just cast a teleportation spell. He twisted toward the entrance where the wiggets had stood.

He jumped to his feet and pointed his wand at Cyann. "Bring them back."

The blue-eyed voga stared at him. "To what end, Master Wizard?"

"You know what end," he said through clenched teeth. "The queen and her assassins are my targets."

"Look behind you. The general is very much alive."

"She's in a ruddy coma!"

"Breathe," she said gently. "If you use your abilities to call her back, the general just might wake."

The wand vibrated to the contrary. He stared at Cyann with an intensity that sent her flying until her back pressed into the wall.

"Return my transport."

Even from her immobile position, her voice remained composed. "Breathe, my dear friend, and remember who you are."

With the help of his wand, he'd become strong and powerful. "All who stand in my way shall perish, beginning with you, old woman, if you don't do my bidding."

She stared calmly back. "That was an impressive imitation. What you've conjured, however, is not Krell."

"I don't need Krell. Watch my wand remove your essence, leaving nothing but a husk."

"Before you remove anything, young wizard, you might want to ask your wand if it knows which herbs and leaves are necessary to restore the general to health."

Reflexively, he peered over his shoulder at Winnie. The brief distraction broke the hold spell. Cyann catapulted from the wall. She muttered a spell of her own. The wand flew from Kip's hand and hovered in the air midway between them.

"Oi!" He reached with hand and mind.

The wand shuddered in place. He gnashed his teeth and willed the wand to obey. It glided closer. Cyann drew a symbol in the air with her finger. The wand immediately reversed direction but only by inches.

Her voice whispered inside his mind. "Remember."

He ignored it and reached again for the wand. Rage calling out to rage. The wand edged toward him. Cyann's power pulled it back. The wand vacillated between the dueling pair, never reaching either.

Willum flapped and squawked. "Master, leave it

be!"

Kip muttered a spell, silencing Willum's voice.

Cyann restored his voice with a nod.

"It's wrong!" the bird cawed and flew out of the cave. His departure broke Kip's focus. The voga commanded the wand to move closer to her.

"You are Kenneth Paul Skyler of Earth," she proclaimed. "Your true self knows that the energy coursing through that bit of wood does not define you."

The wand promised power beyond his imagining. He was no mere boy named Kenneth but a real wizard. Renewed fury gushed into him. The wand flew toward his outstretched fingers. He leaped to catch it. Cyann's counter magic pulled it just out of reach.

He bellowed in frustration.

"You're hurt," she said. "Betrayed by the queen. Hindered by the oracle. You feel responsible for the general's injury. But are you evil? That's the question you must ask."

He most definitely had been betrayed by the queen and hindered by the oracle. In fact, he could have protected Winnie if the oracle had let him. And now he faced the oracle's confounding sister. "I can destroy you."

"I've no doubt you're capable."

The wand quivered between them.

"The real Krell had no conscience," she said. "I believe you do. If you let the ghost of Krell use your hand to harm anyone, the weight of it will end you."

"I want revenge!"

The wand shot closer to him.

"What about Winnie?" Cyann shouted.

The wand halted in the air.

"Do you want her to recover?" she asked.

An unexpected tightness suddenly gripped his throat. Had the wand's power taken over? He fought to speak. "She must."

"Really? Because if revenge is so important, why should you care about anyone?"

He believed in Winnie. He admired her fighting spirit. He wanted to say so, but a force blocked more than his words. He couldn't breathe.

Krell is not dead, a dark whisper spoke in his mind. *He will return. Kill the queen, and the realm is ours to rule!*

His head pounded. His lungs screamed. With what little air he had left, he used it to utter the words that mattered. "Help Winnie."

A tornado of fury churned deep inside. He drifted above it, clearing his head. Sure, the queen deserved punishment, but Winnie's survival mattered more. A feeling of giddy lightness splashed over him. He wanted Winnie to survive because he cared for her.

Kip saw past the levitating wand to Cyann's glowing blue eyes. They radiated kindness and warmth. If this voga was not the enemy, why was he fighting her?

The wand shimmied in the air, then clattered to the stone floor. It stopped pulsing the same moment its connection to Kip blinked out.

"Did you—" He looked to Cyann. "—kill it?"

She smiled. "You conquered it."

Across the room, Winnie groaned.

He ran to the cot. "Winnie?"

"I'm sorry," Cyann said from behind. "She's still lost in a dark place. I'm hoping you'll be able to call her back."

He looked up. "With magic, you mean?"

"I meant she could use the sound of a familiar voice."

Self-doubt crashed over him. How could Winnie ever forgive him for breaking his promise to protect her?

"Go on," Cyann said gently. "Take her hand again and speak to her."

He slid his hand into Winnie's. "I'm so, so sorry," he murmured. "I want to make it right. I have to." With those words, he knew what must be done. "Cyann, I need to go to the lookout post for Winnie."

She smiled. "I've summoned a few friends on the chance you might suggest it."

As if on cue, three robust wiggets glided through the mouth of the cave. The birds landed between Kip and the voga.

"Wigget-wigget, where-to, where-to?"

"Take the wizard to the big beach," Cyann said.

Kip bowed low. "Thank you, Mistress. And…sorry about…"

"Stay true to yourself, young wizard, and all is forgiven."

On the flight to the beach, he correctly pronounced the incantation that reduced odors. Instead of the ocean's rotting stench, a pleasant pine scent encircled his head. His anger had left him, but his increased magical ability had remained.

Far below, a group of palum had gathered on the beach. The man horses waved yellow and green flags while two palum teams bounced and wobbled on the gelatinous ocean, chasing after a round object shaped like a coconut. All members of the tribe laughed and cheered, but with all eyes on the sporting event, none watched the horizon.

"Carry me out to sea," Kip ordered the wiggets.

"No-go, no-go," they honked in unison.

Wiggets never refused a rider unless they sensed peril. Still airborne, he closed his eyes to an inner vision and searched across the sea.

Safe. A little farther…safe. Farther still…also safe. Farthest of all he felt a ripple of movement. The march toward their shore had begun, and no one was keeping watch.

On Kip's command, the wiggets lowered him to the beach. He strode to the tallest palum. "Why isn't this watch post being manned?"

The leader pinned back his ears. "Wizard! You are no friend to the palum. You disrespected our queen's councilmen."

The game stopped. The spectators crowded toward Kip from all sides. He recited a convincement spell under his breath, instantly reducing the tension in the herd.

"Friends," the leader announced, "the good wizard has come for a visit."

Welcoming hands now clapped him on the back.

He smiled indulgently. "Thank you and greetings, palum tribe. I come on behalf of General Windemere to see how things are going. This is the watch post, correct?"

"We remember the general quite well," the leader said. "She brought us a gift."

The leader nodded to a palum youth. The young one ducked out of the circle and returned with Winnie's binoculars. He passed them to the leader.

"We call it the swing-thing." The leader held it by the strap. "When one holds it thusly, it swings in the wind."

"If you think back, just a bit," Kip said, "you might recall it does more than that."

The leader looked more closely at the strap. "It does do more. It can hang about our necks." He tried to put it on, but it only fit halfway down his long nose. "Or perhaps not."

Kip helped untangle the leader from the strap. A simple brush of his fingers over the palum's soft nose gave him insight into the creature's innocent mind. The palum understood skirmishes between their kind, but that related only to one's position in the herd. The concept of battle was so foreign not even the smartest palum comprehended it. No wonder they forgot to watch for an enemy.

The queen's command to keep the palum from battle made sense. These prey animals knew to flee from danger but not to alert the castle. Perhaps if he enchanted the binoculars? An incantation came to mind. It wouldn't help them understand the importance of keeping watch. No spell could do that. It could, however, compel them to do it anyway. They'd even send a warning to the castle upon the first sighting of movement out to sea.

He handed the enchanted binoculars to the nearest palum. The horse man dutifully trained the lenses on the horizon. With the watch post manned, Kip whistled to his wiggets.

On the flight back to the castle, he turned his attention to Winnie's condition. Maybe his increased powers would inspire him to create a potion to revive her.

The wiggets set him down in the courtyard. Four knights clacked up to him.

"Come with us," the nearest ordered. "The queen is stripping you of your powers."

Kip followed, pretending to obey. At the first turn in the corridor, he whispered to the guard at the rear, "Tell Queen Bogen I'm invisible and I'm already in her presence."

He dashed away.

Chapter 25

Winnie floated through nothingness. The dark gradually brightened to a pale haze. Sometimes she heard Kip's British accent, speaking softly. Other times he sang. The more she heard his voice, the more she fought toward those beckoning sounds.

Finally, she returned to her body lying on a bed. She lifted her arm to touch her throbbing head. A cool hand stopped the upward motion, returning her arm to her side.

"Lie quietly, dear General," an unknown female voice said.

Another sharp pain stabbed Winnie's temples. She strained to open her eyes. A blurry gray blob stood over her. Her vision sharpened, turning the blob into a toad woman.

Her groggy mind tried to send a warning that giant toads wanted to kill her, but her muscles had no strength to tighten. The toad made no move to attack. Only tenderness shone from eyes the color of the Caribbean Sea. Without knowing why, Winnie felt safe.

"The pain will leave in time. You took a serious fall."

The voga placed cold leaves on her forehead, easing the ache. Her eyelids drooped closed.

When she woke again, her headache was almost gone.

"Are you feeling better, General?" asked the blue-eyed voga.

"Who are you?"

"I'm called Cyann, Sister of Dawn and New Beginnings. I'm the oracle's sister."

Deep in Winnie's sluggish brain, she remembered hearing the word *oracle* before.

"You'll be pleased to know the oracle explained to the queen your special kinship to Takka. There will be no further attempts on your life."

"Good." Winnie yawned. "How long have I been asleep?"

"Almost five days, General."

"What?" She sat straight up. The sudden movement made her dizzy. She fell back against the pillows.

"Mustn't overexert." Cyann lightly patted her shoulder.

"What about the lurkin?"

"Still no sign from the lookout post."

Relieved by the news, Winnie fell back to sleep.

The next morning her strength had returned enough to climb out of bed. Clutching a blanket around her shoulders, she shuffled to the mouth of Cyann's cave. She expected the scenery outside to be at ground level. Instead of grass and brush, she faced blue sky and treetops. She stumbled backward, caught breathless by the height. She pulled the blanket closer, chilled by the memory of hurtling toward oblivion. She turned from the opening to the calming scene of Cyann putting a kettle over the flames in the fireplace.

"Good morning, dear," the voga woman said.

"Morning. Um, how did I get up here?"

Cyann moved from the kettle to the table. "You were carried by three wiggets."

"Three? Where'd the other two come from? I only had one, and he dropped me."

"The oracle called to them and had them bring you here so that I could cure you."

"I do feel better. Thanks."

Cyann smiled back. "I also had help from the Master Wizard."

Winnie remembered his voice coaxing her from the void. A second memory pushed that one aside. "Wasn't he supposed to catch me before I fell?"

"Some things are meant to be as they are," Cyann replied. "With that said, the wizard came to you every day. He also made frequent visits to the lookout post."

Just picturing Kip trying to explain binoculars to the palum almost made up for him not rescuing her.

After lunch, three wiggets flapped into the cave, carrying the wizard.

"You're awake!" Kip raced to her, arms spread.

His gesture took her by surprise. While she was asleep, had their relationship changed? She took an uneasy step away, not sure she was ready for that yet.

He must have noticed her confusion. He halted and let his arms drop. "So." For half a second, he looked like a bewildered puppy stuck in the rain. Then he straightened his shoulders. In a more formal tone, he said, "Feeling better?"

Why did everything suddenly feel so awkward? She forced a smile. "Much."

"I'm glad. It's, um, so good to see you up and about."

"Me too. I mean good to see you too." She let out a

nervous laugh and looked away. Embarrassment heated her cheeks.

"Why don't you two have a nice visit?" Cyann nodded toward the living room area.

Kip guided Winnie to a stuffed chair. His touch felt so gentle she blushed again.

He sat on the stool facing her. "I'm just back from the lookout post. No sign of lurkin."

Genuine relief washed away her earlier discomfort. "Good. What about the palum? Last time I was there, they had trouble using the binoculars."

"Same with me." He grinned, looking relaxed. "I enchanted the binoculars to help the palum remember how to use them."

"That worked?" She smiled with him.

"I've found that inanimate objects can be quite patient," he joked.

She laughed, finally beginning to enjoy the visit. Then Cyann ruined it by sending him away so Winnie could rest.

After a nap, and Cyann's promise that she'd see Kip tomorrow, she settled into a comfy chair. The voga woman sat nearby, a pair of knitting needles held in her knobby fingers. A ball of dark-blue yarn lay in her lap.

"Making a scarf?" Winnie guessed.

"I am, dear."

Winnie watched her knit until boredom set in. About two minutes. "Thanks again for everything you did for me. But I probably should get back to the castle." She still had general duties to perform.

"Don't rush things, dear. You've got at least a week before you're needed. Why don't you take down that shiny object next to my sewing basket and see what it tells you?" Cyann nodded toward the shelving across the room.

Winnie obeyed. The golden cylinder resembled a miniature telescope and fit easily across the length of her palm. She focused it on the table. The image through the glass didn't magnify or shrink. "What's it supposed to do?"

"It's not a typical spy glass. It's a Frama-scope. Keep looking. You'll find something."

With a shrug Winnie pointed the lens upward. A pair of robin-egg-blue bubbles floated just below the ceiling. When she pulled the scope away, the bubbles disappeared. She put the lens to her eye again, and they reappeared. "What are those things?"

"Have you found a few blue bits up there?"

"More like soap bubbles, but yeah."

Cyann nodded. "They're pinpricks in the time fabric. With practice you can see through them into other worlds."

Time fabric. Other worlds. Mikey had said those exact words ages ago. Did that mean this little device could help her see into her world? On the chance that it might, she eagerly scanned the room and found three more. One hovered above their dining table. Another two drifted beside her cot.

The following day, she found more bubbles but no signs of other worlds. During her recovery, when she wasn't resting or visiting with Kip, she practiced with the Frama-scope. She stared at the same blue bubble, hour after hour, but nothing happened. One afternoon, a sudden downpour outside distracted her enough to let go of her expectations. The opaque bubble cleared enough to reveal a pair of human eyes staring back.

Winnie dropped the Frama-scope. "Whoa! Something just looked at me."

Cyann smiled from her knitting. "That would be a watcher. A guardian of the veil. The space between worlds."

"I think I saw those same eyes inside the time tear. It was kinda creepy."

"Don't be frightened. I suspect they were merely making certain you were worthy enough to enter our world."

Winnie's back stiffened at the thought that anyone, other than the queen, would doubt a warrior's integrity. "Why wouldn't I be worthy?"

"Take no offense, dear General. You're not the first of your kind to visit us. Many stories have been passed down, telling of the Other's trickery. When he first came to us, he offered knowledge we'd long forgotten. We believed he came to aid us. He stole instead."

"I'm definitely not like that."

"Which is why you were freed from the dungeon so quickly. The Other, however, can't be trusted. Throughout our history, he's appeared at random times. He stays away for many years as if believing we'll forget so he might cheat us anew."

"How is that even possible? Is he, like, a million years old?"

Cyann's blue eyes stared deeply into Winnie's. "He stole an item of ours that allows him to open time tears and travel to other worlds at a whim."

Winnie's mouth dropped open.

"Takka's essence traveled to your world because the oracle foretold that the Other would return at a future time. It was hoped that Takka would grow and think as your people do and thus prevent the Other from aiding the lurkin in battle."

Winnie shuddered. "Does that mean I'll be fighting the lurkin and an evil genius?"

"My sister assures me that he won't appear during this timeline."

Winnie's insides still churned. "What if he does?"

"He can't. I believe that was why you were called to come in Takka's place. If we had waited for Takka to grow, the Other would have posed a great threat. Please, General, take a few deep breaths. Remove all needless worry from your mind. I shouldn't have distracted you from your studies."

Winnie's first intake of air was more of a gulp. After a long exhale and a slow inhale, she picked up the Frama-scope and tried again. This time the scope displayed a long, patterned cloth lying on a sandy beach. Winnie recognized its red-and-yellow stripes.

"Mikey's towel. Is that possible?"

The voga nodded. "Extremely possible. Keep looking. A glimpse of home can be very healing."

Beside the beach towel lay a mound of sand. Small hands patted it. When she tilted the scope, her view moved up small tan arms, past yellow short-sleeved pj's, to the little boy's intent face. "It's my stepbrother," she whispered.

"He's waiting by the time tear and won't leave that spot until you return. Victorious."

Winnie lowered the Frama-scope. "He promised me he'd go back to the house. He's supposed to be in the house. I gotta get home. His mom is going to kill me."

"He couldn't leave. He's your anchor. And you've still a task to complete here."

"How can I do anything here when the queen hates my ideas as much as she hates me?"

"General Takka might have your answer."

"He knows how to handle the queen?"

Cyann put down her knitting. "Please come with me. I think it's time."

Chapter 26

Winnie wrapped a blanket around her shoulders and followed Cyann deep into the cave. Her sandals clacked on the stone floor to an eager beat. This passage had to lead to an opening between their worlds. How else could they communicate with Mikey/Takka?

Neither spoke. Every ten yards, Cyann lit a small lantern tacked to the wall. The farther they walked, the eerier the cavern became.

"Is it safe down here?" Winnie asked.

"A bit chilly but otherwise free of danger."

Winnie definitely agreed with the chilly part. The temperature had dropped considerably since they started. Her bare toes were freezing. With each step, the damp air grew colder. At a bend in the passage, the temperature plunged from chilly to frigid. She gripped the blanket tighter around her shoulders.

"How much farther?"

"Almost there."

The tunnel slanted downward. At the next turn a green glow emanated from an opening on the right. Cyann headed toward it. They entered a chamber cold enough to store ice cream. Neon-green light splashed down on them. The room held enough light that Winnie's breath came out in foggy puffs. She glanced upward at the light source and bit back a scream. Thousands of writhing, fluorescent worms clung to the ceiling.

"What are they?" Winnie covered her head with her blanket. If one of those slimy things fell on her, she was out of there.

"They're called orba," Cyann said, steam puffing from her mouth. "They gain nourishment by absorbing heat. We can't stay long, or they'll freeze us too."

"Too?" Winnie shuddered. "Who else did they freeze?"

"They're preserving Takka's vessel."

Winnie swallowed hard. *His vessel?*

"Here we are," Cyann said in a proud voice.

Winnie faced a giant slab of ice, ten feet tall and five feet wide. Something filled the inside. She leaned closer. A frozen beige toad man dressed in a maroon uniform with gold epaulets stood within.

Winnie couldn't look away. "My brother is a—I mean…" She pointed a quivering finger at it. "That's what's living inside his head?"

"Takka's essence resides in the vessel you call brother."

Winnie slowly circled the ice block, studying it from all angles. "But, um. If Takka's essence is inside Mikey"—Winnie was almost afraid to ask—"is Mikey's essence frozen in there?"

"Takka merged with the other form before it could develop an essence of its own."

"What? Are you saying without Takka, Mikey's an empty shell?"

"That's one way of putting it."

A cold shiver, icier than the air around her, rattled up her spine. She took a nervous breath. "What happens when Takka goes back to his original body?"

Cyann looked up at the ice block.

Winnie gripped her arm. "Please. What happens to my brother?"

Cyann gazed back. "No form can live without an essence."

"If Takka takes back his essence, does that mean it'll kill Mikey?"

"Takka's essence was supposed to return in his new, matured form to fight the lurkin," Cyann replied. "After he won the battle, it was never clear which form he might retain."

"But am I right?" Winnie said desperately. "Would Mikey die?"

"If Takka chooses to return to his original form, then yes."

"He can't do that!"

"The decision rests with Takka."

"People from my world are involved now. Not just me. Mikey's mom. Even my dad."

"Remember, Takka also has family here."

Winnie spun away, puffing for breath. Her mind flashed on the memory of Mikey peering up at her with those big sad eyes. *Tell my mom I love her*. She shook her head. "It's cruelty. All of it. He never should've jumped into Mikey's body in the first place. He looks strong enough as he is. Why didn't he just stay and fight like that?"

"It wasn't just about strength. You know that. Besides, vogan don't fight."

She faced the blue-eyed voga again. "I don't care. It's all wrong."

"When the next opportunity arises, I shall contact Takka and remind him of all consequences."

Sudden heat pulsed through Winnie's face. Tears burned her eyes. She refused to let them fall. She gulped for breath. Warriors never cried. "He can't even begin to know the consequences. Dad loves him like a son. He lost my mom five and a half years ago. He can't lose anybody else." Neither could she, but she kept that to herself.

"Things do have a way of working themselves out, you know."

Winnie shook her head. "I'm sorry. Send me back home. I can't help your people." How could she, if her reward for defeating the lurkin was the death of her little brother?

"There are many who believe in you, including my sister, the oracle."

Hot anger shot through Winnie. "Excuse me if I don't trust the oracle. She's the one who messed everything up in the first place by getting the timeline wrong."

"I know it seems like she made a mistake, but I know Maggenta. She might have intentionally sent Takka to the wrong time so that a true human would come in his place."

Winnie folded her arms. "Maybe that makes sense, but if she's so clever, how come she doesn't even know what lurkin look like?"

"Perhaps she does yet refuses to tell."

She scowled. "That's just mean."

"Maybe she wants you to use that clever human mind of yours."

"My clever human mind thinks they're spiders."

"Then prepare accordingly."

"Right now, I'm too busy worrying about him."

She pointed at the toad man in ice. "He'll murder my brother if he comes back to that body."

"You're focusing on the wrong thing."

"I thought we were coming to talk to Takka. Can't we do that now? I'd be able to focus better if I had his word that he'd stay inside Mikey forever."

"I feel certain," Cyann said in a soft voice, "that Takka will do whatever is necessary to ensure your success. That would include agreeing to your request."

"Promise?"

"In exchange for the lurkin's defeat."

Winnie's optimism turned to despair. Mikey's life depended on her victory? She slumped against Cyann. "How can I promise that? We don't have enough manpower. Besides, the queen will probably try to have me killed again."

"Because of your other relationship, your status with Queen Bogen has changed."

Winnie frowned, confused. "I don't get it."

"Takka is your brother, is he not?"

Winnie nodded.

"That had never been made clear to the queen. Takka's preferred title is general. His other title is prince."

Winnie's mouth dropped open. "You mean my brother is…"

"The queen's son. One could say that makes you kin to the queen."

Winnie's head reeled. "I have a toad lady for a stepmother?"

"Not just any toad lady. The queen."

Winnie groaned. "It just gets better and better."

"It does," Cyann said. "Before, Queen Bogen

thought she was turning her back on a troublesome general. Would she do the same to a daughter? I think not."

"If I'm a step-princess, does that mean she'll do things my way now?"

"Gracious no. You still must convince her to strengthen her troops."

Winnie's shoulders fell. "I've been trying to do that ever since I got here. Nobody wants to listen to me."

"Go to the Brothers Ky who guard the spring under the castle. Something there might open your mind to higher awareness."

"Have you ever had a conversation with the Brothers Ky? There's nothing high aware about them."

"Open your mind," the voga repeated, "and you'll find your answer."

Winnie hugged herself and shivered. If she had to rely on help from the Brothers Ky, Frama-12 and Mikey were doomed.

Chapter 27

After two more days of forced rest, Cyann finally declared Winnie fit for duty. Kip joined the celebration and brought three extra wiggets so they could fly together to the castle.

As Winnie bent to adjust the leather straps to her ankles, the voga woman leaned toward her. "Please be kind to the queen. One must always make an effort to get on with one's monarch and one's stepmother."

Winnie shuddered on the inside. Wasn't having one stepmother bad enough? She let out a long sigh. "I'll try. Thanks for everything."

Kip stood by as Winnie slid her arms into her flying vest. She worried more about the upcoming flight than confronting the queen. At least she had Kip and his magic if the birds lost their grip on her.

He winked at her. "Ready?"

She wasn't but gave him a thumbs-up anyway.

The wiggets honked and swooped into the air as one. She clenched her eyes shut, quivering with nerves. The birds flew so smoothly that she reopened her eyes. The puffy green treetops far below tempted her to close them again. *It's okay, it's okay*.

Since the birds showed no signs of strain, she began to trust them. The excitement of sailing through the air returned. She even smiled at Kip flying beside her.

"You might not see much of me once we're back," he called from the air. "I've had something of a falling out with the queen."

She giggled, happy for the chance to tease him. "What did you do? Forget to bow at the right time?"

He flashed a devilish grin. "Froze her councilmen. They took two days to thaw."

She laughed. "Should I ask why you did that?"

He laughed along. "Probably not. I'll be swinging round to the back so nobody sees me."

His birds veered off. Winnie's flew directly to the castle and lowered her onto a stage set up in the courtyard. It reminded her of the day of the hunt. An uneasy twinge gripped her insides. Unlike before, a dozen rows of mel-yew knights, their metal armor gleaming in the sunlight, filled the open space. Mel-yew hunters in leather armor stood behind them. The queen's other non-military subjects, including palum, crowded around the back of the courtyard.

A microphone sat cradled in a stand at the front of the stage. Winnie hoped she wouldn't have to give a speech. Even though lives depended on her, without a stronger army, nothing she might say would help them win a war.

A bugle fanfare played for Queen Bogen. She strutted across the stage at a regal pace, waving to her cheering subjects. Their applause swelled. She stepped up to the microphone, bobbing her head until everyone quieted.

"Fellow countrymen," her voice boomed through speakers set up facing the crowd. "We are gathered here today to honor the one our oracle and our very own General Takka have chosen to lead our army to victory.

General Windemere!"

The crowd roared their approval. Winnie bowed, hoping she looked as confident as the queen sounded.

"We've had recent news about our good general." The queen gave Winnie a brief side glance. "In her world she is more than a friend to the vessel in which Takka now resides. She is known to him as sister."

Surprised gasps sounded from the crowd.

"As it is in Takka's adopted world, so shall it be in this land. Henceforth let it be known throughout the realm that General Windemere has been awarded the kinship title of demi-princess, with all the rights and privileges thereto."

The crowd applauded. Winnie smiled and bowed again, wondering what rights she got.

"Naturally," the queen added, "our new demi-princess is foremost a general. As such, she will continue to be addressed as General Windemere."

Winnie nodded. She'd take the privileges, whatever they were, but didn't need the title. She'd never aspired to be a princess as a little kid anyway.

"As general, Windemere remains in charge of the military. As demi-princess, her first duty is to inspect our springs." She bowed to Winnie. "Carry on."

That was how she ended up following a miniature monk into the lower region of the castle. *Well, Cyann said I'd learn something from the Brothers Ky.*

Kip appeared out of the shadows and fell into step beside her.

Seeing him again sent an unexpected surge of warmth to her cheeks. *Don't blush.* Out loud she said, "Hey, wizard guy!"

He only waved a thumbs-up.

"If it pleases the general," said her guide, "the Brothers Ky are no longer able to see the wizard. He has made himself invisible to us."

"No kidding." She turned from the guide to Kip. "You're invisible? How come I can see you?"

He pulled her aside. "Actually, they can see me just fine." His whispered breath tickled her cheek.

She pretended not to notice. It was just Kip after all.

"The mel-yew, dear chaps that they are, pretend not to see me so they won't get in trouble with the queen if she asks them about me."

"She must be really mad at you."

He laughed. "You've no idea. That's why I missed your ceremony. How was it, by the way?"

She forced a bored tone. "I'm a demi-princess now."

"Ooh, Princess Winnie," he teased. "Did they make you kiss a frog first?"

She laughed and elbowed him in the ribs.

"General," the Brothers Ky said with a bow. "This way, please."

He scuttled onward. Winnie and Kip followed in silence. So help her, she wanted to hold his hand. The same guy who had stolen her locket. What was wrong with her?

On the long march through the dungeon's dark corridor, Winnie distracted herself by gazing at her surroundings. Each cell door stood open. Maybe the queen wasn't so terrible after all. She hadn't imprisoned any of her subjects.

"What exactly is a demi-princess?"

She turned her attention to Kip. "It means the

queen's my step—" Her mind leaped to her last dream visit with Mikey. She stopped short. She'd forgotten to deliver the message to his toad mom. "Crap. I need to go back and talk to the queen."

The Brothers Ky leading the way turned to her. "Please, General, we'll not take up much of your time. If you'll just follow me to the springs."

"Why the springs?" Kip asked.

She rolled her eyes. "Apparently, I'm an inspector now." To the monk she said, "Promise you'll be quick."

The three continued on, descending another stone staircase that brought them toward a thunderous noise. The roaring sound came from an underground waterfall. The monk waved at the gushing water. "Additional power for the castle," he shouted over the noise.

"Rather clever, don't you think?" said Kip.

Clever or weird. They had electricity but used candles instead of light bulbs.

From the waterfall they hiked along a walkway beside an underground river. They followed a side tributary until it ended as a round pool inside a dimly lit room. The place smelled like a mixture of mildew and swampy, sweaty gym socks. The robed monks standing at the water's edge didn't seem to mind. They reverently repeated, "Ahh-tee-ooh."

"Brothers, if you please," the guide called to the others. "We've an exalted guest."

The group stopped chanting.

"The princess general has come to inspect the spring."

The monks bustled past Kip. They crowded around Winnie, offering greetings.

The leader stepped to the front. "When you report

to your mother, the queen, you must tell her how pure we've kept the royal water supply."

"I'm not really an inspector."

Kip nudged her. "Play along. It'll be a lark."

Winnie shrugged. "Okay, let's see the water."

"Ahh-tee-ooh," the monks murmured.

"Come, General." The leader clasped her hand and guided her to the pool's edge. It smelled worse up close. Another monk dipped a crystal goblet into the murky water. He held it up, revealing sludge-colored liquid.

"Ahh-tee-ooh," the monks chanted until the leader poured the water back into the pool.

His scrawny chest puffed outward. "You will report your findings to Queen Bogen, will you not, good General?"

"I hate to tell you this, but I think your water is polluted. That's probably why nobody's allowed to drink it."

"Blasphemy," hissed several monks.

The leader held up a hand. "Stay, brothers. The demi-princess cannot blaspheme."

"Sorry, but I just don't get it. In my world water isn't sacred."

"Some of it is," Kip said, "like in churches. Ya know?"

"Okay, sure, holy water counts as sacred," she conceded, "but basically, water's just water. Everybody drinks it."

"It's scarce in some countries," Kip added.

"I didn't mean it wasn't scarce sometimes. The point I was making—"

"And don't forget the places where you shouldn't

drink the water."

She huffed. He could be so annoying sometimes.

"What I'm *trying* to say is this shouldn't be one of those places. They have solar power and sound systems and alarms and technicians. Why can't they just boil it up so they can drink it?"

"You're missing the point. It's their religion. You can't just come in and tell people to change what they believe. Here, water is sacred."

"I just want to know why it's sacred."

The little monks' eyes bulged in horror.

"Blimey, you've upset them again."

The leader spoke to her in a slow voice, "In Frama-12 the queen's water is sacred because it is so written."

She squinted, still baffled. "Who wrote it?"

"Why the Maker, of course. You may read the holy symbols for yourself."

She followed the procession to the opposite wall.

"Here it is written," the leader whispered reverently.

The monks bowed and chanted, "Ahh-tee-ooh."

Winnie peered at the jagged script slashed across the stone wall in white paint. The symbols read $H2O$.

Kip gasped. "Coo. We're not the only ones to visit from Earth."

Chapter 28

"Have you seen any other people who look like us?" Winnie pointed at herself and Kip.

"I see only you, good General," the leader replied. "You're the first of your kind I've met."

"Remember the wonky timeline," Kip said to her. "When that was written, these blokes' parents probably weren't even born yet."

"Where I come from," she told the leader, "this is the chemical formula for water. Two parts hydrogen to one part oxygen."

The leader gasped. "Brothers, gather round! The general has solved the riddle of the sacred writings. It's a recipe. She can help us make more for the queen!"

Kip snickered.

She glared at him. To the leader she said, "You don't need to make more water. Just clean up what you already have."

"If we could make the sacred water even cleaner, we would, General. But how do you propose we do this?"

"I'd start with your technicians. You could ask—" Out of the corner of her eye, she spotted movement inside the pool. Conversation forgotten, she stepped closer and peered into the water. A black shadow hovered close to the surface before submerging again.

She pointed at the rippling water. "Something's in

there."

"I beg your pardon, good General," said the leader. "The queen's water is free of all heretics. I respectfully request that you report this to Her Majesty."

She grabbed a staff leaning against the wall and poked one end into the water. The monks leaned closer. She gently stirred. Something bumped against the staff. "There it is," she whispered. Whatever it was wrapped around the pole, adding to the weight in her hands. She grunted, trying to hoist the heavy staff. Kip joined in, helping her lift it from the pool.

A shiny black creature had curled itself around her stick. Once exposed to the air, it unfurled and plopped to the stone floor. Its stingray-like pectoral fins flapped frantically.

The monks let out a collective gasp.

"Tainted water," said the leader. "Take up your staffs, brothers. We'll beat it."

"No. Just because it lives in the water doesn't mean it's a heretic. And Mr. Supposedly Invisible, stop laughing."

Kip clamped his mouth shut mid-guffaw.

She knelt beside the flailing ray. She slid her arms under one slippery fin. Its panicked flutters made it hard to grasp. "Kip, a little help?"

He bent over and grappled with the ray's other side.

"What are you doing?" the leader cried out.

"Putting it back," she said. "For all we know, it eats toxins."

"Leave it," said the leader. "For all we know, it adds toxins."

She said to Kip, "We'll lift on three. One, two—"

"General," said the Brothers Ky leader, "because you are royalty, we won't interfere with what clearly looks like blasphemy. However, if any invisible wizard is in the vicinity, he should be warned that if he helps you in any way, he'll become visible to us, and we'll be forced to report him to the queen."

Kip lowered his side.

She strained under the extra weight. "Kip, it's dying."

He looked from Winnie to the Brothers Ky, then back to the ray.

"Please!"

He hesitated a moment longer. Finally, he clasped his side. The creature, desperate for breath, struggled in their arms. After three false starts, they lifted it high enough to throw it back into the pool. It fluttered deeper into the water and out of sight.

"The wizard is here," said the leader. "Brother Clem, inform Queen Bogen immediately."

One of the monks scampered out.

Kip flew after him.

"Stop that brother from going to the queen," Winnie said. "I command it."

"I beg your pardon, General," said the leader, "but the queen's orders take priority over any given by a demi-princess."

"Then at least give him a head start. He didn't do anything wrong. We had to put that thing back. It was helpless. Don't Brothers Ky take care of helpless creatures?"

"That creature was soiling the queen's water."

She stopped listening. The stingray wasn't the only "creature" that needed protection. Her brain flashed to a picture of someone just as vulnerable, waiting beside a time tear. She had a warning of her own for the queen. She sprinted out, past the waterfall, past the dungeon cells, and back up the staircase.

The two knights guarding the royal meeting chamber stepped aside for her. She burst in on the queen and her advisors playing cards.

Queen Bogen slapped down her cards. "Have the lurkin arrived?" she asked eagerly. "Fynn, sound the alarm."

Her military commander leaped to his feet.

"Not yet," Winnie said, puffing for breath.

The queen regathered her cards, and Fynn returned to his chair.

"But first, I forgot to tell you. I heard from your son. He wants you to know he loves you and misses you."

"Thank you, dear," she said in a gentle tone. "We feel the same about him."

"Good, because that's the other reason I'm here. Your son is waiting by the time tear on the other side."

"Your Majesty," said Commander Fynn. "This is excellent news. General Takka can smite the lurkin as they march through."

"He's unarmed."

"Impossible," said the queen. "Takka is always armed. He's a general."

"Seriously? He's armed even though vogan don't fight?" Winnie shook her head to get back on track. "He isn't a general in my world. He's inside another form, remember? There's no way he can fight the way he is."

"Preposterous," said Fynn. "She must be

mistaken."

"Silence!" the queen commanded. "General Windemere was sent in his stead because Takka's current form was unable. Isn't that correct?"

Winnie nodded. "In my world, we call him a little boy."

Queen Bogen gave her a vacant stare.

"I guess you'd call him a...tadpole?"

"That small?" cried the queen. "And he's at the time tear? Alone?"

"I know, right? I told him not to. Apparently, he believes we'll stop the lurkin before they come through. But to do that we need strong fighters."

"Fynn, immediately begin recruiting vogan. We must defeat the lurkin before they reach my son."

The toad man blustered. "But, Your Majesty, royalty in combat?"

"We henceforth decree that no one is deemed too royal to fight."

"Recruit some palum too, please," said Winnie.

"A vogan squadron will be sufficient. We refuse to bring palum into the fray. They protect their young from harriks. That's the only defense they know."

"But, Your Majesty—"

"No palum. That is our final word on the matter. Fynn, begin the recruitment process. This meeting is adjourned."

"General," Fynn said, bounding next to Winnie. "Would you care to assist me in recruiting the vogan army?"

The invitation surprised her. Not too long ago he'd thrown her off a cliff. Maybe one positive thing about this wacky world was nobody held a grudge.

"Thank you." She walked with him into the corridor, hoping to hear his battle strategy since she had none.

Once out of the queen's hearing, Fynn's dark eyes narrowed. "I said that only to please my queen. She might be fooled, but you are nothing more than a meddlesome outsider."

Her mouth dropped open.

"Accidents can still happen, General." He strode away.

Chapter 29

The little blighter named Brother Clem seemed determined to report Kip to the queen. He scuttled through a doorway too small for Kip. If Clem used the castle's hidden passages, every guard could be after him within minutes. He charged up the staircase to the main level, careful to avoid any guards tramping through the corridors.

He managed to zip through the main hall and into the royal kitchen unseen. According to rumor, Queen Bogen despised the smell of raw food being prepared. He hoped she wouldn't think to send the guards there. A passage from the kitchen led to a staircase that reached his lab.

A lone mel-yew cook flattened dough on a kitchen countertop. He winked at Kip. "If I saw you, I'd say greetings."

Kip sidled next to him. "The Brothers Ky think I blasphemed. One of them has gone off to tell the queen I'm visible again."

The cook slapped the rolled dough into a pie tin. "Nobody pays much heed to the Brothers Ky, least of all the queen."

"I'm all right, then."

"That would be my guess." The cook moved to a boiling pot on the stove. He ladled steaming meat and vegetables into the piecrust.

With the threat lessened, Kip munched contentedly on a raw carrot.

"I'd still keep out of sight if I were you, though," said the cook. He slid the raw pie into the oven and pulled out two cooked ones. "I'll let you know when the danger's past."

"Thanks. I'll wait it out in me lab."

"Care for a meat pie to take with you, Master Wizard?"

The words had barely left the cook's mouth when Willum swooped in through an open window. He lit on the counter. "Did someone say meat pie?"

The cook chuckled. "Nothing's wrong with your hearing, is there, Willum?"

Kip carried a tray of food and fruit drinks up the back stairs to his tower laboratory. Willum flew next to him, chattering, "Mind the pies," the whole way despite Kip's efforts to shush him.

After dinner, he carried a history book to his stuffed chair by the fireplace. Since he didn't dare be seen out and about, now seemed a good time to read up on the wizard who had almost led him astray.

According to the table of contents, Krell had an entire chapter dedicated to him titled "The Anomaly of the Wizard, Thaddeus Krell." Kip thumbed ahead to that chapter, hoping for an artistic rendering of the "otherworlder" as he was called. Instead, the author gave a written description of Krell.

During the reign of King Borge, when first he appeared, the passage read, *the Otherworlder, whose height nearly matched that of a voga, bore the body of a mel-yew with bloat and the mane of a palum. During the reign of King Borge IV, ninety years later, his head was covered in black fur. The intensity of his piercing eyes, pale as a blue summer sky, however, never altered.*

"What an odd fellow," Kip said. On second thought, maybe not. Plenty of athletes on Earth stood over six feet. Couldn't "the mane of a palum" simply mean long blond hair? He'd seen that at home as well. And anyone who ate properly would look bloated when compared to a mel-yew's emaciated little body.

He added it up. "Blimey! Krell's from Earth!"

"Earth," Willum spat and went back to pecking at the leftover crumbs in the pie tins. "I know that wizard's story. Popping in long enough to stir up trouble, then vanishing for generations at a time."

"He must have figured out where the time tears are."

"And how to open them," said the bird.

Kip returned his attention to the history book, eager to learn more. The Otherworlder, or "Other" for short, had arrived during a pandemic that nearly wiped out the entire mel-yew population. In a speech, Krell had told the mel-yew people they were being punished for using their Maker's water without permission. If they stopped drinking the sacred water, Krell had promised they would survive. He'd further described rituals that made it acceptable, on special occasions, to drink purified water. Kip's eyes widened. Was that how the Ky Brotherhood had come into being? He'd probably even written the symbols on the wall. If Krell believed the water was polluted, why hadn't he simply suggested a cleanup the way Winnie had?

According to the text, the first King Borge had bestowed upon Krell the title High Priest of the

Brothers Ky. Krell had vanished the next day, along with one Frama-scope and two bags of gold. The people had believed he died trying to jump into an unstable time tear. He'd returned ninety years later and become that king's royal wizard. The "black fur" on his head— or haircut and dye job, Kip presumed—must have fooled them into thinking he was a different bloke. Kip wondered how long it had taken before someone realized it was Krell.

He looked up at Willum. "Wish you were interested in more than just meat pies. We could discuss this Krell business."

"He ruined it for the good wizards, is what he did," said Willum.

A rustling sound came from across the room. A white chef's hat, with the chef attached, poked through the hole in Kip's wall. The mel-yew cook crawled into the room.

"Is it safe for me to come out?" asked Kip.

The mel-yew glanced nervously around the lab. "I apologize for the intrusion, Wizard."

Kip closed his book. "Everything all right?"

The cook sidled toward Kip's desk where his wand and more books lay. "That, I suppose, depends on who you might ask." In a lightning motion, the cook grabbed the wand and pointed it at Kip. It wavered in his trembling hand.

Kip's muscles tensed. His wand packed a wallop if it got waved the wrong way. "I don't understand. Why are you doing this?"

"Sorry, Master Wizard. The oracle's been making prophecies again."

Feet trampled up the stone steps to his tower. Not

the hollow clacks of mel-yew boots, but the heavy slap of giant frog feet treading on the stair. The door crashed open.

"Stay where you are, Wizard," Zyke commanded, "or suffer the consequences."

A battalion of vogan—Kip never even knew they had such a thing—sprang into his room.

"Where is the wand?"

The cook gingerly offered it to the queen's head advisor. In one sweeping motion Zyke cracked it over his knee, snapping it in two. "You'll tyrannize us no more!"

Hands grabbed Kip and hustled him out. They took him to the interrogation room and tied him to a wooden chair.

"It has come to our attention," Queen Bogen said from her side of the table, "that you've been lying to us."

Kip pressed his lips together. Until he knew which particular lie she meant, it was best to say nothing.

"Did General Takka send you from the other world?" Queen Bogen thumped the table with her fist. "Answer truthfully!"

"Yes."

The queen appraised him with one pink eye. "You unleashed the power of Krell and turned it against us. Takka would never sanction such behavior."

He glared. "And what would he say about you tossing his sister off a cliff?"

The queen sat back. "That was an unfortunate misunderstanding."

"Same as me. I only froze your advisers because I thought you killed Winnie."

"We're beyond that anyway. It has been brought to our attention that you might sabotage the good general's work."

"I wouldn't." He tugged at the restraints. "I promised to help."

Queen Bogen rose. "Guards, take him to the dungeon."

"You can't do that."

The queen and entourage whisked from the room.

"You need me!" His claim earned him a cuff on the side of the head by a guard's staff. Two vogan hauled him to the dungeon. They locked him in a damp cell and stomped away, leaving him alone in the dark.

"Do not despair, young wizard," said a disembodied female voice.

He lifted his head toward the ceiling. He recognized that voice. "Maggenta, I'm glad you're here. Could you please let me out? Winnie needs my magic."

"She has all she needs." Her voice faded into the dank walls.

"Wait. Come back! You can't just leave me."

Kip sighed. Perhaps she could. He slumped onto the bench at the back of the cell, folded his arms, and waited. And waited.

Chapter 30

While Fynn trained the army, Winnie spied on him from an obscure corner of the courtyard. She called it observing. Since his last threat, she preferred to keep out of his way. On the plus side he had obeyed the queen's decree to recruit vogan. Thirty scrawny teen toads, dressed in shiny armor, practiced beside the mel-yew. Winnie had requested one hundred recruits.

Under Fynn's direction, the fighters tramped and clanked through their drills. They shot arrows at short mounds of straw. Winnie wanted him to work with taller, moving targets, but his rigid stance said *be silent or die*.

In the afternoon they had sword practice. The mel-yew soldiers paired up with their kind, as did the vogan soldiers. Fynn directed the pairs to *parlay* and *whoosh*. The swordsmen obediently jumped forward or retreated on his commands. Their swords clanged and, as much as Winnie hated to admit it, they also whooshed. But honestly, she'd taken fencing in gym class last year and knew parlay and whoosh were not the proper terms.

What if Fynn's drills weren't enough? She folded and unfolded her arms in frustration. This was supposed to be her battle too. If only she'd paid better attention during the war lectures in history class. At least then she'd have a few strategies to suggest.

She also wished she could talk to Kip. She hadn't

seen him in two days. Even his lab had been empty when she checked. He needed to man up and apologize to the queen so he could stop hiding and help. For now, at least, all Winnie had was her alleged clever human brain.

The first thing her brain considered was how the lurkin had behaved in her nightmares. They'd never sprayed venom or tried to bite her, so they probably weren't poisonous. That would be a plus. They'd looked like tarantulas in her dreams but like daddy longlegs in Kip's crystal ball. Maybe the actual kind didn't matter. The important thing was they had long legs. How well would those oversized legs keep their balance on a springy ocean? For that matter, how well would the vogan army do, marching on a rubbery surface? Could hopping help them keep their balance? Maybe if the royal army bounced on the ocean, they could create waves high enough to tip over the spiders.

"Hey, Fynn," she called out. "How high can your men jump?"

He shook his head and turned away.

She gasped. He did not just turn his back on a general. Just because she watched from the sidelines didn't mean she wasn't in charge. She stormed up to him. "You can't ignore me. The queen said I'm your boss. Why haven't you taken the bouncy ocean into account? Did you know the enemy is a bunch of spiders? And stop saying parlay and whoosh. It's parry and thrust. Parry and thrust!"

He turned to his troops. "Gentlemen, let us show the good general how well we've been doing with target practice." He clasped her arm and pulled her to the courtyard wall. "General, if you'll stand here." He pressed her back into the stone. "Don't move." To the troops, he said, "Men, the object of this exercise is to see how closely you can aim your arrows near the top of the general's head without actually hitting her."

"You can't do that!" She struggled in his grip, but his hold was too strong to escape.

He smirked. "Have no worries, General. I'd say your chances of getting impaled are quite slim. Men, weapons at the ready."

In a fluid motion the entire army snapped up their bows. Hundreds of arrows pointed at her head.

"Oh, and men," he added, "if the general runs, it just means she's testing you to see how well you can aim at a moving target." He strode back to his position at the end of the front line.

She glanced left to right. Nearby stood a barrel, a trough, a few haystacks, and a palum cart. Perfect covers. But could she reach any of them in time? A palum polishing a nearby carriage gave her an idea. If she couldn't run to shelter before the arrows started flying, maybe protection could come to her.

"Aim," Fynn ordered.

"Hey, Pall!" She didn't think Fynn would let the army fire with a palum in the area.

The ground rumbled from galloping hooves. Fifteen man horses rushed to her. She had no idea so many were in the area. Still, they created a protective barrier. All fifteen clamored at once to know what service they could offer.

"Company, halt," Fynn shouted over the noise. "Lower your weapons."

Winnie let out a relieved breath. "Sorry," she told the throng. "Just need four of you." Using the four as cover, she marched to the castle entrance. At the doorway she turned to the palum. "Thanks for walking with me. You're free to go now."

All four bobbed their heads but followed her inside.

"I'm good. You can go back to what you were doing." She pointed to the door, then turned away. She'd barely taken a step when hooves clopped behind her. She sighed and looked back. "Guys, for real. You're dismissed."

"You called my name," said the palum in front. "I wish to help."

"You called my name," the others joined in.

"You already helped. Thank you. Now I really have to go." She sprinted away. Fortunately, they didn't follow. That was when a new battle strategy began to form. She hurried after a passing page and asked for directions to find the queen.

He pointed her to an office where the queen sat, signing decrees. She looked up. "Ah, Windemere. We were just thinking of you."

Winnie bowed. "I came to ask—"

"First, if we may." Queen Bogen lowered her quill. She cleared her throat. "About the hunt." She coughed again. "It might have been a bit rash of us, trying to lose you. We hope you'll forgive us for that."

Winnie's mouth dropped open. She'd never expected an actual apology from the queen. Maybe she wasn't such a pompous old toad after all. Her pink eyes actually looked remorseful.

Her own eyes widened. Had she just found one of those allies her dad had mentioned in her Ferris wheel dream? She stepped forward with her hand out. "Where

I come from, to show no hard feelings, we shake hands. It also means friendship."

"In the name of friendship and kinship."

Her hand clasped Winnie's with a gentle pressure. It felt soft and cool, not warty at all.

"As for our earlier mistake," the queen said, "we wish to make it up to you."

For the briefest moment Winnie considered asking the queen to fire Fynn for almost trying to kill her again. Her main reason for coming to the queen's office, however, took priority. Winnie bowed again. "I do have a request."

"We shall accommodate you."

Winnie's heart fluttered with hope. "Do you think your technicians could build more speakers? Really big ones?"

"They can build whatever we ask. Why would we need them?"

"We could set them up on your ocean, far out to sea, then hide a microphone near the beach. I thought we could…" Here it got tricky. The queen might not do it if she knew what Winnie had in mind. "Scare the lurkin away with loud noises."

The queen gazed thoughtfully at the ceiling. "Do you mean we'd create sounds that would make our army appear much larger than it is?"

Winnie hadn't thought of that, but it sounded better than her original lie. "Yes, Your Majesty."

The queen lowered her gaze from the ceiling. "We are in favor of any tactic that will keep our people from harm. Thank you for your clever suggestion. We shall order it straight away. We'll also command the builders to assemble a special platform in the brush so that we may oversee the battle. Perhaps we'll even employ Polo to insult the enemy with his wit."

"Excellent idea, Your Majesty." Winnie bowed a third time. "With your permission, I'd like to stand by the microphone."

"Shouldn't you be at the front lines, overseeing the battle?"

"Fynn will be with the men. If I'm on the platform, I can tell him what I see." Winnie crossed her fingers for luck.

After a long pause, the queen said, "Granted."

"Perfect. Thanks." Winnie started to leave but turned back. "One more thing. Could you please forgive Kip? We might need his magic if the speaker thing doesn't work."

Queen Bogen pressed her lips into a grim line.

"He didn't mean to freeze your advisors. And they're unfrozen now."

"My son's life depends upon you smiting this enemy. To remove all distractions, the oracle has suggested that the wizard safely remain elsewhere until the war ends."

"But he knows magic."

"Not the kind we need. Carry on, my dear. You've a war to win." The queen waved her away.

Winnie hesitated, wondering if the time was right to snitch on Fynn. Would the queen change her mind about Kip if she knew her military advisor's murderous tendencies were even more distracting? Winnie opened her mouth but closed it again. She was a warrior, not a little kid who tattled. Still, she left the room feeling less confident than she had going in. One of her allies hated her, and she didn't have Kip's magic as a backup. She took a deep breath and straightened her shoulders. Warriors never gave up.

Winnie marched to her meeting about the speakers. To her relief, the royal technicians, comprised of both vogan and mel-yew subjects, accepted her amplifier measurements without question. They even shared how they intended to generate power to the speakers. She didn't understand any of their technical talk. She just smiled and nodded.

For the next two days, while Fynn continued to train the troops in the courtyard, Winnie oversaw preparations at the impending battle site. She sprinted back and forth between the shoreline, where the mel-yew builders constructed the giant speakers, and the vegetation boundary at the beach where vogan worked on the viewing platform. Half a dozen palum hauled equipment and supplies to both places and only occasionally got in the way. All the while, a single palum stood on the rubbery ocean, far beyond the flurry of activity.

Winnie wobbled out and stood beside the palum on guard duty. He stared outward through the binoculars. The two stood so far out to sea that sound from the activity behind them barely reached them.

"See anything?" she asked.

"I see the much-far, good General, but no specks."

"Thank you," she said. The smelly ocean kept her from breathing deeply in relief, but her muscles relaxed. No specks on the horizon meant they still had time to prepare.

On her way back to solid ground, a crowd of tiny mel-yew workers tried to carry the first speaker over the jelly ocean. She hurried to help them, but that only added to the unsteady ground. They stumbled and swayed so much they almost dropped it.

"Go back. Go back!" the mel-yew foreman shouted. "We need a better base."

They unsteadily returned to the beach. The mel-yew engineers scratched their bald heads and pondered. A few minutes later they restructured the speaker bases to roll, instead of tipping over. This time, they employed four palum to heft the altered amplifiers onto a flatbed cart. A group of mel-yew rode along as the palum pulled the cart onto the jellied ocean.

"Keep going," Winnie called from the beach. "I'll tell you when to stop."

Every few yards the palum paused and looked to her.

"Farther." She motioned to them to keep going another two hundred yards. "Right there." She waved for them to stop and set up the speakers.

Once they returned with the cart, a mel-yew handed her the wireless microphone.

"Testing. Test one, test two." Her amplified voice blasted from the speakers with so much intensity birds nesting in the bushes shrieked and flapped away.

She turned to the nearest engineer. "Can you make it louder?"

He bowed. "Indeed we can, General."

She grinned at him. "You guys are awesome."

With the sound system in place, Winnie moved on to the platform hidden by the edge of the forest. The team leader pounded the last nail into place.

She clambered up the wooden staircase to check it out. Protective railings surrounded the platform reminiscent of the open deck at her old lake house. She shook her head. No time to think about that now.

According to specifications, a throne would come later. An opening between the tree branches gave her a view of the ocean and the beach. She nodded. "Looks good."

From her vantage point, the speakers stood so far away they looked like dark blobs. She lowered her gaze to the gray beach and imagined the rows and rows of mel-yew and vogan soldiers. Winnie shuddered and gripped the railing. This wasn't a game. This was a real war, and as much as she wanted to deny it, she was afraid.

She rode back to the castle in a carriage filled with a boisterous group of mel-yew. They laughed and sang about successfully completing their task. She forced a smile, pretending to celebrate with them.

The carriage rolled to a stop in the courtyard. Before Winnie could disembark, a palum galloped past, shouting, "A speck! A speck! There's a speck out to sea!"

Chapter 31

Commander Fynn assembled the royal troops in the courtyard. He barked final instructions, then ordered them to the battlefield. In the hustle, vogan troops leapfrogged toward the beach. Dozens of palum pulled open wagons filled with mel-yew knights in heavy armor. Every available wigget flew additional mel-yew warriors to battle. Queen Bogen, refusing the pomp of riding in the royal carriage, hopped to the beach with her advisors. Winnie had so many jangling nerves a flat-out race to the beach might have calmed her, but the path was too crowded with everyone else.

She huffed in annoyance. "How am I supposed to get there?"

"If you please, good General," spoke a voice from behind. "I've been given the honor of transporting you to the big beach."

She turned to find a lone palum standing by a two-wheeled cart that looked part sulky and part rickshaw. "Better than nothing, I guess," she mumbled. Louder, she said, "Thank you," and climbed in. She nervously jiggled her foot the whole ride, last to leave and last to arrive.

By the time her cart rolled out of the woods, the entire army already stood on the beach, facing the ocean. Winnie walked through the ranks that stretched across the beach toward the ocean. She counted only five rows of vogan who stood nearest the protection of the forest. Directly in front of them stood ten rows of mel-yew fighters, dressed in leather armor. Ten more rows of mel-yew, looking like shiny silver dominos in their metal armor, stood nearest the shoreline.

Winnie stared straight ahead as she passed the miniature knights. She couldn't let them see the uncertainty that shook through her. What if the enemy plowed straight through their ranks, tipping them over?

Fynn stood one hundred yards out to sea with the lone palum on duty. Winnie hoped that, due to the gravity of the situation, he would agree to a truce. She sucked in a deep breath of putrid air for courage and bounced over the wobbly ocean toward him. He acknowledged her with a brief nod, then returned his attention to the horizon.

The palum at Fynn's side continued to watch through the binoculars even though the naked eye could clearly see gigantic daddy-longlegs spiders marching toward them at a slow pace. Kip's crystal-ball prediction had been correct. If only he stood with her now. He would've probably told a joke to take her mind off her feelings of inadequacy as a general. She crossed her fingers for luck.

The enemy moved stiffly, not at all like regular spiders on a stable surface. Did the rubbery ocean make them walk that way or… Winnie took the binoculars from the scout. Under magnification she saw rivets on what appeared to be metal spider bodies.

"They're fake."

"Begging your pardon," said Fynn, "they appear quite real."

She studied them. "I mean they're machines."

Thankfully, no cannons, swords, or other weapons protruded from their spherical "bodies." Still, over a hundred spider-shaped machines headed their way. Winnie's insides churned.

"How long before they get here?"

"We estimate quarter of an hour at the earliest," Fynn said in a grave tone.

A pair of massive black amplifiers, per her request, stood another hundred yards farther out to sea. The metal spiders would reach the speakers first. Winnie turned toward the beach. The queen's army stood stiffly in place. From where Winnie stood, they appeared solid, unyielding. Good. Maybe their sheer volume would give the spider militia second thoughts. She spotted a snag to her plan. The army blocked the opening to the wide path that led into the forest.

"Commander, have your men clear that section of beach in front of the path."

Fynn gaped at her. "Whatever for? They're guarding the trail to the castle."

"Queen's instruction," she lied.

He clamped his mouth shut and scowled.

"Also, the queen will give the attack order over the loudspeakers."

He stomped back to the beach, muttering to himself.

She put the binoculars around her neck and clapped the scout on the shoulder. "You're free to go. Thank you for your service."

The palum bowed and ambled toward shore. Winnie, moving faster, reached the beach first and hurried to Queen Bogen's camouflaged platform. She bowed to the queen and nodded to her mel-yew attendant and to Polo. She peered through the tree branches, relieved that the troops left a gap all the way from the path to the ocean. She silently thanked Fynn for following her instruction.

Queen Bogen rose off her temporary throne to watch. "What's the meaning of this? Why are they moving apart like that?"

"To make room for the palum scout to return to the castle." Winnie used such a firm tone she almost believed it herself.

The queen settled back into her throne. "They're making slow work of it."

Winnie didn't reply. She needed all her concentration to ignore the booming in her chest and the tidal wave roaring through her stomach. She tightened her leg muscles to keep her knees from quaking. She wasn't gangly Winnie Harris anymore but General Windemere. The Great. At least she'd better be. Too many people depended on her to pull this off. She nervously rubbed a thumb over the hilt of her dagger.

Polo, dressed in eye-blinding yellow-and-orange stripes, stepped forward. "Begging your pardon, Your Majesty, will I still be singing today?"

"Most certainly. That's why we brought you."

Winnie squared her shoulders. "Stand by, Polo. You'll sing in a minute."

She lifted the wireless microphone from the arm of Queen Bogen's throne and carried it to the railing. Her army waited. The robotic spiders tramped closer.

"General," the queen said, "they're about to invade us."

The lurkin neared the speakers. Winnie compressed

her lips, silently willing them to keep going without tipping them over. If the speakers fell facedown, this would never work. Her grip on the microphone tightened.

"General, we implore you," croaked the queen. "Sound the charge, or we shall surely perish."

The first row of giant spiders passed the speakers on both sides. Now came the hard part. Waiting. Winnie watched the spider army, afraid to blink, afraid to breathe. Two more rows passed the speakers.

"General!" cried Queen Bogen. "Think of my son. Think of your brother."

A fourth row of lurkin passed. The army on the beach obediently stood at attention, waiting for the command to attack.

"We think you are a traitor!"

"Trust me, Your Majesty. I'm thinking about everybody."

More lurkin marched forward. When the final row of spiders passed the speakers, she raised the microphone, took a deep breath, and shouted into it, "Pall!"

The name blasted from the speakers. It traveled through the forest, echoing off the trees.

"Pall, I need you!" she said over and over.

Her amplified voice made the spiders pause.

"Pall!" With luck, the wind might carry her voice as far as the castle.

A low rumble sounded in the distance. It grew to a thunderous noise. Hundreds of palum galloped across the area cleared by the army and onto the jelly ocean. Rubbery ripples grew as they spread outward. The spiders lurched and staggered as the ground shifted beneath them.

"Pall!"

The palum plowed through the spiders' ranks, knocking the long legs out from under them. Any spiders still standing lost their balance from all the hooves pounding across the jellied ocean.

"I say," Queen Bogen said in amazement.

The stampeding palum raced out to sea. The heaving jelly waves rocked and tilted the speakers, but their rounded bases brought them upright again. By the time the last horse/man hybrid passed, every spider lay on its back or side, legs waving futilely in the air.

"The palum defeated the lurkin," said the queen.

From below, the army leaped and cheered.

Winnie's muscles softened from relief. She laughed out loud. Kip was right. Winning the war was just like agonizing over a test at school that ended up being open book.

The queen smiled back. "We knew you'd stop them. We knew it all the time."

Winnie let out a triumphant, "Ha!" Her strategy had actually worked. Maybe she really was a general. She didn't even mind that Queen Bogen had called her a traitor a few moments ago.

"Your Majesty!" Polo cried out. He pointed at the ocean. Trap doors on the sides of the fallen spiders dropped open.

Tiny humanoids crawled from the openings, weaving and staggering over the residual ripples from the palum. The little men stumbled for balance. Several bumped into each other, which started a shoving match between them.

Winnie zoomed in on them with the binoculars.

The men looked no taller than palum colts but seemed stockier than the mel-yew. The tops of their round heads were covered with orange hair. Their black eyes scowled from beneath bushy eyebrows.

"What tiny fellows," said the queen. "We'd expected a bit more of a threat, didn't we?"

As the queen went on about how silly they'd been for worrying, Winnie saw through the binoculars that each tiny fellow had pulled a spear from his spider-like transport.

"Uh-oh," she murmured.

The lurkin, no longer disoriented, tramped toward shore.

"What are they doing?" the queen demanded. "What have they got?"

The mel-yew fighters remained at attention. The lurkin tramped onto the beach.

"Why doesn't Fynn call them to arms?" cried the queen.

General Windemere jammed the microphone into the queen's hands. "Sorry. You're supposed to give the order to fight."

Queen Bogen spoke into the microphone, "You there!" Her powerful voice boomed through the speakers. "Lurkin. Stop this at once."

The little men's gazes darted left to right, as if searching for the owner of the commanding voice.

"What do you want from these innocent vogan and mel-yew?"

"I am Tudbul, leader of the lurkin," shouted a squeaky voice from the tallest of the little men. "We are here for the doorway. You must know that as well, else your troops would not have greeted us."

"These aren't our troops," the queen spoke into the microphone. "They're royal subjects, merely out for a stroll."

"Fully armed and dressed in battle attire? We think not. Lead us to the doorway of time or die."

The lurkin waved their spears menacingly. Several weapons clanged against mel-yew armor. Three knights fell backward, creating a domino effect, knocking over a dozen men.

"I command you to stop. The doorway has closed up already."

"I don't believe you," said Tudbul. "Our oracle distinctly informed us that the doorway would open when the night winds blew hot and dry over our village."

"Your oracle was misinformed. You should have come when the winds blew cold and wet over your village. Go back where you came from. We don't have what you want."

Tudbul stomped the ground. His face reddened. "You tell falsehoods. And you mock us. The wind always blows cold and wet over our village."

"If I may, Your Majesty," Polo said respectfully, "I believe I know a certain impression that will end this conversation."

The queen offered the microphone with a stately nod.

Polo's impression of distressed colts bleated through the speakers. Suddenly, the air filled with the sound of beating wings and hungry screeches. A flock of harriks shot from the trees. They headed out to sea but quickly turned around and swooped down on the smallest creatures on the beach. The lurkin army. The flying snakes unhinged their jaws and swallowed thirteen before the lurkin realized they were being attacked from above. They shook their spears, but the harriks knocked them away with their tails.

"Go home or be eaten!" Queen Bogen's voice blared from the speakers.

Two more harriks got lunch before the lurkin scampered back inside their metal spiders and closed themselves inside.

The queen nodded in satisfaction. "We are most certainly shot of them now. Pesky little creatures, lurkin."

"With pointy spears," Winnie said. "They still could have hurt Takka if they got through the time tear."

Queen Bogen beamed. "They shan't harm him now."

The harriks circled above the fallen spiders a few more times before flying back into the forest. After the last one flew away, the lurkin crept out of their arachnid vehicles and peered warily at the empty sky. They quickly righted their machines and climbed back inside. This time when the metal spiders moved, they marched back out to sea.

"Open-book test!" Winnie cheered.

"I'm not sure I follow," said the queen.

Winnie smiled. "It was easier than we thought."

In the distance the palum herd headed toward shore. To her surprise they passed right by the retreating spiders without giving them a look. They walked in pairs and seemed to be more focused on conversations with each other. At least they didn't knock into anything on the way back.

"What a jolly clever idea, summoning the palum like that," said the queen.

Winnie's cheeks burned at the unexpected compliment. "Thanks."

"Only someone from your world could have thought of such a creative use of our lowly subjects. You were correct that we needed them all along. They saved our people. You saved our people."

"You helped too, Your Majesty," Winnie said, willing to share the credit. "Good idea, keeping the lurkin talking so they wouldn't attack."

Queen Bogen puffed up with pride. "We found it most entertaining. However, we mustn't forget our quick-witted friend here, who cleverly drew out the harriks."

Polo's tiny ears glowed bright pink. "It was a combined effort that defeated the lurkin, Your Majesty. Commander Fynn's brave army must also be congratulated."

"And so they shall," said the queen. "You are a most wise buffoon, Polo."

"Surely not." His face turned an even brighter red.

"No need for modesty. At this evening's ceremony we shall present you with a special military award. And another to the palum for their valor."

"Just remember not to call out their name," Polo teased, "or they'll trample us."

Winnie laughed just as hard as the queen did. She appreciated the release of tension even if it was from a lame joke.

"You'll have to use that in your next act, Polo," Winnie said.

The tiny jester grinned. "I intend to."

"You must perform for us at the award ceremony," said the queen.

He bowed. "I would be honored, Your Majesty. And I shall include a song extolling our general's brave works."

"Cool. Nobody ever wrote a song about me before."

"We fail to see what temperature has to do with the issue," the queen said, "but that is neither here nor there. Sadly, you'll miss the song, General. The lurkin's oracle was correct. The time tear, or door as the lurkin called it, has opened. You must return to your world."

When the queen's words fully sank in, Winnie's insides pulsed with excitement. She was going home.

Queen Bogen unfastened Winnie's watch from her own wrist. "Our oracle has reset your timepiece to help you. Presently, the time tear is beneath the castle. As the tear rises, you'll hear an alarm."

Winnie eagerly put on her watch.

"A single tone means the door is in the dungeon, cell number five. Your wizard, by the way, is in cell number eight. Here's the key. Kindly take him with you."

Winnie accepted it with a gasp. *That's where he was all this time? Poor Kip.*

Before she could think more about it, the queen continued, "Two signals mean it has risen to the main hall. Three, it's moved to the balcony. Four, the southeast turret. The final warning shall be five tones."

"Where will it be then?" Winnie asked, pocketing the key in her tunic.

"In the sky."

"Not too high, though, right?"

"High enough," the queen said in a solemn voice, "that you would be able to attend our award ceremony as a permanent resident of Frama-12."

Winnie gaped at her.

"We're certain you'll reach the tear in good time. A palum cart is waiting for you."

"Thanks." She turned to go.

"General, if we may."

She turned back.

The queen rose. "You might miss the ceremony, but you needn't miss the award." She removed something shiny and gold from an inner corner of her royal throne. An oddly shaped medallion hung from a wide blue ribbon. "We present this small token, General Windemere, for using human wit to save our queendom and send the lurkin back to their land." She draped the ribbon around Winnie's neck.

Winnie bowed. "Thank you, Your Majesty." She'd add it to all the track medals she'd won at home, but for now, she tucked it inside her tunic. She'd admire it later when she had more time. Cold metal bumped against her skin.

The queen lowered her head in a brief bow. "Thank you," she said in a soft, sincere voice, "for saving my son."

"Well, ya know." Winnie shrugged. "He is my brother."

"That he is," the queen said gently. "That he is."

Winnie recognized the mother love in those bulging pink eyes. Her own mom used to look at her like that. She bowed her head to hide the tears forming in her eyes. Warriors weren't supposed to cry. Or were they? After today, she was most definitely a warrior.

She let a tear roll down her cheek. She sniffed and raised her head.

Warriors also admitted when they were wrong. "I'm sorry about those misunderstandings we had at the beginning. You're a good queen."

"And you, my dear Windemere, are a worthy general and demi-princess." She let out a wistful sigh. "Once again we lose kin to the time tear. You will look after Takka for us, won't you?"

"I promise, Your Majesty."

A single peep sounded from Winnie's watch.

Chapter 32

"Hurry along now," said the queen. "Travel well."

"Thanks again." Winnie strode toward her cart but paused to allow the last of the palum to walk by. She heard them mumbling among themselves about the greatness of the voice that had called them. When the pathway finally cleared, the rows upon rows of vogan and mel-yew troops stood as tall as their commander, Fynn. She'd have to pass him to reach her cart. With breath held, she cautiously moved forward. Her entire body went on alert. Would he let her pass or order her shot?

Their eyes met. Commander Fynn blinked first. He faced his men.

She recoiled. *Uh-oh. Here it comes.*

"Company, salute!" he shouted.

As one, the warriors crossed their arms in front of their chests, fists clenched.

She stopped. Her mouth formed a surprised, "Oh."

A salute? In all the time she'd known him, she never expected that. Well, she'd never imagined the queen might have a good side either. The salute from Fynn, though, was just as good as a medal.

For half a second Winnie considered showing him the way they saluted in her world. But only for half a second. She balled her own fists and crossed her arms in front of her chest.

Fynn gave a curt half nod. One general acknowledging another. She nodded back and hurried away.

Her two-wheeled palum cart stood just where she'd left it. The driver bowed. "Please forgive me for briefly abandoning the cart, General, but a large voice called my name."

She grinned. "It's always important to listen to large voices." She climbed into her seat.

"When it stopped calling, I knew it didn't need me after all, so I came back."

"I'm glad you did. Can you run to the castle? I'm in a hurry."

Pall bowed again. "It is my honor to serve you."

He trotted along the forest path at a smooth pace. She checked her watch. The face was blank! How would she know when the time tear moved?

"Could you go a little faster, please?"

He galloped. Her watch chimed twice. *Oh good, it still works*. But that meant the time tear had just risen to the main hall. She urged Pall to run faster.

He charged around a curve just as a skitter darted onto the path. Pall swerved to avoid it. The cart tipped over, pulling him with it. Winnie sailed out of her seat and sprawled into the dirt.

She rolled over, shaken but unhurt. Surprisingly, the binoculars, still around her neck, weren't damaged either. Before she could celebrate her good fortune, a bent wheel wobbled past.

She turned in the direction it came from. Pall lay on his side, struggling in a tangle of harness straps. "Please forgive me, General."

She hurried to help him remove the straps and sit

up. "You didn't break anything, did you?"

He puffed for breath. "It is only a small pain." He winced. "I shall—" He tried to stand but fell back down. "—be all right."

"You better sit here for a few minutes."

"But, General, you must reach the castle."

"I'll be fine. I still have this." She pulled her wigget whistle from her tunic and blew it twice. "I'll send help as soon as I reach the castle."

Two wiggets soared overhead. They circled her but didn't land. "Sorry-sorry," they squawked. "Too-big, too-big."

"Wait!" she cried out. "I'll call one more."

The birds flapped away without looking back.

She kicked the ground. "Now what?"

"If you don't mind my saying, General," the palum said from the ground, "your own legs look quite strong indeed. Can you run?"

Why hadn't she thought of that? She stretched to limber up. It was time to put her workouts to the test. She started out at a brisk jog. As she warmed up, she increased her speed. She ran through the woods, arms pumping in rhythm with her long strides. She raced down a hill into the valley and through a mel-yew village. Peasant onlookers came out and cheered her on.

Fifty yards from the castle, a muscle knotted in her left calf. She gritted her teeth and kept going. Finally, she burst through the gates. She dashed across the courtyard. A mel-yew doorman pulled open the front door for her. Gulping for breath, she bounded down the staircase to the dungeon.

"Kip?"

"This way," he called back. "It's about time."

His arms waved between the cell bars. She slid her hand into her tunic pocket for the key. Nothing. Her heart rumbled in panic. She slapped her pockets, hoping to feel the outline of the key.

"What are you doing? Aren't you supposed to be letting me out?"

"The key. It must've fallen out of my pocket when the cart tipped over."

"Call a guard," he said calmly. "They carry extras."

"What guards?" she shouted over her booming pulse. "Everybody's at the beach."

He poked his head between the bars. "There's probably a spare on a nail."

She charged back to the alcove near the first cell where a candle gave off minimal light. As promised, a key hung from a hook. She snatched it and raced back to Kip's cell. Her trembling fingers struggled a few times before the key fit in the lock.

Kip stepped out. "If you don't mind me saying so, I rescued you from the dungeon within hours if you'll remember. You took nearly a week."

"Didn't know you were here. Time tear's in the main hall," she said in one breath.

"Oi. You defeated the lurkin, then?"

"Yes, come *on*." She grabbed his hand. "It's moving fast." She pulled him through the dungeon corridor.

"What about the war?"

"Later. We have to go." She tugged harder. "Now."

They raced up the staircase. At the castle's main level, Kip stopped. Winnie bumped into him with an "oof."

"Where's Willum?" His eyes grew wide with

264

worry. "What if they executed 'im?"

She huffed. "They wouldn't. Come on."

He whistled through his fingers.

She yanked his arm. "Hurry up. We don't have *time* for this. What does he come to?"

"Food mostly. Meat pies."

"Willum!" she called. "We have meat pies!"

A black bird flew toward them. "Meat pies?"

"There you are," Kip said in a relieved voice. "Where ya been?"

"Looking for another wizard and meat pies."

"I like that. I lose me wand, and off 'e goes."

Winnie's watch beeped three times. The time tear had risen to the balcony.

"Faster." She panted.

They darted up another long staircase. By the next one, she felt the strain from all the running and slowed to a half jog. At the top she hunched over and clutched her knees. She'd barely caught her breath when her watch beeped four times.

"What's that mean?" Kip asked, gasping.

"Southeast turret."

"Blimey. That's two more levels away!"

She slowly straightened up. "We can make it."

She inhaled deeply, then jogged upward, level by level. He plodded behind her. She stumbled through the open doorway to the southeast turret and into the arms of a female voga. Winnie looked into her glowing, red-purple eyes. "Maggenta?"

The oracle pulled Winnie to her feet. "No time for rest, child."

Kip burst onto the turret and fell to his knees. Willum glided through the doorway.

"The time tear is still moving. You both must return to your world as you came." Maggenta held out two sets of clothes. "Change back into these."

Winnie looked toward Kip. "I can't change with a *guy* up here."

Maggenta mumbled a spell, and two privacy screens materialized. She pushed the clothes bundles into Winnie's and Kip's arms. Each ducked behind a screen.

"There's a wounded palum at the clearing," Winnie said as she changed into her shorts and T-shirt. "Hurt his ankle."

"I'll tend to him after I've seen you off."

"Couldn't you find me shorts and me shirt?" Kip cried out.

Winnie didn't spot her own problem until she jammed her bare feet into her running shoes. "I'm missing a shoelace."

"I did that," Kip said.

She stepped from behind the screen. "I won't even ask. This doesn't matter, does it? No socks and a missing lace?"

"No, child." The oracle draped the canteen straps around Winnie's neck.

Kip edged away from his screen, dressed in green plaid shorty pajamas. Willum sat perched on his shoulder. The sight of them sent Winnie into a laughing fit. Willum flapped into the air.

Her watch beeped five times.

Her smile turned to a horrified grimace. "We missed it."

"It's still within reach," Maggenta said. "You'll have to jump."

"What?" she and Kip said in unison.

"Trust me," Maggenta said.

Winnie climbed onto the crenel. She strained her eyes, searching for the time tear. "I can't see anything."

Kip joined her on the stone battlement. "Neither can I. Is it really out there?"

"Jump," Maggenta ordered.

Winnie cringed at the sight of the courtyard so far below. It reminded her of the time she'd been stuck in a tree. "I don't want to fall."

"The door is still rising," said the oracle. "Jump high. Now!"

Kip gripped Winnie's hand. They took deep breaths, flexed their knees, and jumped together. An invisible web tightened around her, squeezing the breath out of her. Then she began to drop. Her mind cried out with dread *not again*.

Chapter 33

Before everything went black, a pair of green eyes without a face stared at Winnie. The eyes dissolved into her lake dream. She sat on a rocking chair next to her mom on the deck that overlooked the water. Mom wore her honey-colored hair pulled into a ponytail. Her nose and cheeks glowed reddish pink from too much sun, and her eyes sparkled with a vibrant glow, just like the photo in Winnie's locket.

"This is a dream, right? I mean, I didn't die from hitting the ground, did I?"

Mom turned her head toward Winnie and smiled. "You're alive and well."

"Good." Except when she woke from this dream, she'd ache all over again from missing her mom.

"Just enjoy the now, Windy," Mom said, her voice warm with love.

Naturally, a dream mom would say that. Or was it just Winnie's brain saying it? She shook her head. Maybe it didn't matter. "I feel like you're really here. Like when I dreamed Dad was on a Ferris wheel with me."

"Don't overthink it, sweetie. How did you like Frama-12?"

Winnie let her dream mind go with the flow. "I had a kind of stepmom there."

"Did you two get along?"

Winnie grinned. "Not at first. And she was a queen."

Mom smiled too. "Windemere Ellen Harris, warrior princess."

Winnie laughed. "I really was. I even helped win a war."

"I knew you could." Mom kissed Winnie's forehead. Then everything went dark.

****

The hushed sound of rolling waves reached Winnie's ears. She sensed brightness through her closed eyelids. Sand scratched the backs of her legs the way it had when she landed in Frama-12, except this time the granules felt cool. She didn't dare open her eyes in case she found herself in another weird world. A seagull cried overhead. A gentle breeze carried the sweet smell of coconut sun lotion. It smelled like home.

A shadow fell over her face. She blinked several times to clear her vision. A pair of wide brown eyes and a tan face peered down.

"Mikey?" she said in a hoarse whisper. "Am I dreaming again?"

"Nope." He smiled, revealing the gap where baby teeth used to be.

She slowly propped herself onto her elbows. Her canteens and binoculars clanked into each other.

"Something weird happened," she said, still feeling her mom's kiss on her forehead.

"We know," said another familiar voice. Kip, dressed in green plaid shorty pajamas, sat beside her. "I came through a full five minutes before you did. We worried you landed in the wrong place."

"Just Kip worried," Mikey said. "I told him a

watcher kept you back."

"A what?" She sat up all the way.

"Guardians of the veil," Mikey said matter-of-factly.

Kip rolled his eyes. "You've said that twice already, mate, but I still don't know what any of that means."

"Cyann mentioned that." She turned to Mikey. "Can watchers make themselves look like other people, like my mom?"

The little boy shrugged. "I just know they guard the space between worlds. Did the watcher tell you anything?"

She lowered her eyes so the boys wouldn't see her sadness from missing her mom. "Said she was proud of me."

"I'm proud of you too," Mikey said. "You saved two worlds."

She sighed, trying to let her mother go. "I don't know how big the threat was. The lurkin ended up being little dudes inside mechanical spiders."

Kip gaped at her. "They were? Let's hear it all. Start to finish." He squatted in the sand beside her.

Mikey squeezed between them. "Me too. Tell me too."

Winnie gave them a condensed version of the battle. Mikey laughed and applauded.

"That was brill!" Kip said with a wide smile.

"I don't know how brilliant I was. The palum did most of the work, and the harriks did the rest."

Kip shook his head, eyes wide. "Maybe it was a good thing I was in the dungeon after all. If I'd known you were planning to use the palum, I might've used

270

magic to stop you. I agreed with everybody else. The palum are too peaceful for battle."

"Then I guess they needed my wily ways after all," she joked.

Mikey grinned. "Told ya."

She stopped smiling. Mikey wasn't just her little brother. He was a voga. She still remembered Takka's frozen vessel in Cyann's cave. Would he keep his promise and stay as Mikey? Her heart pounded in her throat. "So...Takka. What happens now?" She held her breath, afraid of the answer.

"We'll celebrate with chocolate chip pancakes."

Her heart pulsed to a hopeful beat. "Does that mean you're staying?"

He rolled his eyes. "Windy. Chocolate chip pancakes."

She laughed and gave him a big hug. She kissed his smooth cheeks until he giggled and squirmed away.

"Thanks, bud."

Except for the three of them sitting together on the beach, the day started like so many others. A female jogger ran past. A white-haired man carried a bucket and fishing pole to the water's edge. Nobody knew what Winnie had just done to keep their world safe. The only ones who would ever believe her story were a little boy who used to be a toad and a guy in shorty pajamas who thought he was a wizard. Imagining those two like that made her giggle.

"What?" Kip asked, smiling along.

"Everything," she said, cracking up.

Kip and Mikey joined in. At the height of their hilarity, a woman's worried voice called from farther down the beach, "Michael, where are you?"

Mikey jumped up and down, waving his arms. "Here, Mommy!"

"Crap," Winnie muttered. "Here she comes."

Maria, dressed in her pink bathrobe, stormed across the sand toward them.

"She does not look at all pleased."

"It's okay," Mikey said and skipped to his mother.

Maria crouched to hug him. "We worried about you, buddy." She kissed the top of his head. She straightened and glared down at Winnie. "You took him for a run? In his pajamas no less and didn't tell us?"

"Um."

"When Mikey's room was empty, I thought he wandered off and was alone out here. Anything could've happened."

Winnie opened her mouth to apologize but didn't get a chance.

"He could've been swept out to sea. He could've been kidnapped. And what's all that?" Maria jabbed a finger at the canteens and binoculars around Winnie's neck. "Going on a safari? You didn't even ask to use them."

"Mom, it's okay," Mikey said. "Windy just saved the world!"

Maria took a deep breath and gently rested her hand on Mikey's shoulder. "See how he looks up to you? That's why you have to be the mature one."

The way Maria's lips pressed into a grim line reminded Winnie of Queen Bogen.

Winnie had recently admitted to a watcher that she'd finally learned to accept the queen, toad warts and all. Maybe it was time to do the same with Maria.

Her gaze fell on Maria's hand, lovingly resting on

Mikey's shoulder. The three of them might be different, but Winnie, Maria, and the voga queen had one thing in common. They all cherished the same prince.

"You're right. I should've left a note. I'm sorry."

"That's all I ask," Maria said in a calmer tone. "And who are you?" Her guarded gaze fell on Kip. "Do I know you?"

"That's Kip," Mikey said. "He's a wizard."

Kip waved.

Maria frowned at him. "Are you also out here in pajamas?"

"Loungewear," he said sweetly.

Maria shook her head. "Breakfast is ready. You're welcome to join us, Mr. Loungewear."

"Can we talk to Kip for one more minute?" asked Mikey.

Maria sighed. "One minute only. Then it's time to come home." She faced Winnie. "Your dad wants to talk to you."

Winnie nodded.

Maria turned and headed toward their cottage.

"I am so grounded," Winnie mumbled.

Kip snorted in amusement. "What do you think me dad'll say when I go back without our new tent?"

"Won't he understand we had to leave it on Frama-12?"

He laughed. "Not even a little."

"At least I have some souvenirs." Her fingers touched a thin strap around her neck. She pulled on it, revealing the wigget whistle she'd tucked inside her T-shirt. "And this." She tugged on the ribbon that held her reward. "The queen gave this to me."

A miniature gold telescope hung from the ribbon.

"Frama-scope!" Mikey and Kip said in eager voices.

She gaped at it. It looked the same as the one she'd used at Cyann's cave.

"I've read about these," Kip said. "They're extremely rare."

"Really?" She held the lens to her eye and aimed at the ocean. All she saw were whitecaps and heaving waves. "Probably doesn't even work here."

"It should," said Kip.

She pointed it toward the sky. Still nothing. She turned it toward the beach. A fist-sized orb, in robin's-egg blue, hovered a foot above the sand. "I got one. Not very big."

Kip nudged her. "Told you it'd work. Bigger ones are sure to follow."

She lowered the Frama-scope and looked to Kip. "Think so?"

His grin widened. "Oh yeah. Big enough to walk straight through. I'm ready for another adventure."

"Ya know what, guys?" Mikey said. "So am I."

"Except we're about to get grounded."

Kip leaned so close his soft lips tickled her ear. "I wouldn't let that stop us."

"Oh. Okay," she said, her cheeks pulsing with heat.

"Guys, listen," Mikey insisted. "This time I'm coming too."

She hugged her little brother. "I wouldn't have it any other way. What do you know about Frama-10? Isn't that the world on the other side of us?"

"I think it has mountains," said Mikey.

"I like mountains," said Kip.

Winnie nodded and shoved her whistle and Frama-scope back under her collar. She didn't say it out loud, but more travels with Kip might be fun. And who knew? Maybe another trip through a time tear would bring her close to her mom again, or at least the watcher who looked and acted like her.

"But first, brecky," Kip announced. "I'm ruddy famished."

"Me too," she said. "I can't wait to eat real eggs again."

He laughed. "Agreed!"

The trio held hands and marched toward home, swinging their arms.

Inside her shirt, cold metal bumped against Winnie's skin. An eager flutter tickled its way up her spine. She owned an actual Frama-scope. Oh yeah. They were going places. Definitely.

A word about the author...

Aud Supplee, a reformed reluctant reader, gained a love of words thanks to a juvenile literature class in college. She also has a passion for creating alternate worlds full of characters who face a lot of trouble and a little romance. Her other loves are music and horses. She lives in Southeastern Pennsylvania with her husband, a drum set, and an imaginary pony named Buster. For more information about Aud and her books, visit her website: http://www.AudSupplee.com

Thank you for purchasing
this publication of The Wild Rose Press, Inc.

For questions or more information
contact us at
info@thewildrosepress.com.

The Wild Rose Press, Inc.
www.thewildrosepress.com

CPSIA information can be obtained
at www.ICGtesting.com
Printed in the USA
LVHW010102070722
722768LV00013B/295